To Have and To Hold

Credits

Cover Design © by James Tweedie

Front cover includes detail *of Self Portrait*, Rembrandt van Rijn, New York Metropolitan Museum of Art, altered image created by James A. Tweedie

This is a work of fiction. Names, characters, events and incidents are either the products of the author's imagination or used in a fictitious manner. Any resemblance to actual persons, living or dead, or actual events is purely coincidental.

Printed in USA by Dunecrest Press, Long Beach, WA 98631

LCCN 2016913235
ISBN 978-1-945539-03-9 eBook ISBN 978-1-945539-05-3

To Have & To Hold

A Month in the Life of
Mike Maurison
Private Eye

James A. Tweedie

Dunecrest Press

Contents

Introduction

Two Weeks & Counting

Sunday, June 30

When the Verrazano Bridge begins to fade away in the haze every afternoon it is a good bet that summer is coming to Manhattan. Along with the haze come heat, humidity and hordes of hungry tourists wanting to take a bite out of the Big Apple. This creates the illusion the City changes during the summer. Deep beneath the surface, however, where the real stories of New York are being written, the coming of summer doesn't really change much of anything.

Whether or not the tourists show up like the swallows in Capistrano, babies are born; people die; buildings rise and fall; Broadway musicals come and go; and flowers bloom, wither away, or do both at the same time in the hands of street corner vendors. Every day the vendors sell flowers by the thousands, mostly to men who suddenly remember it is their wedding anniversary, their girlfriend's birthday or maybe all of the above.

The City and I are a lot alike. For example, before I proposed to Mona at Robert and Chia's wedding in mid-May my life had been as constant and predictable as the Thanksgiving Parade every November, but now change was bearing down on me like an avalanche.

June was disappearing faster than Houdini's elephants back in the days of the old Hippodrome and July was about to arrive as a month of destiny; a month when the number "two" would become "one" yet remain "two" in defiance of every imaginable mathematical law, theorem or postulate.

In two weeks, I was going to celebrate a day that would require me to buy flowers from a street corner vendor for the rest of my life. Whether the tourists care about it or not change was about to smush me in the mouth with a piece of wedding cake and, in some inexplicably mundane way, New York City was about to change with me.

For one thing: Mona's landlord was about to lose a tenant.

For another thing: After Mona and her critical eye took a stroll through the toxic wasteland I had called home for seven years it was decided *my* landlord was going to lose a tenant, too.

When the inspection was over and after Mona put the small bottle of Purell back in her purse, we headed over to Neil's Coffee Shop to figure out what we were going to do next.

Mona and I have been an item since we met last August, and getting married has been on our radar for a long time. Yet we both pretended we were too busy to work out the details of what getting married might involve.

For Mona, time has been at a premium. The bookstore where she works takes a forty-hour bite out of her week and she has spent the rest of her time scratching, and clawing herself to within three units of completing her Master's degree in Library Science.

I have been busy too; rushing in and out of an office door on the Upper East Side that has the words "Mike Maurison—Private Eye" stenciled on the front.

When I asked Mona to marry me I felt as high as the observation deck on the Empire State building. By the time we walked into Neil's Restaurant, my feelings were closer to vertigo.

Our sit-down confab started off like one of those Indy 500 races where half the cars get wrecked on the first turn. Once we started talking, we couldn't seem to agree on much of anything.

"Let's see," Mona began after my coffee and her Italian Soda had arrived. "We both want to stay on the Upper East Side, right?"

Although she had phrased her sentence as a question, she rhetoricalized it by moving on to the next point without taking a breath.

"So," she continued, "we'll find a one-bedroom apartment somewhere close by and my parents can back the rental agreement with their income."

Being the easy-going, practical, tightfisted, 31-year old man that I am, I suggested a studio might be a better idea.

"That way we can save the extra $200 bucks a month for something nicer when we have more money."

As it turned out logic and reason came to nothing when Mona started fluttering her eyelashes and flashing her killer smile all over the diner. So of course, I shut up and gave in. We agreed to start looking for a one-bedroom apartment on the internet later that evening.

Mona began rhetoricalizing again by wondering out-loud if Robert and Chia had gotten back from their honeymoon. Our two best friends had wound up going to Puerto Rico for four weeks so Chia could show off the groom to her grandparents, and Mona was getting anxious.

"Listen up, Mike," she said. "We need to have everyone on the same page as soon as possible if we're going to get everything ready before the wedding."

At first, this comment confused me but after I changed all the "we"s into "I"s it started to make more sense.

None of this worried me, though, because for Mona the whole thing was going to be a snap. From what I could tell, she had planned her wedding out in detail by the time she turned thirteen. The only thing missing was the actual guy who would one day show up to fill in the blank where the groom was supposed to stand. Now that she had that figured out she was ready to spring into action and bring the dream into reality.

I assumed she would want to get married in the church she attends on Fifth Avenue. I have gone there with her a few times. I like the pastor but when it comes right down to it, I don't really care one way or the other.

Mona has this strange idea that planning a wedding is supposed to be a collaborative effort involving both the bride and the groom. As far as I am concerned, I would be happy to just walk into City Hall as a single guy and then walk out as a married one.

As it turned out, Mona's pastor agreed to marry us in the church's chapel, a small, elegant gothic space that seats around 100 people. Given the fact my mother abandoned me when I was six and my father died when I was eighteen I figured that, counting my Aunt Lucille, my two cousins and my friends, the side of the chapel reserved for the groom will have enough people to fit into one pew.

So there we were, sitting in Neal's trying to find ways for me to agree with Mona about our wedding.

Mona had just started to ask if I wanted to have little figures of a bride and groom on top of the cake when my cell phone started blaring out Ravel's *Bolero*. Without being polite enough to say, "Excuse me" to Mona I answered the call with a cheery but not especially clever, "Hello."

The caller turned out to be a man in his fifties who had recently lost his shirt to his neighborhood bookie. He thought something smelled fishy so he was hoping he could hire me to sniff around and find the source of the smell.

After taking a quick peek at my watch, glancing over at Mona, and pulling my free Hallmark pocket calendar out of my shirt pocket I said "Sure, why not."

We arranged to meet in front of the Plaza Hotel in an hour but Mona was not particularly pleased with the interruption.

"Look, Buster," she said. "This is our time to talk. We've got some big decisions to make and time is running out."

My mouth opened but before I could shut it, I heard myself saying, "Yep, you're right. I'll cancel the job right now so we can get back to talking about little plastic people slogging through the icing on top of our cake."

There is a time and a place for sarcasm but Mona immediately made it clear that this was neither of them.

"Okay," she said. "Let's forget the cake top thing for the moment. Something came up yesterday that I was waiting to talk to you about this afternoon. It's important and exciting and we really need to make a decision about it before tomorrow."

I figured it probably had something to do with the reception so I said, "Well, I won't be gone long. We can talk about it later this evening while we're looking for an apartment."

"No," Mona shot back. "Not later. We are going to talk about it right now!"

That is how Mona wound up standing with me in front of the Plaza Hotel forty-five minutes later.

"Well?" she asked, as I looked around for a shortish, fifty-year old man with a red, blue and yellow plaid flannel shirt.

Since on any given day there was probably only one person in Manhattan wearing a shirt like that I figured he would be easy to spot if he bothered to show up.

"Well?" Mona asked again. "What do you say? I think it would be fun. You could use some time off, I have ten days of sick leave saved up and, like I said, it wouldn't cost us anything. It has to be the best wedding present ever! So say 'Yes!' I want to hear you say 'Yes!'"

The conversation was cut short for a second time when a man wearing Joseph's amazing Technicolor dream coat stuck out his hand and said, "You must be Mr. Maurison."

"Lucky guess," I said.

"No, not really," he replied. "You were the only person standing around here doing nothing without holding out a box with small change in it."

Mona let out a groan loud enough for the man to ask, "Who's this? Your assistant or something?"

Mona's arms interlocked across her chest and her glare blew a hole clear through his forehead, across Fifth Avenue and into F.A.O. Schwartz.

Mona passed the time using her laser-eye super-powers to melt steel while I absorbed some facts; noted some details; wrote down a few names, addresses and phone numbers on the back of a dollar bill; took a cash deposit and shook the man's hand. After I promised to look into it the next day, he walked away and disappeared into the crowd.

"Well?" Mona asked.

"Well what?" I said followed by an "Ouch" as Mona's shoe connected with my shin.

"Oh, yeah, sure, why not," I said through clenched teeth. "But I'll have to double check to see if my passport is still good."

I had gotten the passport years ago so I could get into Canada when or if a case happened to take me to Toronto or Nova Scotia for some reason. I had not used it for a long time and honestly thought it had expired. It turned out to have four years left so I was stuck with my promise to Mona whether I liked it or not.

Mona's parents had called her the previous evening and offered to give us a two-week honeymoon in Europe as a wedding present complete with stays in London, Paris and Florence. They know how nuts we are about art and figured we would jump at the chance to visit the National Gallery, Louvre and Uffizi up close and personal. Mona had travelled to Asia and South America with her parents when she was a teenager so the thought of travelling overseas did not particularly smite her with the fear of the Lord. As a bonus, she spoke some French and figured that a chance like this was not going to come along again anytime soon. As for me, except for a few random trips to Canada, Boston and Miami, I have tried to stay as close to the creature comforts of New York City as possible. Like anyone else who grew up in Manhattan I've picked up some Spanish and can fake accents from Brooklyn and the Bronx, but when it comes to talking like Napoleon or the Pope, *imbécile* and *coglione* are about all I've got.

As far as I am concerned, French and Italian are things you put on your salad.

But when I said, "Yes, let's go," Mona's smile broke through the sound barrier.

"Hey," she said. "Since we're here at The Plaza why don't we stop by the MoMA and bring your Mom up to speed?"

My mom, of course, had faded away like the Verrazano Bridge years before and as far as I knew, she was dead and probably not likely to be coming back any time soon.

When she left, I projected her persona onto the central figure of Picasso's *Les Demoiselles D'Avignon*, a monumental painting that hangs in the Fifth-Floor gallery of the Museum of Modern Art. The paintings in that gallery have been my surrogate family since as far back as I can remember. Mona loves art, too, and knows how much my visits to Mom mean to me; which is why she gave us each a free pass to the MoMA and the Metropolitan Museum of Art for Christmas.

The museum was only a few blocks down and around the corner on 54th Street so we were there in less than 15 minutes. To our surprise, we were greeted at the front door by "Robert-the-husband-of Chia," my best friend and the front lobby security guard for the museum.

"Hey," I said. "How come you didn't tell us you guys were back already?"

Using his finest oratorical skills, Robert offered the hint of a smile and shrugged.

Mona chimed in with, "I imagine things are pretty busy for you right now."

There was a pause, broken by a slight nod from Robert.

I have to make it clear that Robert isn't deaf or mute or anything. He is simply a man of few words—except when he is with Chia and the words shoot out like water from an uptown fire hydrant in the middle of August.

"Good to see you," Mona added. "We can't wait to hear all about your trip and how things are working out with the two of you crammed into Chia's studio."

Her comment was phrased in a way she hoped would get Robert to actually say something.

In response, Robert gave a soft grunt, fought back the smile and said, "It's all good, thanks."

"Let's get together soon, I said. "There's a lot we want to tell you, too."

We had told Robert and Chia about our wedding plans while they were waiting to board their flight to Puerto Rico. Robert was going to be my Best Man and Chia was going to be one of Mona's bridesmaids just as we had been in their wedding. Mona and Chia were probably going to laugh and giggle through the whole thing. Robert and I were probably going to spend our time staring at the walls and wondering which of us had Mona's ring in our pocket.

We both gave Robert the customary poke on the arm and headed up to the Fifth Floor to see Mom. When we entered the gallery, I could see the corner of Mom's lips curl up a notch and her eyes sparkled just a little.

"Hi, Mom," I said silently in the way we usually speak to each other.

Mona added her regards and together, probably talking at the same time, the two of us filled Mom in on the plans for the wedding, the apartment and the honeymoon trip to Europe. I could see Mom's smile fade just a bit and figured it was because she knew that neither she nor my father could have ever been able to give us a wedding gift like that.

"It's okay, Mom," I said, changing the subject. "You know I'd like to have you at the wedding but that would mean I'd have to spend the next ten years in jail for felony theft. Besides, Robert would never let us get you through the front door."

Mona added that we would be sure to stop and say "Hi" after the wedding and before we headed off to the airport. I thought I could see the smile rise a bit before we said, "Bye." We poked Robert on the way out and caught a cab back to Mona's place just up the street from Neil's on the Upper East Side where we both live and work.

Mona's two roommates were spending the weekend with their boyfriends so we had the place to ourselves for a change. Mona scrounged some dinner from the fridge and we surfed for available apartments on her laptop while we nibbled reheated Chicken McNuggets and fries.

I suppose if I were writing a novel, this particular day wouldn't generate enough interest to lure a reader into wanting to move on to the next chapter. But this is how it is in Manhattan: Real life. Real people.

Really.

Chapter 1
Picking Up Speed

Monday, July 1

After Mona and I decided to get married life picked up speed like an intercontinental ballistic missile as we blazed through the final week of May and soared through the June stratosphere with our nuclear warhead targeted for July 14, a day that was now only two weeks away. The last three weeks of June turned out to be surprisingly productive given Mona's anxiety and my dysfunctional predisposition towards social gatherings of all kinds.

Somehow, through a combination of hard work, dogged persistence, Mona's prayers, and the amazing good luck of having the perfect one-bedroom apartment pop up on Craig's List while we were staring at the screen of Mona's laptop, we snagged the home of our dreams—a third floor walkup on the 400 block of East 81st Street. It was only seven blocks from my office, eleven blocks from *Books and Things* where Mona works, one block from the subway station on Lexington and, perhaps best of all, only four blocks from the Metropolitan

Museum of Art and Central Park. As a bonus, it was only one hundred dollars over our absolute high-end rental budget. Given the cost of living in Manhattan, we had hit a home run. Since we didn't need to move in until after we got back from our European honeymoon we wouldn't have to fork out any dough except the deposit until the first week of August.

The best part about finding the apartment when we did was that it lowered Mona's stress level enough to where she could start enjoying the countdown to our wedding again. As a bonus fringe benefit, the stress level in our relationship ratcheted down a notch or two as well. Life was looking good.

As we headed down the home stretch toward happily-ever-after, Mona was still going to work each day and I was still hot on the trail of a half-dozen low-end investigations. When someone hires me to find something or to figure something out I can usually check it off in less than a week. Take that guy with the eye-blinding shirt who lost his other shirt to the friendly neighborhood bookie. When he told me the whole thing smelled fishy, it brought back the memory of a friend from my college days who stuffed a dead mackerel into an envelope and dropped it through the mail slot in his friend's door. This particular friend was on a Spring Break trip to Daytona Beach and by the time he got back, his apartment smelled so bad he had to sleep at another friend's apartment for two weeks and have his carpet cleaned before he could move back in. I wasn't convinced my client's bookie was going to smell as bad as all that but when I stopped by his shop to see what he was up to I held my nose anyway—just in case.

It didn't take long to decide the guy was as crooked as Lombard Street in San Francisco. I did a quick comparison of the odds he gave on the ponies at Saratoga, Aqueduct and Belmont and found he consistently lowered the odds on the loser horses to make them more attractive to suckers like my client. Since more people would bet on the easier odds, he generated more money on the loser horses than he would have otherwise. If for some reason the horse won or placed, his odds would pay out ten to fifteen percent less than at the track. The whole thing was cash under the table, of course, and the New York Gaming Commission would have kicked him over to Jersey if they had taken the time to sniff him out.

I hadn't been hired to kick anyone anywhere but I did have a short chat with him about what he was doing. He said he was only doing what he was told ("wink, wink, nudge, nudge") and told me to beat it or he'd whistle for what he called "Security." Before I left, I suggested he could make a small donation to help assuage the loss and grief that had been suffered by my client.

His response was classic Manhattan: "Tell the sucker to wise up and find someone else to cheat him out of his money."

As I turned to leave, I could hear him mutter "*Caveat emptor*" under his breath.

I doubt the guy knew any Latin but his ball had dropped between the uprights and the game was over. The only thing left for me to do was hustle over and tell my client that the bookie smelled more like a rat than a fish and that if my client cleaned his carpets he might feel better.

None of this made much sense to my client but he caught the drift, coughed up the agreed upon fee and went back into his flat to take a closer look at his carpet.

And *that* is what I do for a living.

This evening, Mona and I met with Pastor Cheryl for the last of the three counseling sessions required before she will agree to join people together in holy matrimony. The first two sessions had been all about who we were, who we had been, who we were going to be and why we wanted to have a Christian wedding.

"After all," she said, "You spend a lot of time deciding who you are going to invite to your wedding and then you leave out the people you don't really want to show up. Why do you want to invite God to your wedding?"

It had been a good question and I had been perfectly happy to let Mona answer it.

Apparently, we survived the ordeal with enough points to move up to the third and final round. The third round required us to read one of the Gospels before we showed up for the meeting. Mona read every word and I skipped the parts that didn't seem particularly interesting. As I was skimming, I ran across some good stories I hadn't seen before so I actually wound up reading more of it than I had planned.

In her office, the pastor ran us through a Bible study of the word "love." It turns out the way the Bible uses the word is different from the way most of us think it means. It has something to do with putting the other person ahead of ourselves and caring about them even if they do not like us in return. Back in Jesus' day, everyone thought it was a good thing if you were willing to die for your friends, but Jesus died for people who were not his friends. That was something new and strange but the idea started to change the way people acted towards each other. Husbands, for example, were no longer supposed to lord it over their wives like Jesus does from heaven but they *are* supposed to love their wives like Jesus loved people when he was dying on the cross. For her part, Mona is supposed to love me the same way she loves Jesus. When or if I start acting like Jesus we're supposed to go through life together as equals.

The whole *spiel* reminded me of the advice Grandpa Rembrandt van Rijn had given me a few months ago when I went to visit him at the Metropolitan Museum of Art. He had told me to let Mona be the star and for me to take on a supporting role so she could shine as brightly as possible. He then added that I should do the same with God.

I had no idea what he was talking about with the God thing but, after listening to Mona's pastor, it almost started to make sense. I say "almost" because I really like what Jesus and the Bible say about stuff like this but I guess I am just more comfortable leaving Jesus out of it. I know it doesn't make any sense to do it that way but I'm not Mona and I guess I've got to figure it out for myself.

I might have some quibbles about things like theology and doctrines like the Virgin Birth or whether God created everything in seven days but I don't have any problem with the part about loving Mona. On the one hand, it seems to be the right thing to do. On the other hand, I don't think I could *not* love Mona if I tried.

When our session was over, Mona's pastor said she had done everything she could to get us on the right track but from now on it would be up to us and up to God to make it work. Personally, I figured it was going to be easy but I decided I'd try to remember some of the things the pastor said just to be sure. Mona, of course, will remind me if I forget.

We finished up around 7:45 p.m. and were standing at the bus stop across the street from the church when Ravel started *Bolero*-ing in my left front pocket. The voice on the other end turned out to be the lady who owns the street-level beauty parlor in the building where I have my office.

"Mike?" she asked. "This is Bergie. Can you come over? Someone's broken into my shop and . . . well . . . you see . . . I don't want to call the cops . . . at least not right now . . . so I thought I'd call you first. Maybe you can help. I mean I'll pay you and . . . Can you come over . . . like right now?"

I started to say something along the lines of, "Hey, c'mon, Bergie, I'm thirty blocks south having a night out with Mona."

But then I remembered the thing about putting the other person first so I told Bergie to hold for a second while I asked Mona what I should do.

"It isn't a life or death thing but Bergie is sort of my neighbor."

Mona already knew what Jesus and Fred Rogers had to say about neighbors so of course she said, "It's okay. Tell her we'll both be there in thirty minutes."

Bergie had come to New York from Norway about ten years ago. Everyone called her Bergie because her last name was Bergen and her first name was Borghild. Given the choice between the name Bergen and Borghild, everyone had voted for "Bergie" and since America is a democracy the "Ayes" had it and the new name stuck to her like wet sand on a beach.

Bergie's shop only went halfway through the building but there was a narrow corridor leading to a door that opened onto an alley at the back. Whoever broke in had come in that way. The salon was right next to the door that lets me into the building and up a flight of stairs to my office on the second floor. Bergie and I say "Hi" to each other almost every day and we've talked about her life and family a few times, but I had never actually been inside her place to look around until now.

Like most beauty parlors, there were several chairs with cones of silence hovering over them. There were a few chairs with magazines where people could sit while they waited, and there were some other chairs where the ladies could get their faces, nails and other body parts painted, buffed and airbrushed.

There was also a cash register towards the front of the store that looked as though someone had hit it with a sledgehammer. It was totaled so completely that Thor, down at the corner pawnshop, wouldn't have given it a second glance—even if it had been offered to him for free.

"Well?" I asked. "What's missing and what do you want me to do about it?"

Instead of answering my question, Bergie started bawling. She didn't even bother to sit down. She just sobbed and cried to the point where I thought she might keel over from a lack of oxygen. I don't do very well with weeping women so I was really glad Mona had come along for the ride. Mona took control of the situation by walking over and wrapping her arms around Bergie. She also would have been willing to offer her a shoulder if Mona had been two inches shorter and Bergie had been two inches taller. Mona eventually managed to get her into a chair and with a final sob and a few wipes of a tissue Bergie came up for air and started breathing again.

Mona was down on her knees looking more or less eye-to-eye with Bergie.

"It's okay," Mona said. "We're here as friends. Is there something you want to tell us? I mean besides the break in?"

After a long pause Bergie, accompanied by a few lingering sniffles, started talking.

"It's not the cash register," she said. "No, I mean the cash register is why I called you but it's not why I'm so upset. It's me. It's all about me. I'm not supposed to be here . . . in America. It's all a lie and I don't know how to get out of it. I feel trapped and dishonest and embarrassed and afraid."

Mona stood, pulled a chair over in front of Bergie and sat. This reminded me that I had been standing the whole time, too, so I sat and joined them. I braced myself for a long sob story but it turned out to be more like a short story by O. Henry than a novel by Tolstoy.

"I came to America with a tourist visa but I never left. I never got a work visa or an EAD and all of it leaves me ineligible to apply for a Green Card or citizenship. To make it worse, I got my beautician's license by using a fake birth certificate with my name on it. If I'm caught I'll be deported for sure. I have a husband and two daughters at home and they don't know anything about this. Now I've been robbed and I can't even go to the police. I don't know what to do."

The story was over but the tears started flowing again. Mona pulled her chair next to Bergie and put her arm around her for the second time. Personally, I haven't cried much over the years but if I had there would have been no one to put their arm around me; no one to comfort me; no one to care. One of the things that had attracted me to Mona was that she cared about people. She had a shoulder for me to cry on if I needed one and she had two arms to wrap around me if I was feeling down.

Watching her comfort Bergie made me almost forget why we were sitting there. There had been the break-in but now there was so much more.

Being, by nature, a "can-do" sort of guy, it was hard to admit that, just like Bergie, I didn't know what to do about any of it, either. Like a lot of men I tend to want to "problem solve" everything. Mona, like a lot of women I have known, prefers to empathize. Sometimes one works better than the other and right now Bergie needed Mona more than she needed me.

While Mona was empathizing, I put a towel over the cash register and figured out a way to secure the back door for the rest of the night. After she was done crying, Bergie said she hadn't had enough money to pay for an alarm system and the only reason she had discovered the break-in was because she couldn't remember whether she had put the tip money into the lock box and had come back to double check. This meant whoever had done the deed had done it in broad daylight between 6 and 7 p.m. There was no need to check for fingerprints because the only thing the crook had touched was a pry bar, a sledgehammer and the money he took. Since he remembered to take the pry bar and sledgehammer with him when he was finished there wasn't anything left that was worth brushing the dust on.

Mona and I had done all we could for the moment so after I showed Bergie how to secure the back door we stepped outside and said "Goodbye-we'll-check-in-with-you-tomorrow."

For the moment, at least, the adventure was over. While I walked Mona back to her apartment, I filled her in on what I had figured out about the burglary. Her response caught me off guard.

What she said was, "Mike, you are such a patriarchal, misogynist, chauvinist, sexist pig!" After a brief and dramatic pause, she added, "But you knew that already, right?"

The comment left me speechless until I figured out that she was waiting for me to respond. I wasn't sure whether to say something witty, droll, sarcastic, ironic, or to simply say, "What the hell are you talking about?"

In the end what I said was, "Huh?"

"Don't you see?" Mona explained. "You've been assuming the burglar was a 'he.' How do you know that? There are two types of people in the world. God made them both in God's own image and they are male and female. They are equally capable of every sin in the book and as far as I know, burglary is not an exception. Didn't you consider the possibility the burglar might be a 'she?' What kind of a detective are you?"

At that point, although she was through ranting, she managed to keep muttering to herself for at least another ten or fifteen seconds.

I waited until she was done and with a large helping of humility I said, "Oink."

She was right of course. It is a bad habit Mona has—being right about things. Sometimes, like that moment, it comes at the expense of my ego. But what if Mona had it right? What if the burglar *had* been a woman? Male crooks usually prefer to break into places they are comfortable with—like houses, banks, bars, fast food restaurants and places like that. It made sense a woman would be more likely to rob a beauty parlor.

As usual, Mona skipped the part that required logic, reason, facts and statistics and just cut to the chase by saying, "It must have been one of Bergie's customers."

There was a pause before she added, "And I bet it was one of the girls who came in for an appointment earlier today so she could check the place out."

There was another pause but before I could finish the thought she said, "And it shouldn't be too hard to identify which customer would be the prime suspect, right?"

Mona was polite and kind enough to give me the final word.

"Yep," I said. "She would have to be large and strong enough to heft a pry bar and swing a sledgehammer."

The momentum from that conversation carried us all the way to the stairs that go up to Mona's apartment. I gave her a lingering kiss on the lips and before we let go of each other she placed a puff of warm air on my ear as a souvenir.

As I walked away, I turned and said, "Mona. I know you are right most of the time but you were wrong about the misogynist thing. How can I be a misogynist when I'm in love with you?"

I can't speak for Mona but I felt pretty good about things on the way back to my place. Mona was going to be a great partner with me in life and she was also going to be a great partner in crime.

If you know what I mean.

Chapter 2
Flies & Honey

Tuesday, July 2

The next few days moved along like a fly trying to slog through a pool of honey.

On Tuesday, the sweet part was that Bergie had a customer who matched our suspect-description perfectly. Another sweet part was that after I had contacted the police they didn't ID Bergie for anything but her driver's license. The fact she had used her forged birth certificate to get the license didn't put a blip on the cop's radar gun so in the end she didn't get deported.

Later, after the police looked into the case they found that the lady in question was as innocent and pure as a Great White Shark. She didn't have the teeth but she did have a long record of thefts, burglaries and break-ins under her belt. Bergie's salon was not her first foray into crime and it most certainly would not have been her last except for the fact the cops busted her fair and square and the judge was kind enough to give her free room and board for the next two years.

The sticky part was working out the honeymoon details with Mona's parents. They had planned the whole thing out, made all the reservations and put together a day-by-day and hour-by-hour schedule of what we would be doing, where we would be going, what we would be seeing and when we would take time out to eat and breathe. Even "lights-out" and "rise-and-shine" were neatly chiseled onto the stone tablets.

Mona didn't want to rock the boat but I felt as though I was on the *Lusitania,* being torpedoed by an enemy submarine.

"What's with this?" I asked. "How come they never bothered to ask what sort of trip *we'd* like to take? It's supposed to be *our* trip, isn't it? If they want to work out every detail without talking to us about it why don't they just take the trip themselves and we can say good-bye to them at the airport . . . 'Have a nice time, folks! We can't wait to hear all about it when you get back!'"

Deep down Mona felt the same way as I did so she sucked it up and didn't make a single snarky comment about my sarcasm. As it turned out, the trip Mona and I had dreamed about wasn't much different from the one her parents had planned for us so when we suggested that maybe we could spend one more day in Paris and one day less in Florence they were happy to make the change. When we said "Thank you" to them for the hundredth time, we really meant it.

Another small slog was Mona and her roommates, Brin and Corrine. The three of them had been together for over four years and, unlike most people randomly thrown together into a small space, they actually got along with each other. They took turns cooking meals and cleaning the kitchen and bathroom. They had a white board where they wrote down when they would be having friends over, when they wanted the place for a private rendezvous, or when they would be away for a day or two. They shared the stories of their lives, provided counsel and advice, and helped each other limp through hard times. Through it all, Brin and Corrine had shared the large bedroom and Mona had the small one to herself.

Mona's roommates weren't surprised when they heard she was moving out. They had seen it coming for a long time and, not so secretly, each of them hoped they would one day find a man like me or maybe better. They also felt a little betrayed as though there had been some sort of lifetime commitment for them to stay in the apartment together. Shakespeare said that "parting is such sweet sorrow" and there were plenty of tears flowing as they laughed and planned out the wedding together.

Mona asked her sister-in-law Pam to be her Maid or Matron of honor. Pam had been married to Mona's brother, Nathan, until Nathan died early in the morning on 9/11 while repairing a fallen electrical wire in the Bronx. Their son, Danny, was Mona's nephew. After talking it over Pam and Mona decided the title "Matron of Honor" would be best since it would be one more way to remember Nathan at the wedding.

At Mona's suggestion, I asked Danny to be my groomsman; the only other person who would stand next to my Best Man Robert and me during the service.

To fill out the wedding party Mona asked her two roommates to be bridesmaids along with Chia. That made the girl-boy ratio somewhat unbalanced at four to two so Mona assigned me the task of figuring out how to get them all in and out of the ceremony in a neat and tidy manner. I felt honored that she had entrusted me with such an important detail and spent a whole fifteen seconds deciding how to make it work.

Mona's father was tapped to walk his little girl down the aisle and Mona's mother was put in charge of the rehearsal dinner. As for the reception and the wedding itself, Mona had sunk her teeth and claws into each of them so deeply it would have taken the Four Horsemen of the Apocalypse to pull her away.

As for the rest of the preparations it only took me about one hour to arrange for the tuxedo rentals but it was taking Mona, Pam, Chia and the other two Musketeers weeks to figure out the costumes and bouquets for the bridal party. As for the *tour de force,* Mona and her mother were having fun finding the perfect dress for Mona to wear as she walked down the aisle to "Here Comes the Bride."

In an attempt to keep things from getting even more complicated than they already were Chia and Robert teamed up and managed to schedule Mona's bridal shower and my Bachelor's Party for the same time on Friday evening. Each of us was looking forward to spending a few hours kicking back with our friends and relaxing while they put on the show.

July 2 turned out to be a day when we were able to pretend we didn't have a care in the world. There would not be another day like it until we grew tired of enjoying the pleasure of getting adjusted to living together as husband and wife.

In other words, there would never be another day like it again.

Chapter 3
Rings
Wednesday, July 3

On Wednesday after work, Mona and her ensemble headed off to buy the dresses and shoes the four maids in waiting would be wearing. I had already given Mona an engagement ring I had picked up for a good price at Thor's Pawn Shop and together we had found a wedding band that matched it perfectly. So while the girls did their thing Robert and I headed over to the jewelry store to haggle the lowest price possible for the circle of gold that would tie our nuptials into a knot.

The manager of the store turned out to be a man for whom I had done some sleuthing a few years back. His brother had been the executor of their parent's estate and my client had hired me to help get back his share of the inheritance. The brother turned out to have committed so many moral, civil and criminal violations that I could have nailed him to a wall in Federal Court if my client hadn't had a heart of gold and settled the matter by blackmailing his brother into signing everything over to him for safekeeping.

As manager, he had the discretion to sell certain items in the store for as low as "at-cost plus ten percent." By the time we had finished reminiscing and were leaving the store, I not only had the ring but I had a lot of spare change jingling around in my pocket.

All Robert could say was, "Sheesh, I paid full price for Chia's rings."

To which I replied, "Heh."

I couldn't tell whether Robert said anything back at me or not because my phone started ringing. It turned out to be a dame who was looking for a P.I. to help her out of a jam. Being a *film noir* buff I sometimes get a kick out of pretending I am Humphrey Bogart pretending to be Sam Spade. Mona thinks talking like this is disrespectful to the feminine species but occasionally I talk that way in front of her just to hear her get passionate about something besides me.

The dame on the phone had only gotten out one or two sentences before my cell started buzzing and vibrating. I am smart enough to know this means I am getting another call on top of the first one but I am not smart enough to know how to put the first call on hold while I take the second one. Even then, if I get lucky enough to pull that off I have no idea how to get back to the first one again. So of course, I punched one of the options on the display and disconnected myself from both calls.

After a few moments, my phone rang. It was the dame. Before she could even finish saying, "Hey, what happened?" the buzzing and vibrating started up again.

This time I handed the phone to Robert and said, "You figure it out."

Robert told the lady to hold while he took the other call.

He tapped something on the screen and handed the phone back to me saying, “Here you go.”

As I have said before, Robert is as full of surprises as a bowl of *chioppino.*

The voice on the phone turned out to be Mona, phoning from a dress shop on West 38th Street.

“Hey,” I said. “Make it short ‘cause I’ve got a client on the other line.”

“No,” she said testily. “I can’t make it short,” and she hung up.

I handed the phone back to Robert.

He tapped something else on the screen and handed the phone back to me saying, “Here you go.”

The dame was back explaining she wanted to hire me to do some investigative work.

Out of curiosity I asked, “Why out of all the Private Eyes in Manhattan did you choose me?”

After a short pause she said, “Because the “I” in P.I. stands for Investigator and I figured if I wanted someone to investigate something they had better have the “I” after their name. As for you, I just closed my eyes and stuck my finger in the Yellow Pages under the listing ‘Private Investigators’ and you hit the jackpot. It’s up to you whether you want this to be your lucky day or not. If you agree, I’ll pay half your fee in cash up front and if you can pull this off I’ll pay you the rest—flat out with no add-ons and no questions asked. If you’re not smart enough to take the offer then I probably called the wrong guy.”

I had been waiting my whole life to work for a dame like this so of course I said, “It’s a deal” before I had the common sense to check her out first.

She agreed to come by my office on Friday morning at 9:00 to lay everything out on the table. I started to say I didn't have a table in my office but fortunately I remembered the difference between rhetorical and literal in time to keep my mouth from being invaded by my foot.

After the imaginary dial tone came on, I remembered Mona and called her back.

Picking up where we left off I said, "Hey."

It turned out to be one of those "Houston-we-have-a-problem" moments.

Mona started talking so fast I couldn't catch my own breath until she finished. It seemed Corinne had tripped and fallen as they got off the bus. Her leg was broken and she was already being chauffeured by ambulance to Lennox Hill Hospital just a few blocks from their apartment in the Upper East Side. Mona wasn't sure what to do. As she put it, this was probably the only time all of them could be at the store together and the staff at the store were waiting for them because they had made an appointment and the wedding was only eleven days away and would Corinne be able to walk down the aisle in a cast and . . . .

I cut her off and said, "Take a cab to the hospital. Right now. All of you. Nothing matters now except for Corinne. Robert and I will meet you there. Now go! Just go!"

As though something had just rebooted in her brain Mona said, "You're right. Of course you're right. Bye."

Maybe some of Mona's bad habit of being right was beginning to rub off on me . . . and maybe the gap between empathizing and problem solving wasn't as wide as I had thought.

As far as emergency rooms go, things turned out to be relatively uncomplicated at Lennox. By the time Robert and I arrived, Corinne had already had her leg x-rayed and her cuts and bruises attended to by the ER staff. Mona and her entourage were sitting in the waiting room staring at their feet while trying to decide if the magazines were sterile enough to be picked up and touched with their hands.

Someone with an ID tag engraved with a name too small to read came in and said Corinne was going to be all right. It was a simple fracture and they would have a cast on it in less than an hour. Unlike most hospitals and doctor's offices, they were true to their word and we all got out of the place by 9:30 p.m.

It wasn't easy to fold Corinne and her crutches into a cab but even with all of us tripping over each other trying to help we managed to get her down the block, around the corner, and up the stairs to her apartment. It was, of course, summer in New York and the apartment was more than a little hot and stuffy with two men and five women standing around and not enough chairs for everyone to sit down at the same time.

Pam spoke first and said it was getting late and she still had a long ride to get home to Bayswater. Corinne was sitting in the recliner looking miserable with her leg elevated and her brain floating around like oil in a lava lamp from all the painkillers they had given her at the hospital. Pam went over and gave her a kiss on the forehead. Robert, who is more gallant than I am, offered to walk her to the subway.

Pam said "No thank you" and "Good night" and left.

Robert and Chia were the next to leave, followed by Mona gently steering me out of the door behind them.

"Thanks," she said. "You were wonderful."

I had no idea what she meant by it and I didn't ask.

Instead, I said, "Don't forget . . . 'With God nothing is impossible.'"

I knew those words meant something to Mona and after everything that had happened during the past year they were beginning to mean something to me, too.

Mona didn't say anything else and neither did I. As the apartment door closed, she smiled and I thought I saw a tear in her eye.

Chapter 4
Sparking
Thursday, July 4

By the end of the week, Corinne was back at work cruising around Manhattan as easily as one of those red, double-decker buses that give tourists the illusion the Chrysler building is sitting in the heart of downtown London. As it turned out, she didn't miss any work at all because the day after her accident was the Fourth of July and she would have had the day off anyway.

Corinne's mother came down from Poughkeepsie to spend the day with her, so Mona and I were free to take some time off by ourselves. As usual, the Fourth was chaos. People were shopping, rubbernecking, and coming and going to see family and friends up and down the entire East Coast—including Manhattan.

To beat the crowds we walked over to Central Park, stood in a long line to get a couple of dogs and sodas, and found a less-congested trail that wound its way over to what's now called the Jackie Onassis Reservoir. With the Great Lawn on our left and the back of the Metropolitan Museum of Art on our right, we walked past the Obelisk and paid our regards to the tragic figure of Alexander Hamilton.

Just for fun, Mona and I stood in front of his statue while I asked a dozen people if they could guess whose picture was on a ten-dollar bill. I got answers ranging from Abraham Lincoln and JFK to Bill Clinton and Whoopie Goldberg. The person who guessed Whoopie was, as it turned out, the only one to get at least part of the answer right—that the person on the ten-dollar bill had never been a president.

Choosing this particular path had steered us clear of the crowds, but to beat the heat we needed to find some place inside, preferably with air-conditioning. Although we hadn't said anything about it to each other, we both knew where we were headed next. We took the nearest path to Park Avenue and then turned south to the front entrance to the Met Museum.

It gets confusing sometimes in New York with all the things that have the word "Met" or "Metropolitan" in them. Depending on who you are and what you are interested in the word "Met" could mean the Metropolitan Opera at Lincoln Center, the Metropolitan Museum of Art, a player on the baseball team, the private club, the hospital, the playhouse, the correctional center or the mental health facility on the Upper West Side. For Mona and me it's the Met Museum, and the words "ropolitan" and "of Art" are simply assumed.

As usual, I led the way upstairs to the rooms with Grandpa van Rijn and Frieda hanging on the walls. Grandpa was a Rembrandt self-portrait who had given me advice and support since I was a kid. To most people walking past he probably looked sort of distant and cold. If his clothes were changed and someone kicked him onto the street he might easily pass for some homeless man staring blankly at nothing in particular as people walked by.

To me, however, he is the embodiment of someone who looks you straight in the eye and takes the time and interest to listen to what you have to say. That is why I call him Grandpa; and that's why I head straight for the Met Museum when I need to talk out something that seems too hard for me to figure out on my own. During the past year, he had kept me on track with Mona and I doubt we would be getting married if he hadn't helped me get my life's priorities straightened out.

It had taken Mona a long time to feel comfortable around this particular painting. Part of the reason was that she couldn't get past the fact it had been a print in one of her parent's art books when she was growing up. For Mona, the painting had been more of a thing than a person. With my help, she had begun to feel almost as comfortable around Rembrandt as she did with my Mom over at the MoMA. Mona never seemed to hear what Rembrandt had to say very clearly but that was probably because Grandpa was more interested in talking to me than to her when I was in the room.

While we were there, we gave our regards and told him about how things were going with our wedding plans. For some reason he didn't seem to be particularly interested in any of it until I mentioned we were going to Europe on our honeymoon. When I mentioned London, Paris and Florence, I could see his right eyebrow lift a little.

As far as anyone knows, Rembrandt never travelled outside the Dutch Republic his entire life and from what I could tell, Grandpa didn't seem to feel he had missed anything by not visiting those places himself. On the other hand, he did seem pleased we were going to go and were excited about it.

Our next stop was to see Frieda, the name I have given to the young woman in Vermeer's painting *Woman with a Pitcher*. Until I met Mona, I had considered Frieda to be my best girl. We are still on friendly terms and she is always glad to see me come by for a visit but her eyes seem to look down at the floor even more than usual when Mona is with me. So this time we simply said, "Hi" and moved on.

We strolled through the rest of the other European galleries, spent time with some of the American art in honor of the holiday and then walked downstairs to the Egyptian exhibit where Mona likes to look at the little boats from the 12th Dynasty with all the figurines rowing, fishing and otherwise enjoying themselves out on the Nile. Before we left, we splurged and split a Chocolate Molten Cake in the Petrie Court Café.

Last year on the Fourth of July, I spent the entire evening sitting alone in my apartment eating a frozen potpie and watching the Macy*s Fireworks on TV. This year, however, I was with Mona, and I couldn't help but think that for "as long as we both shall live" I will never be alone on the Fourth of July again.

Personal fireworks are illegal in New York—not just Manhattan but the whole state. If I could have found any, I would have bought a couple of sparklers so Mona and I could set them off in the alley behind my apartment building or some other place where no one would ever think of going after dark. Instead, back at Mona's place we shared a couple of pizza's with Corinne and her mother and sliced up an apple pie so we could all feel as patriotic as possible. The mother and daughter team were sitting in the living room watching the fireworks on TV when Mona and I slipped into her miniature bedroom to celebrate with some privacy. As Mona sat on the bed, I made sure the blinds were closed as tightly as possible. I handed Mona a small candle I had carried in my pocket all afternoon and turned off the light.

Getting as close to Mona as possible I popped a Wintergreen Certs in my mouth and started chewing with my lips pulled back as far as possible. It was probably my imagination but I thought I saw Mona's face light up just a bit when sparks shot out of the Certs as it broke apart between my teeth. Mona started laughing so hard she started to hiccough. She reminded me of an evening, years ago when I was seven. My babysitter's boyfriend started tickling me to see what would happen. I begged him to stop but he kept it up until I laughed so hard I ran into my bedroom and shut myself in the closet. If I remember it right, I was so embarrassed I didn't come out again for the rest of the evening. As a result, my sitter and her boyfriend had the apartment all to themselves. Later I heard giggling but at my age, I figured they were just fooling around. When I got older, I realized I had probably been right.

When Mona stopped laughing, she begged me for one of my Certs. So face to face, we chewed and sparked until there were no more Certs left to chew. It had been fun but there was more to come. I asked Mona if she still had the candle handy. When she said "Yes," I pulled out a lighter and lit both of our candles. After telling her to do everything I was going to do we waved our candles around and began whistling *Yankee Doodle*, followed by the *Stars and Stripes Forever* and then the *Star-Spangled Banner* which started us both laughing again when we realized the high notes were only coming out of our lips as little, noiseless puffs of air.

When we stopped laughing I quietly blew out Mona's candle and then my own. With our arms around each other, we laid down on the bed as close together as possible. It would be another ten days before Mona's pastor would declare that the two of us had become one but we felt like it was already a done deal. It was a good feeling and it got even better when Mona started giggling.

Chapter 5
Bub & Bubbette

Friday, July 5

When I woke up the next morning, I was still lying on the bed next to Mona. She was already wide-awake and looking at me with a curious smile that seemed more mischievous than lascivious. After I had given my eyes a good rubdown, I smiled back and moved closer to give her a kiss. Mona pulled back, rolled off the bed, picked up a small plate and handed me a toasted bagel with a butter and cream cheese *schemer*, just the way I like it.

"Happy Fifth of July," she said. "I tried to find an old birthday candle to stick in it but . . . well . . . sometimes you have to take what you can get."

"That," I said, "is why I am taking you as my bride."

"What?" Mona asked with a smile that was now definitely mischievous. "Is that the only reason you're marrying me? Because you can get me?"

I tried to smile back as mischievously as possible but the effect was probably lost as I sank my teeth into the bagel. Mona pointed out that there was some cream cheese on my face but before I could reach up to wipe it, she bent over and kissed it off.

"Mike," she said, loudly and dramatically as she smacked her lips, "you might think you got the better deal but personally I think you taste good."

She reached down and pulled me off the bed.

As we stood facing each other she put her arms around me and said, "I think I'm going to really enjoy the part of the wedding where we promise 'to have and to hold as long as we both shall live'. If I didn't have to go to work today I'd be happy to have and to hold you like this for the rest of the day."

"I'd like that, too," I said, "But, regardless, we would have had to quit before this evening when Robert and Danny pick me up for my Bachelor Party."

Then, emoting as best as I could, I added, "Mona, I love you a lot. You know that and so do I, but a man has only one chance to attend his own Bachelor Party. With you, there will always be another day!"

As I had hoped, the soliloquy went downhill as fast as the man who tried to ski down Mt. Everest.

"Don't count on it, Bub," Mona retorted. "I'm a busy girl, too, and my calendar fills up real fast. If you're lucky I might have a few minutes free to squeeze in a hug sometime . . ." she opened her calendar " . . . on Sunday afternoon a week from now."

She looked at me for a moment and since I could tell she was leading up to a grand finale I waited for her to wrap it up.

Mona checked her calendar for a second time before saying, "Oh, dear! I am so sorry. I'm already booked for that afternoon. You see, I'm getting married and so I guess we'll have to reschedule something after I get back from my honeymoon."

After I had faked disappointment she added, “That’s the sort of thing that happens when men leave their women in the lurch and crawl off into dark corners to sweat and spit with each other.”

“Wait just minute there, Bubbette,” I retorted. “It seems to me that you and your bridal pals are going out to do some spitting of your own tonight. I just hope you’ll have enough energy left over to make it to the church on time when July 14 rolls around.”

Mona started to reply with another masterful snippet of witty repartee but I put up my hand for her to wait while I tried to remember something that had started banging on my brain like a woodpecker.

Even though the sun was already up, or maybe because of it, it suddenly dawned on me that I was going to have a client prepared to lay it all out on the table arriving at my office at 9:00 a.m. I glanced around the room looking for a clock.

”What time is it, Mona?” I blurted.

“Eight forty-two,” she said. As an afterthought, she added, “In the morning in case you can’t tell.”

I put the half-eaten bagel back on the plate, grabbed everything I had brought into the room with me except the candles, gave a startled Mona a kiss on the lips, and ran out of the apartment faster than a snag in a silk stocking.

Instead of enjoying my customary, leisurely, earth-friendly, non-polluting, zero CO^2-emitting, cost-effective, health-conscious, and time-tested stroll from Mona’s apartment to my office, I increased the global temperature two degrees by catching a cab and telling the driver that if he didn’t take the corners on two wheels I wasn’t going to give him a tip. I usually don’t give tips to anybody if I can help it but this guy got me where I wanted to be in less than four minutes. Even though it hurt to do it, I tipped him well enough to keep him from honking his horn at me as I walked away.

I threw a haphazard wave at Bergie and ran up the stairs to my office just in time to hear the downstairs door buzzer go off. Two weeks ago, my landlord was good enough to reinvest some of my rent money in a wireless intercom system next to the downstairs door. Now I had a small speaker with some buttons sitting on my desk where my old dyspeptic tabletop fan used to be.

I punched the button that had the word "Talk" on it and said, "Who is it, please?"

"It's me and if you don't know who that is then you're not good enough to get paid for doing what you claim to be able to do. Let me in or I'll take my money somewhere else."

There was no doubt in my mind as to who was attached to the voice. I buzzed the dame into the building and sat down behind my desk, hoping she would make an entrance worthy of an Academy Award nomination.

I wasn't disappointed.

She was curved in all the right places. Her dress was tight, mid-calf and red. Topping it off was a hat—a large, black hat with red feathers that flickered and flamed like a campfire on a dark, moonless night. The hat sat above her face, lips gleaming with dark red, high-gloss lipstick, eyes hidden behind a pair of high-fashion *Illesteva* shades, and all of it framed by a mass of thick, blonde hair. The only things missing were a pair of white gloves and a long cigarette holder.

"Mister Maurison, I presume?" she said with her hidden eyes no doubt inseparably locked on my own.

"How'd you guess?" I asked.

"Your name is written on the door," she answered. "Mind if I come in? Or do I need some sort of a ticket to gain admission?"

The sarcasm was palpable but I did my best to act as though Lauren Bacall walked into my office once or twice a week on a routine basis.

"Sure," I said. "Take a chair." I was going to add " . . . and take a load off your feet" but the whole scene was a cliché already and too much of a good thing would have knocked it down from a "B" movie to a "C".

After she sat in the chair across from me, I said, "All right. Tell me: What's the score?"

The question didn't make a lick of sense. I was trying my best to keep in character but I could tell that I was already starting to lose my grip.

"Ten to four in the bottom of the sixth," she said without missing a beat. "Yankees on top. Red Sox underneath."

The dame was sharp. But not sharp enough to realize it was only 9:00 a.m. and the Yankee game wouldn't start until 7:05 this evening.

"But that's not why I'm here," she continued. "I'm Esther Ramone and I'm here because life is cheap and so is my ex-husband. He's a cheat and a chump, too, if you want to keep score. He's out to get me. He says he won't let our marriage end until one of us wraps it up by fulfilling the part of the wedding vow that says, 'Until death do us part.' He says that if the two of us are going to part then one of us is going to have to . . . well . . . he says it's not going to be him.

"I have a restraining order but he's always been a snake in the grass. He's hiding somewhere just waiting for a chance to strike. Sometimes when I'm walking down the street or standing in a subway station I can feel him watching me. I can't take it any more. I want you to find him and I want you to find enough dirt on him to put him away for a few years so I can get on with my life . . . without having to look over my shoulder every minute . . . every day . . . forever."

She laid a large, thick envelope on my desk.

"Here's the skinny on Bert. In this envelope is everything I know about where he's been hanging out and who he's been hanging out with. There are phone numbers, addresses, his Social Security number and some photos. Bert started paying me alimony six months ago and told me there is only one way for him to get out from under it."

She paused for breath.

"He says there are no other options left because he knows I won't murder him and he has no plans to commit suicide."

She laid a smaller, much thinner envelope on my desk.

"Here is half of your fee up front like I told you over the phone. If you find him and get the dirt, I'll give you the rest and we'll be square. If you get enough dirt to put him behind bars, I'll double it. If you are as stupid as you look then go ahead and say 'No.' Otherwise surprise me with a handshake."

When she had said what she had come to say she stood up and . . . well . . . she just stood there; waiting, apparently, for me to respond one way or the other. I wanted to stick out my hand but my guts had put up a sign that read, "Warning—Drive Slowly—Dangerous Road Conditions Ahead." My guts have the same bad habit Mona has: They are right . . . at least most of the time.

I reached across my desk. With one hand, I pulled the large envelope towards me and with the other hand pushed the smaller envelope back in her direction.

"Tell you what," I said. "I'll look through this stuff and give you my answer tomorrow morning. I already have your phone number on my cell from when you called me the other day. If I decide to say 'Yes,' I'll take the money. If not I'll give you this envelope back."

I stood up and faced her eye to eye—as well as I could through her dark glasses.

"Okay," she said. "But if I don't hear from you tomorrow I'll hire another P.I. to track you down and get my envelope back."

There was another pause; one that was broken when I said, "Deal."

Probably out of habit, she started to stick out her hand but after a small twitch, it went back to hanging limply at her side.

With the hint of a smile, she turned and walked out of the office. She didn't bother to close the door behind her.

As soon as she was gone, I opened the envelope and rummaged through the legal forms, photocopies, typed pages, pictures and handwritten notes that had been crammed into it. At first glance, it seemed Robert Ramone was as cheap as his wife had said. He had moved up to East Inwood and was staying in a low-end hotel unit with a shared bathroom down the hall. He worked part-time as a floor trader with the NYSE so, even with the long commute, he would have plenty of opportunity to hang around Esther's place a couple of blocks over from where I live. With a job like he had I figured he had more than enough dough to pay alimony and still afford to squat someplace else a bit more upscale: like in a room at the Ritz-Carlton or an apartment at the Dakota with a view over Central Park.

After thinking it over and knowing I was getting married in just nine days, I could not decide whether to take the job and get the other half of my fee or to let it go. But the Lorelei started singing and the lure of a double payment turned out to be enough incentive to pull me onto the rocks.

Within minutes I called Edith back. I said "Yes" before she had walked up the stairs to her brownstone apartment.

I spent the rest of the day researching the credit rating of a man who was negotiating the purchase of a warehouse over in Hell's Kitchen. The bank that was handling the transaction had looked into it and found him legit but the seller had a bad feeling about him and hired me to do a double check. Finances and credit ratings are not really my thing, but I made a few phone calls, did some checking on the internet and went on a pilgrimage to places where I hoped to find the faces behind the names that seemed to be connected to his.

The faces I met all seemed to be clean and legit. Some knew the man personally and others had bought or sold property from him. They all said he seemed honest enough and that they would not hesitate to do business with him again. On the other hand, I tripped over something that suggested he had been investing heavily in a large IOU with one of the Atlantic City casinos. It was not up to me to decide whether this compromised his credit rating or not so I just passed the facts on to my client, took my check, and let him figure it out.

I got back to my apartment around 5:30 p.m., just in time to put on a shirt that didn't smell as if it had been worn two days in a row.

At six o'clock sharp, Robert and Danny arrived as the chaperones for my final night out on the town as a single man. They were both wearing clean slacks and Hawaiian shirts. Danny had come by train from Bayswater and Robert had slowly wandered over from the MoMA after the place closed down at 5:30 p.m.

I had gotten to know Robert pretty well since we had met several years earlier, but Danny and I were still feeling each other out. As far as nephews go, he was not very much younger than Mona. Because of this, I always had a hard time trying to figure out whether I should treat him like a brother or like a son. Mona told me I should just treat him like a friend and forget about splitting the hairs. Although I had known Danny for seven months, this was going to be the first time we had ever done anything together without Mona.

I knew Robert had really put out for me by scheduling the party on a Friday evening. If it wasn't for me and the bachelor tradition, he would have already been on his way to Long Island for his weekly dinner with his parents, followed by a few well-chilled games with his curling team at the Long Island Curling Club. With the exception of Chia, the curling league was the one thing he looked forward to more than anything else. No matter how the evening turned out, I knew I would never be able to repay him for giving up the curling just for me.

I had spent the last few days wondering what Robert and Danny would come up with for my bachelor outing. The one thing I didn't expect to see was a cheesy-looking girl popping out of a cheesy-looking wedding cake. Robert was quirky but not especially "over the top" crazy. So I was thinking that maybe he had set up something like taking the subway uptown to the Yankees' game with all the trimmings; or grabbing a take-out burger on our way across town to a cheap-seat 7:30 p.m. concert at the Lincoln Center. Then, on our way back, we would stop by an upscale bar for some drinks and dessert. Either of these would be classic Robert.

I was wrong about Robert and I was wrong about the rest of the evening, too. It turned out that Robert and Danny were both more "over the top" crazy than I had ever imagined.

As soon as I let them in Robert handed me a bag with the words, “Tommy Bahama” tattooed on it. Inside was one of the most eye-blinding tropical shirts I have ever seen. To my sincere disappointment, it was exactly my size, and both Robert and Danny started unbuttoning the shirt I already had on before I could crawl out of the window and head down the fire escape.

After my costume change was finished Danny said, “Grab a jacket and let’s get outta here.”

After I had pulled my windbreaker out from under the dirty laundry in my closet, we headed out and down to street level.

Out of habit, I started walking west towards the Lexington subway station, but Robert grabbed my arm and steered me in the opposite direction. Like in a scene from an old gangster movie, I was shoved through the open door of a green mini-van that looked vaguely familiar. If I had been paying closer attention I would have noticed the word “Thor’s” written on the front door and the words “Pawn Shop” written underneath in smaller letters.

Sure enough, the van belonged to Thor, my Vietnamese buddy whose pawn shop had been the only place in town willing to loan me money when I was first starting out in the P.I. business. Thor was driving, of course, and Robert climbed into the seat next to him. Danny sat down next to me in the middle seat and I almost went through the ceiling when four hands simultaneously grabbed my neck and shoulders from the back. The hands turned out to belong to Thor’s nephew Zach, and Sid, a pal and former client who lets me borrow his car every now and again.

“Okay,” I said, directing the question to no one in particular. “What’s going on?”

Everyone in the car started chanting in near-perfect unison, "We're going to have a party, a party, a party. We're going to have a party, a pa-ar-ty for you!"

Everyone seemed to have a noisemaker of some sort and the noise in the car was deafening. Danny thought I was feeling left out, so he handed me a small kazoo to join in the concert, but he had it all wrong. It wasn't that I felt left out *in* the car, it was that I wanted to be let out *of* the car.

I felt a little goofy when I realized my best friends were kidnapping me. I decided I would just have to make the best of it, especially since I was supposed to be the guest of honor. As we drove along, the music started to sound noticeably better once I joined in with my kazoo.

Before long, we were zipping through the Holland Tunnel. When we emerged into Jersey Thor took a quick turn south and, after another minute or two, we came to a full stop in the Liberty Harbor Marina parking lot. I had heard about the place but I had never been there before. When we were all out of the car, Robert took charge and led us on a parade that snaked through several gates on our way out to the docks.

When we came alongside one of the nicer boats, Robert made an about face, pulled a sailor hat out from somewhere, gave a full salute and said, "All aboard!"

One by one, we stepped onto what turned out to be a 60-foot cabin cruiser owned by a friend of Robert's father. The owner, decked out in a full ship captain's outfit, greeted us warmly. Robert's father and mother were there, too; something that made me wonder what sort of a bachelor party this was going to be.

I didn't have long to wait before I found out.

From across the gangplank I heard a feminine voice shout out, "All aboard."

Suddenly, with Mona in the lead the entire bridal party including Corinne on her crutches appeared on the boat, complete with their own noisemakers and paper hats.

I heard Danny say, "Oh, rats, I completely forgot," and in less than a minute, all the men were wearing paper party hats, too.

Mona and I looked at each other, each of us wondering if the other had been a part of the conspiracy that had set this thing up. Not knowing what else to do, I walked over to where she was standing at the stern of the boat. When I took her hand in mine and gave her a short, soft kiss, everyone on the boat broke into applause.

Robert shouted, "Break out the Champagne!" but the Captain said, "No, not yet. There's something we have to do, first."

What we had to do was walk through all the emergency safety and life jacket drills. It seemed obvious we were not going to be spending the evening tied to the dock.

The yacht had enough room to hold at least thirty passengers so the fourteen of us had plenty of room to move around. The main deck had enough chairs and tables for everyone and there was a well-stocked bar on one side. Below decks was the galley, the bathroom and several sleeping cabins. There was also a spacious upper deck where the wheel and the navigation and communication equipment were located.

It wasn't long before we cast off and headed into the darkening twilight of New York Harbor. Robert's father explained that "starboard" was to our right. In that direction we looked past Ellis Island to where the Statue of Liberty stood tall and green on the smaller, twice-named island of Liberty/Bedloe. "Port," apparently, was to the left, and in that direction we were looking straight up the Hudson River with the skyline of Manhattan looming like a wall on the east side of the river.

The sound system came alive as the Captain's voice said, "Welcome to New York Harbor. For the next two and a half hours, you will be celebrating the final days of Mike and Mona as bachelor and bachelorette on the good ship, *La Dona E Mobile*. Have a good time. Enjoy the food, and enjoy the view. *Mazel tov,* everybody! "

Everybody on the boat shouted, "*Mazel tov*" and the party began.

When all the food had been set out, there was white cheese and garlic pizza with imported German beer for me and the boys, and silver trays full of petit fours and canapés served with china teacups and lots of tea for Mona and the girls. As the evening sped along I saw some of the gals drinking beer but I can't say I saw any of the guys holding a teacup.

As we quietly slid past the soaring buildings and bridges of New York, the men stood by as Mona opened her gifts from the ladies and then the women stood by as I opened the gifts from the gents. Thor's long and narrow gift turned out to be the fake Samurai sword I had hocked at his shop six years earlier. The cufflinks Robert gave me were two matching Scottish thistles made from Sterling Silver and studded with small, green emeralds.

"Wear them with your tux," he said.

With his last name being Frasier, it was clear the cufflinks stood in as symbols for the real gift, which was Robert's gift of himself to me as a friend.

The cruise was a big success. It was more beautiful than words and it was more than wonderful. Robert and his parents had exceeded my wildest expectations, and, after having such an enjoyable evening on the water with Mona and her friends, I have sworn I will never, ever grump or complain about co-ed bridal showers again.

Several days later, I found out Friday had been a "bye" week for Robert's curling league. I still owed him big-time, but not as much as . . . oh what the heck, I still owed him big-time.

Chapter 6
Gravel

Saturday, July 6

After trying and failing to sleep in late, Mona and I spent the following morning trying hard not to fall back asleep. When we weren't yawning we were deciding what furniture and kitchen things we were going to keep and what we were going to pile up on the sidewalk for folks to take. Most of my stuff was going to wind up on the sidewalk except for the twin masculine necessities of my flat screen TV and microwave. Mona had already opened up an on-line wedding registry at Macy*s and figured by the time we moved into our new place we would have everything we needed except for the living room furniture.

After lunch, on the way over to my office, my cell phone started ringing. Lately I have noticed the phone in my office never rings anymore, especially when I am sitting there. Everyone is in love with smart phones and I am still trying to sort out all the texting, voicemail, email and Facebook accounts that keep causing into my phone to beep, bleat or moo. Some mornings I don't even need to wait for my alarm to go off. Instead, I wake up to a text message arriving at 4:00 a.m. accompanied by the sound of birds chirping.

With my phone still ringing out Ravel, I made a mental note to ask Robert to turn all the sounds off the next time I saw him except, of course, for *Bolero*. Then I punched the button that said "Answer." The voice that came out of the phone was Edith's.

"Bert tried to kill me this morning," she said in a voice that seemed somewhat too calm and cheery for the occasion. "I had finished breakfast at the Waldorf with my girlfriend and was standing in the 51st Street station, waiting for the train to take me home when I was pushed from behind to the edge of the tracks. I was standing too far away to fall in front of the train but I could see Bert disappearing into the crowd after I'd caught my balance and turned around."

"Go on. I'm listening," I said.

"Well, I don't think he was trying to kill me, exactly. It seemed more like a warning shot across my bow, if you know what I mean. As if he was trying to let me know he could knock me off anytime he felt like it."

There was a pause as if she was waiting for me to say something.

"So," I asked, "Did you make a report to the station cops? Are the police going to do anything about it?"

"No," she said. "I don't want the police involved. That is why I hired you. I want him put away for good, not just for violating a restraining order. I couldn't prove it was him anyway and I'm sure his face was shielded from the security camera. Bert's no fool. Like I told you yesterday—he's a snake in the grass."

"So what is it you want from me?"

"Make Bert your priority. Make him the only reason you have to be alive. Be consumed with the desire to take him out of circulation. Do it now. I don't know how much time I have left. Do it and I'll pay you even more than we agreed on. I've got plenty of money but it won't do me any good if I'm dead."

And she hung up.

My guts told me to raise the white flag, surrender the ship and hand my sword over to the police. But the thought of all that money left me deluded into thinking I could wrap the thing up in a couple of days with plenty of time left over to get ready for the wedding and the honeymoon.

It turned out I was wrong.

After lunch, I stopped to get the first half of my fee money from Edith. I spent the rest of the afternoon in Inwood casing out Bert's apartment. I phoned him and got lucky when he answered right away.

"Hi," I said. Is this Robert Ramone?"

"What's it to you," he said.

In as formal a voice as I could make up on the spot, I said, "I am representing IBM in an upcoming stock transaction and was wondering if you were at home. There are some details I'd like to check out with you in person."

Ramone took the ruse like a shoplifter takes a pack of gum from alongside the checkout counter.

"Yeah, I'm at home, but I don't have time to meet with anyone today. Call me again next week."

There was a click. I looked up at what I guessed was his apartment window, trying to look as invisible as possible while I waited to see if he would come outside and do something or go somewhere.

There was a coffee place nearby so I grabbed a cup without taking my eyes off the building. Sure enough, I had just picked up my change when he hit the sidewalk and started heading towards the nearest subway station. He turned out to be a fast walker and I began to break into a sweat. The afternoon heat surrounded me like the Indians used to do with wagon trains in the old westerns they don't show on TV anymore because they aren't politically correct.

I was only fifty feet behind him when he disappeared down the subway steps. Not wanting to lose him, I hurried even faster to catch up. By the time I reached the bottom of the stairs he was nowhere to be seen. The station was not very crowded for a Saturday afternoon and yet he had disappeared completely, just the way a coin disappears when you drop it on the kitchen floor in what you thought was plain sight.

Just to be sure I hadn't missed something, I turned around to look behind the stairs and found myself face to face with Bert. He was not smiling and did not look as though he was planning to initiate a transfer of stock into my name.

I noticed a bulge in the front of his jacket and was not at all surprised when he whispered, "You're the jerk Edith hired, aren't you. I was watching when she went up to your office yesterday and then I checked you out when you walked home. You're a real loser, aren't you? You think you're smart. But you're stupid dumb and you're going to pay for it.

"So far you're doing very good. You're not talking and you look the same shade of gray as the stairs. So why don't we just take a little walk back outside. Feel free to yell or run away if you want. That is if you like collecting bullets as a hobby."

Since I do not consider myself to be stupid dumb enough to try and outrun a .38 the two of us walked side by side and played "Simon Says" with him being Simon.

After a block or two, we turned away from the sidewalk and stepped behind a bank of garbage bins. After both of us had gotten comfortable, Bert opened his jacket and broke into a big smile. His laugh sounded as though he had swallowed the soundtrack from the Wizard of Oz at the scene where the Wicked Witch of the North cackles at Dorothy.

"See?" he said. "There's no gun. It was a joke. Get it? I was just teasing you . . . pulling your leg. No harm done, right? Here, let's just shake on it like good friends."

I took a swing at him but missed. Bert swung his foot up between my legs and walked away while I was busy noticing just how interesting those little pieces of gravel can be when you are looking at them from close up.

Three days ago, Mona had been worrying about whether Corinne would be able to walk down the aisle with her broken leg in a cast. Now it was my turn to worry: about whether or not I would be able to perform my half of the entertainment we had scheduled for our honeymoon.

After five or maybe ten minutes, I stood up and noticed my half-full cup of coffee lying on the ground. Like a good citizen, I picked it up and dropped it into one of the bins. It turned out to be the only productive thing I did for the rest of the day.

Before it got too late, I phoned Edith and said that from what I had seen so far, her ex-husband did not appear to be a very nice man.

She responded by saying, "For *that* I've given you money? You're going to have to do a lot better if you want to see any more of it."

Chapter 7
Snake In the Grass

Sunday, July 7

When I woke up the next morning, the Sunday sunrise was starting to reflect into the air-well outside my bedroom window. For once, the birds had not flown into my cell phone and started chirping. I was glad to have the extra hour of sleep. When I got out of bed and stood up most of me felt just fine. The rest of me felt . . . well . . . the rest of me felt tender.

It was 6:45 a.m., which gave me plenty of time to eat, dress and get to Mona's so we could go to her 10:00 a.m. church service together. Since we were getting married the following Sunday afternoon, and because Mona would be missing church that weekend, I knew she would want to be there today. When I volunteered to go to church with her, she gave me a hug that would have broken my back if I had been suffering from a bad case of osteoporosis.

If she noticed I was walking a little stiffly, she didn't say anything about it. This saved me the trouble of having to make up some sort of lame half-truth sufficient to deflect the conversation in another direction.

Worship was more or less as usual. The organ played, the people sang, and, since the choir was on vacation during the summer, they didn't. The sermon was probably good as well but I was too busy thinking about Bert to pay much attention to it.

Every Sunday towards the beginning of the service, everyone says the Lord's Prayer together. After going to church with Mona off and on and off again during the past year, I have actually memorized most of it. Thinking about Bert made me think of the place in the prayer where it says, "Forgive us our sins as we forgive those who sin against us."

As I have said before I really like most of what Jesus says about things but this particular part of his Prayer isn't one of them. How was I supposed to forgive a pathological, psycho-maniac whose idea of a good time is to threaten people with pain, suffering and death? I had already been introduced to the pain and suffering part of the equation, so I decided Jesus would just have to take a seat this time around.

I had not yet figured out how I was going to get even with Robert Ramone but imagining the possibilities gave me far more pleasure than singing the hymns that morning. As for the part about having my own sins forgiven? Well . . . that would just have to wait until later.

Mona had a date with her mother for lunch. Afterwards they were going to pick up Mona's wedding dress from the bridal shop where it had been, 1. Chosen off the rack; 2. Paid for, and; 3. Retrofitted to Mona's exact size, shape and form. All of this is so Mona will look and feel as spectacular as possible when she makes her entrance at the wedding. As far as I am concerned, she could walk up to the altar wearing

Bermuda shorts and I would still be convinced she was the most beautiful girl in the world.

Robert and Chia had gotten tickets to a Mets game and, seeing how busy Mona was going to be that afternoon, asked if I wanted to go with them,. I haven't been to a Mets game in years. In fact, I haven't been to a Yankees game in years either. Or, for that matter, a Jet's game, a Giant's game, an Islanders, Devils, Rangers, Nets or Knicks game. Soccer and women's sports are off of my radar completely, but the price of a ticket to any of these events has been out of my league since they closed the Polo Grounds in 1963, twenty or so years before I was born.

I might have been tempted to go with Robert and Chia except for the fact there were only a few days left before the wedding and there was this pressing need to get even with Bert. So in an elegant and graceful manner, I demurred.

With Edith's consent, I spent the afternoon following her up and down and back and forth across Manhattan. The lady is apparently unable to stand still for more than three minutes without experiencing an uncontrollable urge to spend money somewhere. At one point, she took the #6 Train from Grand Central to 51st Street, purchased a truffle at Godiva's, ate it on the spot, and took the A Train back to Grand Central again. I considered the possibility that being a moving target might be giving Edith an edge, assuming duck hunting was not among Bert's collection of sordid talents.

Around dinnertime, Edith headed back towards home. She seemed to handle her five or six shopping bags with a well-practiced ease. As we rode north, I spotted Bert's face peering through the door windows that separated our car from the one behind us. He was staring directly at me. When our eyes met he didn't try to duck down or hide, he simply smiled, gave a little wave and slid his hand sideways across the front of his neck. I did my best to offer him a smile in return, but found it difficult not to blink or to start looking at the front-page headlines of the paper being read by the person sitting next to me. Bert had wrapped me around the same finger he was giving me. I felt as rotten as the six-week-old, half-eaten banana I had found in the back of my refrigerator the day before.

As we got off at 86th Street, I walked up to Edith and said, "Bert was on the train."

Edith did not even bother to look at me when she answered in a matter of fact way, "I know."

Just to be nice I walked her home and when she was more or less safe inside, I went into a nearby pizza place and ordered my usual white cheese and garlic pie. As I was taking my first bite, I looked up and saw Bert sitting down in the chair across from me.

"Hi," he said, with a grin that was a total knock-off of Jack Nicholson's in *The Shining*.

When he added the words, "I'm back," I almost choked on a piece of crust.

Somehow, I regained my composure enough to switch on the digital recorder I had put in my pocket before I had left for church.

"So," he continued, "you're still running interference for Edith? Of course you are. Do you like her? Is that why you are willing to put your life on the line for her? Or is it the money?"

There was a long, long pause.

"What does Mona think about all of this? Have you talked to her about it? Is she jealous?"

The grin grew a little bigger and I could feel his breath on my face as he leaned across the table.

Mona? I said to myself. *How does he know about Mona?*

"Accidents happen sometimes," he hissed. "It's sad, but sometimes they happen to someone you love; like Edith, maybe . . . or Mona. Who knows? One could even happen to you!"

There was another, shorter pause.

"No, wait . . . I almost forgot . . . you've already had one accident, haven't you?"

One nice thing about a digital recorder is that it does not make a whirring noise. If the settings are configured properly, it can pick up words spoken in a whisper from clear across a room. Since I already knew what my own voice sounded like, I kept quiet and let Bert go on with his little speech.

"They say lightning never strikes twice, right? But I read about a man who was hit by lightning three different times. Do you think this could happen to someone else? Like maybe to . . . you?"

One bad thing about a digital recorder is that it does not make a whirring noise, so it's impossible to tell whether it is actually on or not when it's in your pocket.

Oh, God, I said to no one in particular except maybe to God, *make the damned thing work. Please!*

"Don't get the wrong idea," the speech continued. "I'm not threatening you or Mona with anything, but stuff happens. Sad things that can interfere with a person's pulse, or breath, or things like that. So let me give you a piece of medical advice. Back off. Retire from your employment with Edith. Get married to your lovely bride—and you will agree with me that she is pretty, right?—and live out a long, healthy and happy life. Doesn't that sound nice?"

An envelope, looking a lot like the one I had pushed back to Edith two days earlier appeared on the table.

Bert kept smiling as he slid it in my direction and said, "I know Edith has offered you a lot of money to pay for your trouble. Since her money is, by all rights mine, I thought maybe I would just pay you myself for the fine work you have already done . . . and for all the fine work you won't be doing from now on.

"So, what do you say? Consider it a gift . . . or maybe a down payment on your future. There is plenty of money in this envelope . . . enough for you to take another trip or two to Europe and with more than a little left over. Unless, of course, you would prefer to hang around here doing the same-old, same-old until you die and have your ashes scattered in the East River."

"Is this a bribe?" I asked.

"No, it's not a bribe," came the reply. "It's simply an offer to lure you away from one employer to another. One employer who pays you to engage in dangerous and deadly work, and one who pays you to do nothing at all, safely, and without any need to worry about all the bad things that might happen to you otherwise."

Bert might have been a slime ball and a snake in the grass but he was very good at what he was doing. When I was little and going to school, there were kids who were a lot like Bert; pushing other kids around, taking their lunch money, pulling down their pants, and telling them how nice their Daddy's plate-glass window was and what a shame it would be if a brick went through it.

I had survived all of that, and I knew I could survive Bert's bloviations as well. But it was the stuff about Mona that made my blood temperature drop to below freezing.

I sat there staring at the envelope, not exactly sure what to do. On the one hand, I had a professional, contracted obligation to protect and serve the interests of my client. On the other hand, I had a moral and transcendent responsibility to love and cherish Mona for as long as we both would live. I wanted that loving and cherishing to go on for as long as possible so I took a brief time-out to see what my guts had to say about it. All I heard was a rumbling sound, as though Mt. Doom, in the *Lord of the Rings*, was about to explode. The image of Mona walking down the aisle ran through my mind as though it was on a tape loop; her radiant face floating towards me over and over again, like a scene from *Groundhog Day*.

After carefully considering my options and after considering the best interests of my troops, I raised the white flag, accepted the terms of surrender, and handed my sword over to Bert. I had lost the battle and withdrawn from the field with my head bowed in shame.

Throughout it all, Bert's smile never flagged. He watched as I took the envelope in my hands and I watched as, without saying a word, he stood up and walked out of the restaurant. I had taken only one bite out of my pizza the entire time. I left the rest behind and walked out into the warm, comforting, midsummer evening air of Manhattan. I slowly made my way back to my apartment where, as soon as I walked through the door, I threw up.

Chapter 8
Sing Sing
Monday, July 8

On Monday morning, I ate an egg I soft-boiled in the microwave. Cooking eggs in a microwave is an art that cannot be mastered without having first exploded two or three dozen of them over the span of several months. With practice, I have now learned to poach them, hard boil them, soft boil them, scramble them, and even create recognizable versions of sunny-side up and over-easy. Milk goes bad after a week, but eggs last long enough for me to eat most of them before the last few start to fall apart and smell when I pick them up. For this reason, and because they are relatively cheap, eggs are what I eat for breakfast most of the time.

After I finished doing my best imitation of a contestant on *Chopped*, I phoned Edith and told her that from now on she was going to be on her own.

At 9:00 a.m., I stopped by her place to return the money she had paid me. I also gave her the digital recording I had made of Bert's speech at dinner. I figured I was still working for her when I taped it so in a sense it was hers. I guessed she would probably add it to her "skinny on Bert" envelope where it would be available to whomever she hired to take my place.

Edith handled my retirement with the same practiced ease with which she had carried all those shopping bags the previous afternoon. As it turned out, she had been rehearsing my retirement for some time. I was, in fact, the third P.I. who had quit on her after having met Bert personally. She thanked me for the recording and apologized for whatever it was that Bert had done to me.

Before I left, she insisted on paying me for the time and trouble I had already invested in her case. I accepted the offer. When I left her apartment, I noticed I was not walking as stiffly as I had when I went in. A visit to Lourdes would not have brought about a quicker or more miraculous healing.

Mona and I had already decided Wednesday would be our last day of work. After washing my hands of Bert and Edith, I only had one or two small matters to clear up today and Tuesday before my calendar become clear for the next two weeks. I had already composed a new message for my call waiting and answering machines that said, "Thank you for calling Mike Maurison. Mike will be out of town until the first week of August. If you leave a message, he will get back to you after he returns. In the meantime, I hope you are having as good a time as Mike is having."

One of the things still on my calendar was to help a woman whose brother was about to be released from the Sing Sing Correctional Facility up-River in Ossining. He had completed serving twenty years of a fifteen-year sentence for armed robbery. Five years were added to his original sentence after he found a rock somewhere, carried it into the exercise yard and used it to beat another prisoner unconscious. It came as no surprise he had not received any time off for good behavior.

The sister's name was Maureen Sandler and the brother's name was Billy Cantor. Maureen and her two daughters were the only family members Billy had left so she felt obligated to meet him at the prison where he was about to be released. If no one came to pick him up two of the guards would escort him to the nearest bus station in handcuffs and hand him a ticket before letting him go. Maureen had visited him from time to time while he was in prison but she was not comfortable about him becoming a part of her life once he got out.

In her words, "I never trusted him before he was arrested and sentenced and, after all these years, I really don't have any reason to trust him now, either."

She wanted someone to be with her when she picked him up and to be there when she talked to him about what was going to happen next. Even though she had told her brother over, and over she would not take care of him in any way, he continued to insist he would stay at her house until he got a job or found something else to do with his life.

The thought of him living with her and her two teenage girls was a constant nightmare. Even the thought of him showing up on her doorstep terrified her. The local police and the State Corrections Department explained to her that once released there was nothing they could do to prevent him from going anywhere he wanted. A friend had urged her to apply for a restraining order but since she didn't have any evidence that showed him to be a threat her request was denied.

Maureen not only didn't trust her brother but she didn't trust herself, either. To make sure she wouldn't be tempted to cave in to his demands, she arranged to meet me at my office at 10:30 a.m. and leave whatever cash she had in my desk drawer, along with her credit cards, debit card and checkbook.

Maureen arrived right on time and, after a full and complete separation from her spendable cash, we got into a car I had rented for the occasion. We headed north up FDR Drive and followed I-87 all the way to Ossining. The trip took a little less than an hour. Billy's release time had been set for 12 Noon so, by the time we had checked in and parked, we only had to wait five minutes before he appeared.

Billy was dressed in a new pair of jeans, an off-white button-down shirt and a pair of well-worn tennis shoes. He was clean, his hair was trim, and a tattoo of what looked like the tip of an ocean wave crept up the side of his neck. Maureen walked forward to meet him. There was an awkward moment where neither of them could decide whether to hug or shake hands. In the end, the hug won out, although it turned out to be both brief and sideways.

Maureen then introduced me as a friend who had offered to drive her up and be with her for the day. Billy shook my hand but looked me over carefully, as if I had been a new addition to his cellblock.

Maureen added that we could only stay in Ossining for a couple of hours, so she wanted to make the best of the time they had. Billy looked down at the ground for a few moments when it sank in that his sister was not planning to take him home with her.

"How about some lunch," I offered.

"Good idea," Maureen chimed in. "Where would you like to eat, Billy. Lunch is on me."

There was another awkward pause as Maureen realized she didn't have any money to pay for lunch. As for Billy, he hadn't made a decision about where to eat lunch in over twenty years.

"I don't care," he said. "Let's just go anywhere. I want to get as far away from this place as possible."

He had a very small gym bag with him. I reached to take it but he pulled it away and wouldn't let go of it. Getting in the car was awkward, too. I was driving but no one had figured out who was going to sit in the front passenger seat and who was going to sit in the back. After a moment or two, and without saying a word, the two of them got into the back seat together.

While they talked about all the red tape that had to be unraveled before his release, I headed over to Highland Avenue where I had noticed a few pizza places, a diner and a McDonald's.

"Take your pick," I said.

To my surprise, Billy pointed to a Chinese restaurant and said, "That looks good. I haven't had Chinese in a long time."

We sat in a booth and Billy ordered four things from the a la carte menu while Maureen ordered Sweet and Sour Pork and I ordered Cashew Chicken with Pork Fried Rice . Billy's food would have been enough to feed three or four people but he somehow managed to eat all of it before we left.

The conversation quickly turned to what Billy was planning to do next.

"I don't know," he said. "Try to land a job somewhere--if I can find anybody willing to hire an ex-con."

"Do you have any money to get started with?" I asked, as Maureen shot me a look that would have frozen kerosene.

"Yeah, a little," he replied, "enough to live on for a few days or so."

Maureen broke in.

"The Warden's office told me they had arranged three job interviews for you in Yonkers over the next three days. If you don't have the list with you, you can have mine. It shows when and where they'll be taking place. I think these interviews are as good a place to start as any."

Billy didn't offer any response so she kept going:

"I also looked around on the internet and found a shelter where I was able to reserve a bed for you. There are long waiting lists everywhere, but I got lucky and found a place where I was able to work something out. Billy, I want you to know there aren't a whole lot of places where you can go. The place I found in Yonkers isn't the Ritz-Carlton, but it's the best I can do. I'm not able to help you with much, but I have left enough money at the shelter for you to be able to eat and sleep there for at least a week. After that, I guess you'll be on your own. Is that okay? . . . I mean, what I did . . . Is it okay with you?"

"Yeah, sure," he said. "What choice do I have? Hell! I don't even remember where Yonkers is. I don't know anybody in Yonkers. I don't know anybody anywhere except for the cons, crooks and rapists I've lived with for the past twenty years. To hell with Yonkers! To hell with all of you!"

The other folks in the restaurant were staring at us, but when the headwaiter started walking in our direction, I put my hand below the table and waved him off.

"To hell with you, too, Billy," I said with as much conviction as I could muster in a small, crowded public place.

Maureen shot me another glance; this time a glance that would have melted all the ice in Antarctica if it had gone off-target.

Billy looked surprised, too. "What the . . . ?"

From somewhere deep down in his soul, Billy managed to control his tongue in a way he hadn't had to do in a long time. I took this as a good sign . . . a sign that maybe he might make it after all.

"Hell is where you are headed," I continued, "unless you suck it up and decide what you want to do with the rest of your life. Maybe you just want to go back to jail. That would be the easy thing to do . . . the coward's way out. Or maybe you can be a man for a change. A real man. The kind that earns a living, pays for his room and board, and feels as though he has accomplished something he can be proud of."

I paused for a moment to catch my breath. Billy tried to say something but I cut him off by adding, "It's up to you. Be a man or go to hell."

As soon as I stopped talking, I began counting to myself, a habit I have whenever I get put on hold during a phone call. I was up to twenty-seven before Billy broke the silence.

Speaking slowly and softly he said, "I've been in hell before. Some of it was in prison and some of it was before I went in. I don't know . . . maybe that's where I belong. Me and hell . . . in for life . . . together."

"Please, Billy," Maureen pleaded. "Don't think that way and don't do anything to hurt someone just to get back in prison. Give this a chance. If it doesn't work out then you can go back to, well . . . back to hell if you want. But if it works out, then maybe you'll start to think differently about yourself. When you were growing up, nothing seemed to come easily for you, but I always knew you had talent. You were playing the guitar like a pro. You wrote lyrics for the songs you composed. And you could run faster and further than all of the other boys, except for maybe Bobby Williams."

She took a deep breath and Billy seemed to be paying attention to what she was saying.

"Billy, you have it in you to do something with your life. I want you at least to try. But you're going to have to do it on your own. I won't be able to help you with anything more than I already have. I'll give you moral support from a distance but I don't want you coming to my home for any reason. I'll be happy to keep in touch with you by mail, by phone or by email if you can find a computer to use."

There was another pause.

"That it, Billy, that's all I have to say. We're going to drop you off at the shelter in Yonkers and then . . . well good luck to you."

Billy sat there and said nothing while he finished eating his Chow Mein with pan-fried noodles.

When he was done, he stood up and said, "That was good. Thanks. I'd like to go now."

"To Yonkers?" I asked.

"Yeah," he said. "Where else have I got to go?"

The drive to Yonkers took about half an hour. When we pulled up next to the shelter, Billy got out of the car and stood on the sidewalk, holding his gym bag, and staring at the building with his back to us. Maureen walked over and stood next to him. She whispered something in his ear and when he didn't respond, she walked back and got into the front passenger seat.

"That's it. You can take me back."

So I did.

There wasn't much more to say, so I let Maureen play with the car radio until we got to Manhattan. First, we stopped by my office to pick up the things she had locked in my drawer. Then I dropped her off at a subway line that would take her south where she would be just a transfer or two from home. She asked me what my expenses had been, including lunch, and added them to the fee on which we had agreed.

After handing me a check she said, "Thank you, Mr. Maurison. You were a bigger help than you can imagine. And you were worth every cent of it to me."

She closed the car door and disappeared into the station. It was only 4:15 p.m. I called Mona at work and asked her out to dinner.

"I had a payday again today," I said, "and I'd like to spend some of it on you."

An early dinner at the Heidelberg gave me the chance to splurge on *Weiner schnitzel*, washed down with a good German beer. Mona had Hungarian Beef Goulash with a *schnaps*. A good time was had by all, and when it was over we still had the whole evening free to talk about what we were going to do on our honeymoon.

Chapter 9
Headache

Tuesday, July 9

Tuesday I woke up with a headache. Headaches are something I never have unless they involve an annoying client. Even in those situations, the headache isn't really in my head; the headache is the client.

After pushing things around in the medicine cabinet and after looking under the bathroom sink, I finally found an expired bottle of ibuprofen. It was in the kitchen where I keep the salt and pepper. The bottle was sitting in one of the empty margarine tubs I use for storing food before I throw the food out. Even though the pills had expired, I took two of them anyway figuring if they didn't do any good they probably wouldn't do any bad, either.

I had used up my last egg the day before and a cup of caffeine was the last thing in the world I needed for a headache. I threw on some clothes that were hanging in the closet instead of lying on the floor and went downstairs and outside.

At the corner market, I said, "*Buenos dias*" to Juan, and looked around for a pizza pocket.

Juan is the man who stands behind the cash register and takes my money. I'm not certain, but I think he owns the place. His English isn't as good as mine and my Spanish isn't as good as his so we usually just smile at each other and say "Hello" in whatever language comes to mind. Juan's English, however, is very good when it comes to money. Maybe he's not able to say "How about those Yankees" in a way I can understand, but he can say "That will be fourteen dollars and eighty-seven cents" better than I can. People sometimes say that money talks but I know better. It's not the money that talks; it's Juan.

Even after the *Weiner schnitzel* the night before, I was hungry enough to inhale a pizza pocket and a burrito. I have noticed that pizza pockets eventually get digested but corner store bean burritos are good for at least six or seven hours before they stop being a lump in your stomach. I figure that starting my day at the corner market saves me a lot of change since I never feel the need to each lunch after I've had a burrito for breakfast.

It was 9:00 and my last appointment for the next two weeks was not due to come in until 11:30. I decided to kill some time with a short walk, hoping New York City's version of fresh air might do my headache some good. Since the East River is only three blocks from my apartment, I figured I could get there and back to the office with plenty of time to spare.

I walked along 87th Street to John Day Park and watched the mothers and nannies keep their eyes on the toddlers as they played on the slides and the few other things the insurance companies still consider safe for children to play on.

Looking through the bars in the park fence made me think of Billy, and thinking of Billy reminded me of Sing Sing. Maybe the children were the ones who were locked up this morning: guilty of being children and sentenced to spend two hours behind bars, surrounded by armed guards (each of them having two of them . . . arms, that is), with no way out and with no hope of escape.

Then again, maybe I was the one behind the bars; locked up like a caged animal at the Bronx Zoo. Maybe, just maybe, it was the children who were on the outside looking at the monkey and tossing peanuts at him when no one was looking.

Strangely enough, the thought of munching a roasted, salted peanut sounded good to me; even with the burrito still lying in my stomach like a lead weight. While pondering where I might find some peanuts, I continued my walk for another hundred feet, went up and over the pedestrian overpass that crosses FDR Drive, and came back down onto the East River Esplanade. It was a beautiful summer morning. The sun was clear and bright as it hovered over Roosevelt Island, warming the air around Manhattan and probably melting the polar ice cap at the same time.

My headache had not gone away so I headed for the nearest bench and sat down with my chin in my hand, looking and feeling like Rodin's *The Thinker* but with clothes on. Appropriate to the pose, I was thinking—thinking about Mona and the next five busy, hectic and stressful days leading up to our wedding. When the reception ended and we drove away from our old way of life into a new one, I still had no idea whether Mona was planning for us to be pelted with rice, birdseed or bubbles. Whatever the guests threw at us would be the send-off to our European honeymoon. The wedding would be at 2:00 p.m., the reception would probably wind up around 6:00 p.m. and our flight to London was scheduled to depart from JFK at 10:55 p.m. that night, arriving at

London/Heathrow at 10:50 the next morning—English time. It was going to be a grueling day, and the first night of our honeymoon was going to be far less physically intimate than I had originally planned.

As I looked at the sparkling water in the East River, it seemed almost surreal to think that in just a few days I would be standing in London with Mona, looking across the Thames. Soon, there would also be the Seine, the Arno and the Tiber, each of them oozing with history and romance. Oddly enough, I could not recall a single American poet who had ever described the East River as being the quintessential apotheosis of passion. Even so, as I turned to retrace my steps I couldn't help but notice an elderly couple strolling hand in hand along the Esplanade. It crossed my mind that one day, many years from today, that couple might be Mona and me.

As I turned back to look at the East River a final time, I decided it didn't matter what river I stood alongside. If I was with Mona then every river would not only be beautiful but also a reflection of my love for her.

I got back to my office at 10:45 and began spring-cleaning two weeks behind schedule.

After transferring a half-dozen disposable coffee cups, a Styrofoam take-out food container, and a couple of stained and crumpled paper napkins from the top of my office desk to the bottom of the wastebasket, I paused and looked around. Except for the dust, there wasn't very much left to clean up or move around.

A year ago, my landlord provided a cleaning woman to come around and clean up my office every two or three weeks. The cleaning thing had been a sort of incentive to lure tenants into signing a lease in what was otherwise a marginally inhabitable building. Once all the rooms and offices were rented, the only real incentive for me being there had been laid off. Whenever a blue moon had signaled it was time for Rita to appear, I would put a cookie or a donut on my desk along with a can of sweetened tea and a thank you note. I really meant the "Thank you," but I was also hoping the gesture would serve as a pre-emptive strike against her asking the Board of Health to stop by my office for a visit.

Times had changed. Like the Shawn Desmon song puts it, "She Ain't Coming Back No More," which is one way to explain why I was standing alone in my office looking at all of the dust.

My reverie was interrupted when the buzzer on my intercom started to do what it does when someone is trying to get in through the outside door.

"Is that you?" I asked, fully aware that no matter who they were, they would say "Yes".

Instead of "Yes," I heard a woman's voice saying, "Who else would it be."

As I buzzed her in, I made a mental note to award her two points for originality.

The woman who entered my office looked somewhere between forty and sixty years old. It was hard to tell her age because she didn't look well and her head and hair were covered by a rather shabby, rainbow colored knit cap. She didn't say anything until after she had sat down. I started to offer her a bottle of water but remembered I had already taken the last one over to Mona's as part of my farewell-to-the-office celebrations.

Instead of offering the water, I said, "Good morning, Sarah—or should I say, "Ms. Sheehan?"

"Call me whatever you want. You can even call me late for dinner. At this point in my life I really don't care one way or the other."

My guts immediately slipped into gear and announced that the lady was not having a good day. Sometimes my guts are helpful and insightful in pointing out things I otherwise might not have noticed, but sometimes they are just annoying. This was not one of the helpful moments.

After telling my guts to "shut it and stuff it" I said, "It sounds as though you are not having a good day."

When she heard that, she pulled off the knit cap and revealed a head that was completely bald.

"A bad day?" she said, or asked, I wasn't exactly sure. "Every day is a bad day, and last Sunday was the worst of it. That's why I'm here, because of what my step-son did to me on Sunday."

"Well?" I asked. "Is that all? Or is there something more you want to tell me?"

Most women who come into my office and are having a bad day would have started crying at this point in the conversation but Sarah's eyes looked as dull and dry as a pair of dead scorpions in Death Valley. Even so, there was a fire hidden inside of her, and when it came out, I wasn't quite prepared for it.

"Crap," she said, as she actually spit onto my antique, un-vacuumed carpet.

"Sorry about that," she added, without the slightest hint of remorse. "The little loser hates me and the feeling is mutual. I've been married to his father for the past three years and the boy has wanted me dead since the first time we met. I can't really blame him for being angry. His mother lost the custody case and can only visit him for two hours each week with supervision. He blames his father Jerry for everything and takes it all out on me. It's not fair to me, of course, or to Jerry, but life isn't always fair, is it?"

She looked at me for moment and added, "I suppose doing what you do for a living . . . you already know that, don't you?"

"Yeah," I said. "If life was fair then I'd probably be out of a job. But what's the thing? I mean, why are you here and what do you want me to do?"

"I want you to find my wigs."

With that announcement, my guts joined me in a duet as we both said, "What?" in perfect harmony.

Sarah gave us the answer by saying, "I already mentioned that Carter—that's the kid's name—Carter wants me dead. When I was diagnosed with stomach cancer last January he acted as though his prayers had been answered.

"But there's more. He's been stealing my things. My jewelry, pictures of my family, things like that. He takes them when I am at the doctor's office or having my chemotherapy appointments at the hospital. Whenever I come home, something is missing."

I cut in by saying, "What about your husband, Carter's father? Why isn't he putting the kid in handcuffs and locking him in a closet whenever you both have to leave the house?"

"Because we'd both get arrested for child abuse you idiot," she replied.

It quickly became clear to me that sarcasm was not on her radar.

"Actually," she went on, "Jerry has gotten Carter hooked up with an adolescent psychologist for counseling. Carter treats it as though it was a joke, and I'm not convinced that any good will come from it.

"That's not why I'm here. It's about my wigs—fourteen hundred dollars worth of wigs. Because of Carter, I've been reduced to wearing this stupid knit cap that I took from his bedroom. Fair's fair, even if it isn't fair. I don't really want the cap. I just want my wigs back but I don't know where he put them. I can't believe he would have pawned them or thrown them away. They're hidden somewhere, I'm sure of it, but I don't know where to look and Carter isn't saying anything about anything. When I talk to him, he just sits or else he stands with his hands in his pockets and a big, leering sneer on his face. Sometimes, when I'm through talking and turn to walk away he actually laughs at me out loud.

"I've told Jerry if Carter doesn't wise up and come clean, I'm going to demand he be turned over to Family Services and placed with a foster family."

I had noticed her dull, dry eyes had begun to get all misty. As soon as she said the words "foster family" the waterhole in the desert oasis sprung a leak, and it took four of five of my ever-present tissues to keep the tears from joining the spit that was still soaking into my carpet.

After getting her eyes looking dull and dry again, Sarah summarized the whole thing by saying, "I want my wigs back. I will pay you to find them. Jerry knows I'm here. He asked me to tell you that under no circumstance are you to slap Carter around or threaten him with anything. That is the only restriction I'm putting on you. I need those wigs and I want them as soon as you can find them.

"Well?" she asked. "Do you want the job? Is it something you can do? 'Yes?' or 'No?'"

I looked at my watch. I looked at my pocket calendar. I pulled out my smart phone and I wished the lady had never come into my office. I didn't need the money at the moment but, for no reason I could think of, I figured I could check the wig thing out this afternoon and, if necessary, tomorrow morning, too. If nothing turned up, I would just have to call it quits.

I told her what I was thinking and noted that the time limitation was the only restriction I would be inscribing on my half of the contract.

"So," I concluded, "if you say 'Yes' then I'll say it, too."

She nodded, we shook hands, we discussed my fee, we both signed a boilerplate form with the details scribbled on it, and then she left.

I phoned Mona and told her I would be tied up until Noon the next day and she said, "Just get it over and done with. I don't want to wait until the rehearsal to see you again. How about if you drop by the store when I take off for lunch tomorrow?"

"Sure," I said. "I'll be there."

She couldn't see it, but my fingers were crossed when I said, "Sure."

The burrito was still doing its thing so there was no reason to grab lunch. My headache, however, was still on full volume. I thought about closing my eyes, getting down on the floor and lying on my back for a few minutes to see if that would help, but Sarah had spit in the middle of the only place in my office where there was enough space for me to lie down. So I closed my eyes and leaned back in my desk chair, instead.

When I work, I do not multi-task very well. One thing at a time is all I can manage. When I'm in my office I'm always doing something like sorting the mail, making calls or talking to clients. Sitting at my desk with my eyes closed opened up the possibility of noticing things I usually tuned out. Sound, apparently, was one of them.

As I sat with my eyes closed doing nothing, the sounds of the building began to vibrate in my ears. I could hear the sounds of feet going up and down the stairs; the sound of voices in the neighboring rooms; the sound of my battery-powered clock ticking across the room on the wall next to my office door.

It wasn't long before other sounds began to drown out the sounds of the building. The sounds of the street outside my office window began to pulse and throb in perfect counterpoint to the pulsing and throbbing in my skull. The sound of cars, trucks and busses with engines revving, horns blaring and brakes squealing joined with the sound of bicycle bells, police whistles and sirens of all kinds. There was the sound of someone trying to whistle down a cab and there was the deep, subterranean rumble of the subway, rolling like thunder two blocks away.

I was surrounded by life . . . a magical and almost mystical sort of life that only cities like New York are capable of generating. As if in a moment of enlightenment or cosmic consciousness, I saw myself as being part of something larger, wider, deeper and higher than I had ever imagined before.

As John Donne once said, "No man is an island, entire of itself."

I had read those words many times. I had memorized them, and I had honestly believed them to be true, but until this moment, I had never actually *felt* the truth of those words.

Everything, it seemed, *was* connected to everything else in a complex tapestry of . . . of . . . of what? Of essential nothingness? Or, like an actual tapestry, a purposeful creation of some transcendent, cosmic weaver? A Creator? A maker of the heavens and the earth? A "Ground of All Being" that . . . or *who* . . . had woven Mona and me into the story and had then set us free to add our own chapter to the collective whole? Were we sub-plots in a novel that was so vast and complicated that *War and Peace* would, by comparison, not even qualify as a short story? or as a single comma? Is this what Mona and her

Pastor talk about when they talk about God? Is this who St. Augustine confessed as "the One in whom we live and move and have our being?"

I opened my eyes. The headache was still there and the sounds of the city were still there, but my world, in those few moments, had changed. I had caught a glimpse of something that had been hidden from me for my entire life. Now it was too late to go back.

Either because of my headache or in spite of it, I had seen the soul of the universe and it had seen me. There was nothing to be done. I no longer thought. I *knew*.

If I had been in a movie, the script would have called for me to fall down on my knees with tears streaming down my face. That, of course, didn't happen. Instead, I checked to make sure my handgun was still safe and secure in my desk drawer. I turned off the lights. I locked the door behind me, and I set out to see if I could find Sarah's wigs.

As I headed over to her place on the 200 block of East 61st I started thinking about the "connectedness of all things." I started thinking about what sort of connectedness there was with her family—the threads that wove them into their own private tapestry. There was Sarah, of course, and Jerry. There was Carter and there was Carter's mother . . . .

That was it. She was the missing thread. Carter's mother was the one person who tied all the pieces together. As Yogi Berra once said, "It was *déjà vu* all over again."

For the second time in the last few minutes, I was no longer thinking—I was knowing.

Carter's mother either had the wigs already, or was going to have them very, very soon.

There was something I needed to know as soon as possible. I called Sarah as I was walking across 65th Street.

When she answered, I asked, "This is Mike Maurison. When is the next time Carter meets with his mother?"

The timing turned out to be perfect.

"They meet every Wednesday. When school is in session, they meet for dinner. During the summer they get together somewhere for brunch."

"Are they scheduled to meet tomorrow?"

The warp and the woof of the tapestry merged seamlessly together as she said, "Yes, as a matter of fact they are. Is that important for some reason?"

"Yes," I said. "I think it will turn out to be very important.

"By the way," I added, "do you have any idea where they are going to meet? Or when?"

"Not exactly," Sarah replied. "But the last few Wednesdays, Carter has left the apartment around 9:30 and has gotten back by Noon or a little after. I get the feeling they don't always meet at the same place. If you want to know, you can ask Carter. He's right here if you want to talk with him."

"No thanks," I said. "Don't tell him I called. Don't even tell him I exist. I was going to stop by and look around your apartment this afternoon but I think I'll wait and see what happens tomorrow at brunch. Thanks."

A few minutes later, I was walking along 61st Street in front of the building Sarah, Jerry and Carter lived in. The street was one-way heading west and there was overnight parking on the left-hand side. Parking, however, was only allowed until 11:00 a.m. which would be fine if Carter happened to be picked up by his mother in a car and I could follow them in mine. On the other hand, if I had to leave the car in order follow Carter on foot my car would get ticketed and towed before I got back. It seemed the absence of a place to park was putting a crimp in my list of options.

Most of the buildings on the street had steps leading up to the front door. The steps that were not under trees were, of course, cleaner than the rest. After looking around, I found one that didn't need to be scraped with a putty knife and sat down to think.

This is what I thought:

The person designated to supervise the visits would probably have a stopwatch to keep the time within the allotted two hours. Unless the supervisor was sitting in the same car as Carter's mother there was no legal way the mother could pick him up at the curb by herself. It was also unlikely the mother would want to waste the little time she had by driving to and from a restaurant and trying to find a place to park. Because of these two things, I figured the place they were going to eat had to be nearby and within walking distance.

If that was true, then I wouldn't need a car to follow Carter to wherever he was going to have brunch. Since he had never met me before—and didn't even know I existed—it would not be a hard thing for me to follow him down the street on foot. I could even sit at a table right next to them and eavesdrop if I wanted to. If the rendezvous for brunch didn't solve the case then I would just tell Sarah I had done my best, that time had run out, and that it was time for me to turn my attention to some important personal matters such as meeting Mona for lunch.

I decided I had done everything I could do for the moment. This gave me lots of time to get back to the clothes in my apartment and start separating the wheat from the chaff, while putting the wheat safely away in what the old Dutch hymn calls a "garner." I have no idea what a garner is, but if the wheat is supposed to go into it then that's where I figure I should put mine.

It was only two o'clock and to my surprise, I could no longer feel the burrito hibernating in my stomach. Since I had the time and still had the desire, I walked over to Lexington, bought a package of roasted, salted peanuts at a pharmacy and ate them on the way back to my apartment.

After putting all the clothes that were not on hangers into a big pile on my bed it didn't take me long to decide which ones I wanted to keep, which ones I wanted to give or throw away, and which ones I wanted to take on our honeymoon. The clothes hanging in the closet were another matter altogether. The fact they were hanging in my closet did not necessarily mean they were my best clothes. What it means is they are not the clothes I wear most of the time. Most of them are too worn out, or they don't fit, or they are so out of style I could put them on consignment at a retro clothing store.

By the time I was finished, almost everything in the closet had found its way into the throwaway pile. I kept most of my t-shirts and underwear except for the ones that had so many holes they were no longer safe to wear. As for socks, I kept all the ones that matched and set the rest aside to use as rags when I started cleaning the place up before I moved out.

I inherited most of my pots, pans and other kitchen things from my father. There were a few I could remember my mother using so I decided to keep those. As for the rest, except for two professional quality knives and a nearly new, heavy-duty grater I had purchased on a whim from Broadway Panhandler, Mona's stuff was a lot better than mine.

I also wanted to keep most of my books, my music collection, my parents' dresser and, as I mentioned earlier, my flat screen TV and microwave. There were toiletry items I needed to keep, but everything else had to go, including all of the pre-packaged consumable items in the fridge and the cupboards. This was an easy decision since most of them had long outlived their expiration dates anyway.

My apartment was a relatively large studio with the bed set apart from everything else in a back-wall corner. Since I was going to be sleeping in the bed for a few more days, I left it where it was. I pushed all the disposable furniture together in the living area and started stuffing the clothes and other things into boxes and bags I had collected since Mona decided she would rather swim across the Atlantic than move into my apartment after we got married.

When I looked at my watch, I was surprised to find it was already past eight o'clock. Rather than eat out I micro waved a fried chicken TV dinner and ate an ice cream sandwich for desert. As always, I was profoundly grateful for my freezer. Without it, I would never have survived all these years as a bachelor.

After killing time watching an old movie, I turned in for the night. To my relief, my headache had disappeared. As I was falling asleep, I could hear the muffled sounds of my building intermingled with the all-transcendent sound of Manhattan, living, moving, and being what it is.

Six blocks away, knotted alongside me in the tapestry of creation, was Mona. Although there was no way I could have known it, Mona was also in bed, thinking of me. We fell asleep within minutes of each other; each dreaming dreams that joined our smiles together as one.

Chapter 10
Of Beds & Sofas

Wednesday, July 10

I skipped breakfast figuring I would probably eat something while Carter and his mother were having brunch. After a quick shave, I grabbed a box filled with junk and threw it in a dumpster on my way out.

I arrived at 61st Street at 9:00 sharp, hoping Carter hadn't broken his routine and left for an early breakfast instead of a late brunch. At 9:40, I was starting to get anxious. Just as I was thinking about calling Sarah, the front door opened and Carter came bounding down the steps wearing a small backpack.

He headed west in the same direction I had walked the day before, but Carter turned south on Third Avenue for two blocks before heading west on 59th. Halfway down the block he slipped into Bloomingdale's and stopped to talk with two women outside the entrance to the Burke Bar Café. One of the women went in and sat down at a table by herself while the other woman and Carter found a table on the other side of the restaurant. Lucky for me, the place had just opened at 10:00

and there was a vacant table next to the one occupied by Carter and the woman I assumed was his mother.

As soon as I sat I tried to listen, but there was too much clattering in the place to hear what they were saying. To make it even more difficult they were leaning across the table with their heads close together, whispering. They ordered first and the waitress took my order next. In a surprisingly short amount of time, Carter was digging into a stack of Belgian Waffles and his mother began nibbling on the same omelet I had ordered.

My watch said 10:35 when Carter bent over and picked up his backpack. After unzipping it, he pulled out a bag that looked as though it had barely fit inside the pack. With a big smile on his face, he reached in the bag and pulled out what looked like a wig. He held it up for his mother to see and pointed into the bag as if he was describing what else was there. After he handed the wig across the table, Mom put it on her head and the two of them started laughing. As they stood up, Carter's mother dropped the wigs in into a large Bloomingdale's bag she had brought with her. Carter put on his empty backpack and after leaving some money on the table, they walked out of the restaurant followed by both the visitation supervisor and me.

As they wandered through the vast expanse of Bloomingdale's I waited until they passed within ten feet of a store security guard. As I walked up to Carter and his Mom, I caught the attention of the guard and waved at him to come over.

As the two of us converged, I stepped up and said, "Good morning. My name is Mike Maurison. I am a Private Investigator and I am placing you both under arrest. Carter, I am arresting you on a charge of theft, and you . . . " I turned to his mother, " . . . I am arresting you for receiving stolen property."

Carter and his Mom looked like the proverbial deer caught in the headlights.

Turning to the security guard I said, "Sir, if you will be so good as to assist me in holding them in custody until the police arrive, I would be most grateful."

The guard had a direct line to the NYPD and called for someone to come over right away.

The visitation supervisor came up demanding to know what was going on.

What I said was, "I am so sorry, but it looks as though their time together might be longer than two hours this morning."

In just a few minutes, two police officers arrived and listened to what everyone had to say. They looked at the wigs, checked everyone's ID and issued us all an invitation to join them at the 19th Precinct Station whether we wanted to go or not.

After Carter and his mother had their rights read to them, the police cuffed and placed them in the back of a squad car. While they were driving away, the security guard met with his boss who gave him permission to join the visitation supervisor and me in following the squad car to the station, eight blocks north on 67th just off of Lexington.

We found a cab, and while we were turning right onto Lexington, I called up Sarah and asked her to meet us at the station as soon as possible. Since the wigs were hers, she needed to identify them in order to confirm they were stolen.

"Thank God you found them," she said. "And what a mess this is going to be."

Before we hung up, I encouraged her to phone Jerry at wherever it was he worked, and if he was close enough, she should ask him to come over to the station, too.

By the time I hung up, our cab had pulled up to the curb. I insisted on paying the tab and, since I was going to be reimbursed, I added a decent tip.

It took about two hours for everybody to sort it out. Soon after the Bloomingdale's guard and the supervision lady left, Carter was booked for theft and his mother was booked for receiving stolen property. Then the two of them were placed in separate holding cells until someone decided what to do with them.

The police eventually released Carter to his father's custody in time for dinner, and after calling her lawyer, Carter's mom enjoyed an overnight stay in the pokey.

It was now 1:00 p.m. and once again, I had stood up Mona—this time leaving my bride-to-be standing at the sidewalk altar in front of the bookstore. I knew Mona well enough to know she wouldn't bother to give me a call to ask where I was or why I hadn't shown up. In any case, I suspected that with her super-powered eyes, she had seen me cross my fingers when I had set up the date over the phone and never really expected me to show up in the first place.

While we were still at the police station, I called her. When she didn't answer I left a lame message saying I was sorry.

"Mona, I love you, and I'll take you out to dinner tonight to atone for my sin if you're free to go."

Sarah, the wigs and I went back to her place to settle accounts. By three o'clock, I was finished.

With four un-cashed checks in my pocket, I felt wealthy enough to call a cab instead of walking the twelve blocks to my bank on 79th. I had negotiated three of the checks with my clients and already knew what they were. The fourth check was from Bert "the Intimidator." When I had first taken it out of the envelope it came in, I had stuck it in my wallet without even looking at it.

Now that the check was sitting on the counter in front of me, it became clear Bert hadn't been joking when he said he was willing to pay me a lot of dough if I would stop bothering him. Even if Mona and I used the check to pay for our entire honeymoon there would still be enough left over to cover the cleaning deposit and the first and last month's rent on our new apartment.

Maybe Mona would forgive me after all.

After putting some of the money in our checking account, some of it in our savings account, and some of it back in my wallet, I decided to walk the three blocks over to *Books and Things* to see Mona.

When I got there, she was gone. When I tracked down the manager, she told me Mona left for lunch and never came back.

"I thought she was having lunch with you. At least that's what she told me before she left. What happened? Is everything all right?"

All I could think of to say was, "I don't know. I really don't know."

"Well," she added, handing me a gift with a card on it. "We were going to have a little going-away party for her at the end of the day but it looks like we'll have to eat the cake by ourselves. If you'll wait a minute I'll give you a piece to take with you."

I waited until she came back with not one, but two pieces of cake lying side-by-side on a wedding shower paper plate wrapped in cellophane.

"Here's one for you, too. Tell her we love her and we'll see her at the wedding."

I thanked her and said I would give the gift and the cake to Mona when I found out where she was.

Outside the store, I tried phoning Mona several more times but she didn't or wouldn't answer. In a near panic, I scrambled over to her apartment, buzzing and banging to no avail. Not knowing what else to do or where to go, I phoned Corinne, hoping against hope she knew what was going on.

Corinne, apparently, had put my name and number on her phone because she seemed to know who had called before I even had a chance to say anything.

"Well hello there, Mike," she oozed, "how nice of you to call."

I could tell from the tone of her voice that as far as she was concerned I was no longer the most popular groom in the greater New York metropolitan area.

"How nice of you to answer," I shot back. "Do you know where Mona is? Is she all right?"

There was a long pause before Corinne was ready to give an answer.

"I suppose if you had shown up for lunch you would have known where she was. Afterwards, she would have gone back to the store and finished her final shift and you would have known where she was then, too, but you didn't and so she didn't either. I think it's all right for me to tell you she's not dead, drunk or in a hospital, but it's up to Mona to decide whether to tell you anything else. So good-bye. If Mona decides to come I'll see you at the rehearsal . . . if you're able to make it."

When Corinne hung up I was still breathing, but the conversation was DOA.

Curiously enough, when I had started talking to Corinne I was standing on a public sidewalk in the middle of Manhattan. When I had finished talking to Corinne, I was sitting in a doghouse.

New York . . . what a town.

After considering the possibilities, I began to suspect Mona had left to be with her parents in New Jersey. The way I saw it, Mona realized she was under more stress than she could handle. She may have imagined she was coming down with a case of cold feet, maybe even questioning whether getting married was what she really wanted to be doing.

The more I thought about this the more I became convinced that whatever was going on with Mona didn't have very much to do with me at all. She had shown me in so many different ways she loved me and was eager to marry me warts and all. When I failed to show up for our lunch date it all must have come crashing down on her. My guess was there was something important she needed to tell me, something she wanted to discuss right then and not later. Maybe she panicked and felt desperate enough to climb onto her own personal fire escape where all the ladders led directly to her mother.

If I was wrong about any or all of this it didn't really matter. But, if I was right, then I needed to be as gentle and patient and supportive of Mona as I could. Just as Bergie had needed Mona more than me the night her beauty salon was burglarized, Mona probably needed her mother more than she needed me. I had always hoped I would be all things for Mona. But even though I have become the most important person in her life, I am beginning to realize there will always be other people important to her in ways I can never be.

Ever since I met her, Mona has been all I have ever wanted and everything I have ever needed in my life. This may be true for me, it isn't fair to assume she feels the same way about me. There is nothing wrong with the way either of us feel about each other. I am just going to have to learn to live with it. *Vive la difference.*

I wound up deciding the best thing for me to do was to send a text message.

Mona, Corinne wouldn't tell me where you are but she did tell me you were all right . . . at least physically. I want you to know how much I love you and how sorry I am I didn't get back in time for lunch. I have now cleared my calendar and have cleaned and locked up my office. I have also started getting ready for our trip and getting my apartment ready for when I move out. I want you to know the next three weeks of my life belong entirely to you. "I can do all things through him who strengthens me." You can too. Love, Mike

After I pushed "send," I started thinking that maybe I have been getting too religious lately. It is, of course, all Mona's fault.

For me, at least, her faith has been like a communicable disease. It's not as if she's trying to convert me or anything, it's just that the closer I get to her the more it seems to rub off. But so what? If that's the price I have to pay for being with Mona then I can't think of any reason to complain.

After sending the text, there was nothing more I could do but wait for Mona to call me back. In the meantime, my hands and arms were getting tired from trying to juggle the cake and the gift without dropping one or both of them all over the sidewalk. I waved down a cab and crawled back to my cluttered and unkempt cave.

The first thing on my agenda was to wash my clothes. There were too many of them to do all at once so I did some triage and stuffed the dirtiest ones into a duffle bag. The laundromat was just around the corner from Thor. After the wash, rinse and spin cycles were over, I decided that walking over to see what Thor was doing would be a better use of my time than watching my underwear spin around through the little window on the drier,.

"Say hey, Mike," Thor said as I made my entrance. "Wassup?"

"Nothing much, except that I'm getting married and going to Europe in four days. How about you?"

"About the same," he said, "except for the part about getting married and going to Europe."

"Thor, I want to thank you again for giving me my Samurai sword back. It has always been a highly valued part of my life."

"Sure," said Thor, "just like all those fake diamonds you foisted on me last year. If you remember, I gave those back to you, too."

"The diamonds didn't cost you anything," I reminded him. "They were a gift of love to you from the bottom of my heart. The sword, however . . . if you remember . . . you paid me for the sword. That's why I was glad to get it back. If I ever need another loan, I know I can count on you to take it back in exchange for some cash like you did the last time."

"Forget it," Thor grumbled. "The thing sat in my window for four years and nobody even made an offer for it. The only good thing about it is that, for a fake sword, it has a decent edge on the blade. You might be interested to know that last Thanksgiving I used it to carve the turkey."

I groaned at the joke. The blade was a dull as a commencement speaker. I knew it would have been easier for

Thor to tear the turkey apart with his bare hands than to try hacking and sawing it to pieces with the sword.

"Nice talking to you," I waved as I turned to go back where I came from. "I have an important appointment to collect my clothes from the laundromat."

I turned my head in his direction and added, "Will I see you at the wedding on Sunday?"

Thor looked up from the tray of old coins he had been sorting through when I had walked in.

"Since you took the trouble to have a reception, I've decided to go to the trouble of showing up. Oh, and before I forget, thanks for not bringing anything in to hock."

I turned to leave for the second time, but Thor wasn't done.

"By the way," he said, "remember the sledgehammer that's been sitting next to your sword in the front window? Last week I actually sold it to a lady who looked exactly like Brünnhilde in *Seigfreid*."

"Would you like it back?" I said. "I don't think she wants or needs it anymore."

"No hurry," he said. "I can wait 'til the fat lady sings."

With another groan I let him have the last word and went back to get my clothes before I started seeing them walking down the sidewalk on the backs of complete strangers.

As I carried the laundry back to the apartment I looked at my watch. It was well past dinnertime and I still hadn't heard from Mona. I was feeling sorry for her, feeling sorry for myself, wishing I had been able to meet her for lunch, and feeling responsible for being part of whatever had caused her to ride off into the sunset and disappear.

When I opened the freezer, I couldn't find so much as a bag of frozen peas. I was faced with the choice of starving to death, pretending I was fasting for Lent, calling in a pizza delivery, or eating out. The decision was too much for me so I folded the laundry, wiped the dust from the top of the coffee table with an unmatched sock, and stacked my folded clothes and underwear where the dust had been.

At that point, my guts started grumbling and commanded me to go get some food ASAP. I walked down the street to a sushi place and washed down a half-dozen California Rolls and a half-dozen assorted tempura vegetables with a Japanese beer. I was just adding up the bill when my phone rang. It was Mona.

"Mike," she said. "I'm sorry I dropped out of sight. I guess what I really did was run away. I've been feeling so overwhelmed by everything. I thought I could do it all but I was wrong. I was going to talk to you about it at lunch but when you didn't show up I panicked. I needed to talk to somebody and the only person I could think of was my Mom. I didn't even phone the store to tell them I wasn't coming back and they had a party planned for me and I feel so stupid I don't know how I can ever go back."

I could hear her crying. I wanted to take her in my arms and love her. I wanted to wave a magic wand and make everything happy and beautiful again. Yet I knew the only thing Mona needed was for me to be with her. She didn't need words, she just wanted me.

Because I love her so much I found myself doing the impossible. As I stood leaning against the back wall of a Japanese sushi restaurant holding a phone to my ear I did nothing and said nothing while I listened to the most important person in my life weep tears I could not wipe away.

After a few minutes when the weeping stopped and all I could hear was random sniffling I said in a voice that was as soft and gentle as possible, "Mona. When you feel you are ready, come home. I will be here. I will be waiting for you. And I will love you."

There was another sniffle and then a pause.

"Mike, I love you, too. I think I'll spend the night with my parents. I'll be in my old bedroom and my old bed. There is something calming and reassuring about that, but you're right. My home isn't here anymore. It's with you. I'll come back in the morning. We can talk then. Did I say that I love you? If I didn't . . . I love you. Good-night Mike, and thank you for being . . . for being you. Bye."

"I love you, too, and I'll see you tomorrow. Bye."

When I got back to my apartment, I stood inside the door looking at a scene of domestic destruction that would have made Oscar Madison proud. The whole place was a mess. There was no doubt about it. But it was *my* mess. The idea that it would soon be gone was a hard thing to grasp. In a sense, the mess was the closest thing I had to a photo album. Each piece of detritus triggered memories of my past . . . memories soon to be lost and gone forever . . . swept away by a broom.

In the middle of the mess was my sofa. For some reason, during the mindless sorting of my stuff into "sheep" and "goats" I had failed to put it into either one flock or the other. Now that I thought about it, there was no doubt in my mind it was a lamb that had strayed and needed to be brought back into the fold.

My sofa has been an important part of my life since I was eighteen. After my father died, I couldn't afford the rent he had been paying on our two-bedroom apartment so I was forced to move out and look for someplace smaller. I found the sofa where someone had abandoned it on a sidewalk in front of an apartment building on West 94th Street, about 22 blocks north of where I had been living on the Upper West Side

One of the reasons this sofa is still so special is because of its association with those formative years. My father had a deep and passionate love for music and for all things theatrical. Because our home was close to Lincoln Center, my father and I became a familiar sight at the low-cost dress rehearsal performances of the New York Philharmonic and the Metropolitan Opera.

Just to the east of us was the Museum of Natural History where because of my age I had free admission. It was there, under the posthumous spell of the museum's legendary Director and paleontologist, Roy Chapman Andrews, that I enjoyed a short-lived love affair with fossils.

As the years passed, a love of art replaced my interest in fossils. It didn't take me long, even as a child, to discover it was easier to have a conversation with a pastel by Cassatt or an oil by Manet than with a dinosaur egg from Mongolia or a pterodactyl from Bavaria.

Even so, the dinosaurs taught me what a magical place a museum can be. I have been an inveterate denizen of museums ever since.

When I began living on my own, the sofa was the only bed I could afford. Now, thirteen years later, it is an over worn, malodorous shadow of its former self. Still, it is what it is. It is my teddy bear and my comfort blanket all rolled into one. It is my place of refuge, my tower and my strength. Mona once pointed out that those are attributes of God. Her comment has stayed with me, and even now, as I stood surrounded by memories, the image of God as a sofa made me smile.

The day had been long and emotionally draining. The wedding, the honeymoon, and Mona's disappearance had taken their toll on me, so without even thinking about it, I pushed everything off of the sofa, climbed on, curled up, and fell asleep with my clothes on. Mona had her old bed to sleep in and I had my . . . well . . . you know.

Chapter 11
Coming Clean
Thursday, July 11

I woke earlier than usual and after getting up, I put all the junk back on top of the sofa. I changed my clothes, dropped the used ones onto the "honeymoon" pile and took the pile down to the Laundromat. My plan was to get the clothes clean so I could practice trying to squeeze them into a suitcase that wouldn't require a forklift to put it on the plane.

During the wash, rinse and spin cycle I backtracked past my apartment and went down the street to Juan's corner market to pick up some breakfast.

"*Guten tag*" I said when I spotted Juan standing in the chips and dips aisle.

"*Halle tosis*," he shot back with a smile.

I wasn't sure if he had mangled something or whether he was pulling my leg so I just said, "Same to you, Juan."

As I stood at the counter paying for coffee and a box of powdered sugar mini-donuts, I asked him if he wanted to come to a wedding on Sunday afternoon.

"Who is having a wedding? He asked.

"Me," I said. "I'm getting married. If you want to come, you can be my guest."

"Oh," he said. "That is really good. I am happy for you. How do you say . . . congrat . . ."

I helped him finish the word by saying, " . . .ulations. Why thank you very much, Juan. Can you come?"

"Sunday I work. Seven day a week I work except when my cousin come. Then I can have time with my family. Mike, sorry I can't come. Here's your change. Congratulations."

"*Halle tosis*," I said as I walked out the door.

I was sorry Juan couldn't make it to the wedding. He might have helped my family and guests spill over into a second pew.

Mona phoned while my clothes were in the drier.

"Where are you?" she asked.

"Washing my clothes," I said.

"It's about time," she poked.

That's when I knew the old Mona was back.

"I just had breakfast."

"Oh," Mona said with a sigh. "I thought we could meet at Neil's. Isn't it a little early for you to be up and around and eating breakfast already?"

"Not when I'm eager to rendezvous with my bride-to-be. Let me finish what I'm doing and I'll be there in a half-hour. I will be there. I promise, promise, promise and no fingers crossed."

I expect Mona was somewhat baffled by the "fingers crossed" comment, but she came through like a trooper when she said, "Okay. Bye."

Since the clothes I had just washed were the ones I wanted to take on our European honeymoon, I didn't want to stuff them back into the duffel bag, so I folded them as neatly as I could and put them in a cardboard box someone had left behind. When the box was full, whatever was left went into the bag. The box went on top of the bag and I carried the whole pile up to my apartment before heading over to Neil's and Mona.

Mona was already sitting in a booth when I walked in. After bending over and giving her a kiss I sat and told her about all the money I had raked in during the past few days.

She was so impressed that she stood up, leaned over the table, and gave me a kiss, too.

"It sounds like you're going to treat for breakfast. Am I right?"

Mona didn't look like someone who had just missed a nervous breakdown by a few inches. In fact, she was smiling a smile that would have put the other, more famous *Mona* to shame.

I ordered an orange juice and a toasted Danish with butter. Mona ordered a bowl of plain yoghurt with fresh fruit.

"I've got to make sure I can fit into my dress on Sunday," she explained.

"My tux comes with an elastic waistband and suspenders," I replied. "I'm looking forward to the reception so I can expand my horizons."

"Just don't overdo it or I won't be able to squeeze in next to you on the plane."

"Well?" I asked. "What did your Mom say that brought you back from the dead?"

Mona's smile faded a bit when she heard the question, but instead of dumping her yoghurt on my head, she did her best to answer it.

"Mom let me cry, and she let me say everything that I had to get out of my head and my heart. She calmed me down and made me feel safe. I guess that's what moms are for."

Her smile faded even more as she looked at me with sad eyes. I knew she was thinking she had really screwed up with the "that's what moms are for" comment. Mona knows how my Mom dumped my Dad and me and then disappeared . . . just like Mona did yesterday, but with one difference: Mona came back. My mother never did.

"Mona," I said. "It's all right. What you said is all right."

"I am so sorry," Mona said. "I shouldn't have said that, or I shouldn't have said it that way. I'm . . . ."

"I said, 'Its all right.' What your mom did is what moms are *supposed* to do. Mine just wasn't able to do what moms are supposed to do, and I sort of struck out before I even had a chance to swing a bat. But you, Mona, you and your mom hit a home run, and that's good. It's okay. I'm glad for it, and I'm glad for your mom, just like I'm glad for you.

"So, tell me more about what your mom said that changed you back to the old Mona?"

"That's just it," she replied. "I don't think I am the 'old Mona.' The old Mona hadn't made up her mind about a lot of things, including getting married. That doesn't mean I've been putting on an act or trying to mislead you or anything like that. I really do love you and want to be married to you and share in all the things that go along with it. I guess it was just the whole idea of marriage I wasn't sure about. I wasn't convinced I was going to be any good at it. I wasn't sure I was going to be good enough for you.

"The thing is," she continued, "it wasn't my Mom who helped me get through this, it was my Dad. You see, after Mom calmed me down Dad came over and sat next to me. Dad is a lot like you, Mike. He doesn't do well when other people are crying. Especially when the person is me. So, after I stopped crying, that's when he came over.

"After he sat down he didn't say anything at first, but then he turned and looked me straight in the eye and said, 'Mona, you don't have to be the best wife or be good at being married and you don't need to get all stressed out about whatever it is that marriage is supposed to be. You just have to be Mona. That's all Mike wants. He doesn't want you to be a good wife, he wants you to be Mona. That's all. And since you are already Mona, well there you go! You're already there!'"

"That was it," Mona said in a soft, almost inaudible whisper. "That's all he said. It all sounded too easy to me—too simple, maybe, but that has been my problem all along. I've been making everything too complicated: the wedding, the reception, the dresses, the flowers. It was messing me up and keeping me from just being me. Dad was right. It took me most of the night to figure it out, but when I woke up this morning it was as if I was Mona for the very first time in my life. Am I making any sense?"

As Mona was talking about her mom and her dad, I was fighting back tears. I had said "It's all right," and in some sense it was. In another sense, though, it wasn't all right at all. I never had parents who were able to do what Mona's parents had done for her last night.

All I have for a family is a collection of imaginary people hanging on walls; people without arms to hold me or hearts to actually love me. I had always thought these paintings had become more or less just like me: alive, wise, and kind, but as Mona was talking I realized that instead of the paintings becoming more like me, I had been denying who I was by trying to become more like them. I had become good at being as two-dimensional as possible. I liked being that way: Being invisible to everyone; being alone as much as possible; being as distant and impersonal as possible while boxing myself into my own personal picture frame; being liked and admired, not for who I am, but for the image I have created of myself, flat and shallow, with no depth, and going nowhere.

Maybe Mona's Dad was right about me, too. Maybe it was time for me to step back into the world of three-dimensions and learn how to be as comfortable with people as I have been with those paintings.

Without being aware of it, ever since we met, Mona has been drawing me out of my fantasy and back into life and love in a world I had turned my back on for far too long. I, on the other hand, have been trying to drag her down into my world of brush strokes, daubs of paint and ancient, aging canvas. Because she loves me so much, Mona has been willing to step into that world with me, but that isn't where she belongs. Although it's not easy to admit, it isn't where I really belong, either.

Maybe there needs to be a new Mike who can stand next to the new Mona. When we say, "I do" to each other, maybe the old can pass away and the new can come. Maybe it's time for me to leave my past behind and start a new future with Mona.

Something touched my shoulders and gave them a little shake. I had drifted off into a sort of mind-meld with myself and needed a poke of some sort to bring me back. As it turned out it wasn't a hand that shook me or poked me, it was a question; but what was the question?

I looked at Mona and said, "I'm sorry, but did you just ask me a question?"

Mona didn't seem to miss a beat. "I just asked you if I was making any sense?"

I had no idea if she had been making any sense or not but I remembered that what she said about her father had made more sense than I could handle.

So I said, "Yes. You made perfect sense," even though I might have fudged my answer just a little.

Now that Mona had finished her yoghurt, I pulled out the piece of cake from a bag I had brought with me.

"This is what you missed yesterday," I said. "I don't think there is enough of it to pop any buttons on your dress. Besides, you owe it to your friends to eat it."

Mona smiled a big smile and said, "Maybe they like me after all!"

That was when I pulled the gift and the card out of the bag.

"I think they like you even more than that!"

Mona grabbed the gift and ripped it open with the same refined decorum that a cheetah displays when taking down a zebra on the African savannah.

"Ooooohhhh," she said excitedly as she held up a somewhat mismatched pair of salt- and peppershakers.

The saltshaker seemed to bear some resemblance to Marian the Librarian, with horned-rimmed glasses pulled down on her nose and an open book in her hands. The peppershaker was, of course—and without any doubt—Nigel Rathbone as Sherlock Holmes.

"Oooooohhhhh," she said a second time. "These are perfect! They're going to go on top of the wedding cake! They're perfect!"

"Why don't we walk over to the bookstore so you can say "Thank you" to your friends in person?"

"After yesterday," Mona replied, "I don't really want to, but you're right. I might as well get it over with."

Less than five minutes later we were standing in the bookstore surrounded by the whole staff who were giving Mona hugs and kisses and whatever else women give each other when they are really, really glad to see one another.

While Mona was saying "Thank you" to her friends, anyone with larcenous intent could have pulled up a van and packed out the entire "Mystery and Suspense" section without anyone noticing.

Someone asked Mona if I had given her the piece of cake from her party and then someone else asked if she would put pepper in the librarian figure if she was having a bad day.

There was lots of laughing until Mona put up her hand and said, "That's probably enough. Remember, we're supposed to be paid for selling books. Mike and I have lots to do before Sunday, including the rehearsal on Saturday, so . . . I hope to see you at the wedding! I love you!"

All the staff yelled, "We love you, too."

At that point, the love-in ended and the Woodstock farmlands returned to their usual bare, boring and muddy glory.

As we walked back to Mona's apartment I purchased a single red rose from a man selling flowers on the sidewalk.

Quoting one of Shakespeare's sonnets I declared, "As the noble Bard of Avon once said, 'My love is like—' like this!" and I handed the rose to Mona with a flourish.

Once again, Mona's degree in English Literature helped make my wooing a winner! My reward was a kiss in broad daylight with a standing ovation from ten or twelve otherwise indifferent, nearby pedestrians.

Back at the apartment, Mona had already sorted out her things in the orderly, practical way women are known for. All the clothes she was taking on our honeymoon were either hanging in her closet or folded on a shelf. The clothes she was not taking were already packed away in boxes neatly stacked along one side of her room. The clothes she wasn't going to keep had already been picked over by Corinne and Brin and were sitting in the living room stuffed into 50-gallon garbage bags. Her bedroom furniture and her living room chair were all clean, empty and dusted.

The whole thing was amazing. Mona was all ready to go. She had already packed her suitcase for the trip to make sure everything fit, and had taken all the clothes out again so they wouldn't get more wrinkled than necessary. If I was Oscar Madison then Mona was Felix Unger. Mona and Mike: *The Odd Couple*.

Corinne and Brin had already arranged with their landlord for Mona to overstay her lease by a week while we moved our stuff into our new apartment. My landlord had also been kind enough to give me an extra three days to stay in my studio after we got back from our trip.

I asked if Mona would come over and help do the same fine, professional packing at my place that she had done at hers.

"No thanks," she said. "I feel good about myself because of what I've done. I would hate to steal that same sense of satisfaction away from you."

"How's the rehearsal dinner coming together?" I asked, realizing I had allowed myself to fall completely out of the loop from all the wedding preparations Mona's family and friends had been working so hard to put together.

"Mom has it all set. When we're done with the rehearsal we'll all walk over to Rothmann's Steakhouse and eat a preordered dinner of steak, pasta and salad. We'll all have a good time together and then . . . ."

" . . . and then," I interrupted, "we all go home and everyone sleeps like a baby except for the groom, who spends the night sweating bullets out of fear he'll forget to zip up his pants before the ceremony."

“Exactly right,” said Mona.

“What about the wedding decorations and the reception afterwards?”

“I’m glad you asked. I already told you I was so stressed out over those things that I almost took an AmTrak to Pittsburgh yesterday afternoon,”

“I don’t remember you mentioning that part of the story. Why Pittsburgh?”

“That’s not the point!”

Mona can’t stand it when I shift the subject in the middle of a conversation.

“The point is that yesterday afternoon my Mom said I should just forget about all of it. She said I had done everything I needed to do and that if there were any loose ends she and Pam would take care of them. And that is one reason I am a new Mona today!”

I offered a small burst of applause for the brief but inspirational message and kissed her until she pushed me away to keep from suffocating.

“That,” she said, “was disgusting!”

“Yes,” I said. “and I cannot think of anybody else I would rather be disgusting with than you!”

Mona gave me a series of shoves until I was outside her apartment door.

“Go home, clean up and pack right now . . . today. I want you to be ready to fly away with me at a moment’s notice. I do not want to travel with you if you have all your things stuffed into that stinky duffle bag you use with your dirty laundry. Now get out and go home!”

Before I could offer a good comeback, the door was closed in my face. The fact it hadn’t been slammed left me feeling somewhat encouraged as I headed back to my personal mess of memories.

On the way, I grabbed a premade tuna salad sandwich from Juan's place along with a soda and a small bag of chips. Juan was kind enough to give me the chips for free.

"Congratulations. It's a gift for your wedding," he said.

"*Muchas gracias,*" I said, realizing that for Juan, the chip thing was a genuine gesture of affection.

"*Y que tongo a buenos días,*" I added as I left.

Juan knows my Spanish isn't as good as his English, so I could only hope he'd be able to figure out whatever it was I had tried to say.

Yesterday, when I was sorting through my clothes and waiting for Mona to call, I phoned Robert and asked if he could come over today after work and help me clean up my apartment. He said he would be happy to help. I knew he meant it because Robert has been inside my apartment on several occasions and he said "Yes" anyway.

Before he hung up the phone, he asked if I wanted him to bring a shovel. What a pal.

At two o'clock, there was a buzz at my door and Robert walked in.

"I thought you didn't get off work until 5:30." I said.

"I told the boss that something important had come up and I had to leave. One of the guys said he could cover for me so here I am, sleeves rolled up and everything."

"How come you're talking so much when Chia isn't around?" I asked.

"I guess it's because she's here, too." He turned around and yelled, "Come on, Chia. Hurry up and say 'Hi' to Mike!"

Between the two of them they had brought two buckets, a mop, glass cleaner, scrub brushes and a whole bunch of other cleaning stuff I had never seen before."

"We assumed you had a broom," said Chia. "You do have a broom, don't you?"

"Sure, I've got a broom, and I have a vacuum cleaner too, if you really want to know. I'm just not sure where it is . . . ."

Both Robert and Chia looked at each other as if saying, "This is going to be harder than we thought."

"Just kidding," I said. The vacuum is in the closet, on the floor where my clothes used to be.

The next five hours were just as much fun as the proverbial bamboo under the fingernails.

When we were about halfway through, I asked Chia why she was so good at cleaning. She said working at a beauty salon means everybody has to keep busy cleaning and re-cleaning everything over, and over again all day long, every day.

When Robert refused to clean my bathroom, Chia put on her rubber gloves and scraped it clean in no time. What a pro!

While Robert and Chia cleaned, I finished sorting through my clothes. Mona's garbage bag idea turned out to work for me, too. Not only did the old clothes go into the bags but a lot of the old kitchen stuff wound up going into them, too.

When 7:00 p.m. rolled around, the place actually looked as though there might be an outside chance I would get some of my cleaning deposit back when I moved out.

I offered to take them both out to dinner but they said there were lots of things they had to do before the rehearsal and the wedding.

"The excitement starts in just two days, and besides," Chia added, "both of us have to work tomorrow."

When they mentioned the wedding rehearsal, I started to feel nervous and anxious about the wedding for the first time. The rehearsal was just two days away and the wedding the day after that! How could the time have melted away so quickly!

If I had a mom, I probably would have run over to her place like Mona had done with hers. I pictured myself breaking into the MoMA after-hours so I could talk to the mom of my imagination. After remembering I had decided to move myself back into the real world, I dropped the idea of heading off to the museum almost as quickly as I had picked it up. More tempting was the all-embracing comfort of my sofa, but I needed something to hug, and even my sofa wasn't magical enough to pull that one off.

Robert and Chia left, carrying their cleaning things with them. I figured they were probably taking a cab back to their place since carrying all that stuff onto a bus or the subway would probably have looked like something out of a Keystone Kops comedy.

I was glad I had already purchased a small gift to thank Robert for being my Best Man. It was a winter wool scarf, made in the Hebrides and bearing the tartan plaid of the Fraser Clan. I was tempted to put an English penny in the box with a string glued onto it but, to my great relief, I was able to exercise enough self-control to tell myself, "No."

As it turned out, I fell asleep on my bed instead of the sofa. I was so tired I had completely forgotten about dinner. Later, when I realized I hadn't eaten I reckoned I would simply compensate for it by eating more at the rehearsal dinner.

Chapter 12
Exuent Stage Left

Friday, July 12

I woke up in a strange and unfamiliar room. Even before I opened my eyes, there was an odd hygienic smell in the air. Earlier, when I had gotten up during the night, I had, without knowing it walked around clothes and furniture that were no longer in my way. It was, I suppose, the sort of thing that happens when your apartment has been cleaned for the first time in three years.

When I walked into the bathroom, I was surprised to discover I could actually see my face in the mirror. Somehow, instead of looking like the familiar Jackson Pollack forgery painted with accumulated toothpaste splatter, it was clean and clear.

In the kitchen, I noticed my feet didn't stick to the floor anymore, and my carpet had been vacuumed so thoroughly that the stains now stood out clear and bright like the colors in old paintings gleam after the layers of old varnish have been removed.

It seemed a shame I was going to be moving out of my apartment just when the place had become inhabitable again.

Mona and I had arranged to meet for lunch and go over some final details about our trip. What that means is that she will go over a checklist of all the things I'm supposed to have ready. Things like: "Do I have my passport in a place where I won't forget it and so I will have it when we get to the airport?" "Do I have my shaver and did I check to make sure it had a built-in adaptor for direct current?" "Did I contact our credit card company to tell them we would be charging things in Europe for the next two weeks?" That sort of thing.

One thing I have never had to do is make a list of things for Mona to do. Mona always seems to be one or two steps ahead of me with things like that.

One thing she is light years ahead of me is our honeymoon trip. This is because she has been in constant touch with her parents concerning all the details they arranged for us. Things like: "Where we are going to stay in London, Paris and Florence and how we are going to get there from the airport and back again." "Where are the museums and other attractions and how we are going to get to them." "Where are the good places to eat, the best bargains on museum passes, city tours, boat tours, and so on." Those sorts of things.

If I made a list to remind Mona of all the things she needed to do, it would be five or six pages long and it wouldn't matter because she would have done all of them already. I may taste good but I will be the one getting the best deal out of this marriage.

As far as the museums go, I am way ahead of Mona. I have been studying and memorizing them room by room and painting by painting since I was fifteen years old. Mona may know more about Madam Tussaud's Wax Museum but I can tell you all about the massive painting of Monet's *Water Lilies* that overwhelms everyone when they see it for the first time in the Tate Gallery in London.

I am also better at directions than Mona. That is about all I am good for—museums and directions—unless you count my ability to carry more suitcases at one time than she can.

There is one other thing I am good at: I am good at taking pictures. My small pocket camera will be Mona's to use. I, on the other hand, will be carrying my 56 megapixel digital SLR, fully capable of capturing every treasured moment in an image clear enough to serve as evidence in a court of law—which is why I bought this particular camera in the first place.

My big chore in the morning was to rendezvous with the Salvation Army truck scheduled to stop by and pick up all my disposable stuff at 9:30 a.m. At 9:00, I received a phone call telling me the truck would be at my place within the next hour. Thirty minutes later, the truck pulled up in a loading zone just down the street from my building and two of the largest men I have ever seen outside of Sumo wrestling climbed out.

After I let them into my apartment, they carried every piece of furniture down the stairs and into the truck except my sofa and dresser. When they were finished with the furniture, they came back and completed the job by taking the bags of clothing and kitchen stuff. The reason I kept the sofa was because I still had two more nights to sleep in my apartment before the wedding and even though the carpet had been vacuumed, it still wasn't clean enough for anyone but a beagle to lie on it without regretting it immediately.

By 10:15, my apartment looked as empty as a hospital operating room, except instead of an operating table there was a sofa. *A propos* to an operating room were my two professional quality culinary knives sitting on the kitchen counter next to my super-duper grater. What a grater was doing in the operating room I have no idea.

The clothes I was leaving behind, along with a few miscellaneous items, were neatly stored in a small line of boxes on the floor next to my TV, microwave and bedroom dresser. The stuff that was going to Europe was on the sofa next to the suitcase and carry-on bag I would be taking on the plane. I spent the time left before lunch trying to fold and fit everything into the suitcase without turning the pants and shirts into two-dimensional reproductions of wrinkled prunes.

To my surprise, everything fit on the first try. Once again, Mona had been right: As I surveyed my apartment and the zippered suitcase, I felt as satisfied and excited as a 10 year-old boy feels when he is left at home alone without a babysitter for the first time. Except for picking up my tux the next morning I was ready to get married, fly to Europe and start a new life with Mona without a chaperone or a babysitter in sight.

We met for lunch at the same sushi place where I had eaten dinner the day Mon disappeared. I ordered the same thing I had that night and Mona ordered shrimp Teppanyaki.

"Where do you get off ordering Teppanyaki at a sushi restaurant?" I asked incredulously. "It's not even on the menu."

"Because," she said, "the chef, Millard Yoshida, is a friend of mine. He told me he had a Teppanyaki grill in the back that he uses to fix food for the staff when they get tired of the sushi. 'It tastes good,' he told me. 'Next time you come in for lunch, just order it and I'll fix some for you.'

"I've had it before and he's right. It *is* good. And if you're nice, I'll let you have a shrimp."

Sometimes I forget Mona has lived in the neighborhood almost as long as I have and knows her way around town as well as I do.

As usual, Mona didn't start talking in earnest until after she had put the first bite of food in her mouth. It was obvious that since she finished her own packing and had turned the final details of the reception and the wedding over to her Mom, she was feeling as relaxed as anyone can be just two days before they are scheduled to sail over the horizon and fall off the edge of the earth.

When I mentioned that I had finished my own packing, she was so caught off guard that a shrimp, gently caressed in her chopsticks, never made it to her mouth.

"Wow, am I impressed," she exclaimed as she retrieved the shrimp from her lap. "Underwear and everything?"

Just as I started to say, "Of course," I realized I had completely forgotten to pack that particular necessity—along with my socks and an extra pair of shoes. I caught myself in time, however, and aside from a brief hesitation, all Mona noticed was my saying the words, "Of course."

During the conversation, I brought up the possibility of taking a day trip from Paris to Amsterdam to visit the Rijksmuseum instead of our scheduled bus tour to Versailles and Monet's home in Giverny.

"Imagine the canals, the windmills and the Rembrandts," I teased.

"Mike," Mona said as she placed a shrimp on my plate, "Between the National Gallery in London and the Louvre, there will be more than enough Rembrandts for this trip. Trust me on that."

I knew she was right, of course, and I didn't really want to miss Giverny or Versailles, either, but there was so much I was hoping to see and two weeks was simply not going to be enough time to see all of it. I felt like I was standing in front of a vast buffet and having someone tell me I could only choose one entrée.

Like my client Sarah had said, “Life isn’t always fair.”

“Maybe,” I said to Mona, “we can use some of the money I got from Ramone to make a return trip like maybe next year or something?”

Mona was busy scraping the last few pieces of rice off her plate with a fork but looked up long enough to say, “Maybe. But don’t you think we should put our children through college before squandering their future so we can tilt at windmills?”

Mona’s habit of being right was starting to get on my nerves. Reluctantly, I deep-sixed the plans for a return trip to Europe and tucked them into a mental file folder labeled, “Walter Mitty.”

Mona went on to remind me to pick up my tuxedo the next day and to make sure Robert did, too.

“Dad decided to wear his own tux and Danny picked his up yesterday so that’s taken care of. Tomorrow Corinne, Brin and I will be tying the wedding favors together.”

“Favors?” I asked. “What favors?”

By the look on Mona’s face, I figured if we had been standing up she would have kicked me on the shin again.

“The favors we both agreed to have at the reception. What do you mean, ‘What favors’?”

“Oh, *those* favors!” I said, desperately trying to cover my tracks. “I thought you said you were going to *do* some favors for someone tomorrow. Of course I know about the favors,” I lied.

Not wanting to be completely ignorant, I went fishing for information like the kids do for bluegills in Central Park.

"And how did the favors turn out?" I asked, hoping she would remind me what they were.

"The little magnifying glasses didn't come with holes them so it's going to be hard to tie them onto the little books. But the tiny print in the books with our names and the wedding date on them turned out really well; assuming everyone can figure out what to do with the magnifying glass."

"So," I said, relieved at having my memory refreshed, "the favors and the top of the wedding cake will cover the P.I. and Librarian angles. That is so cute."

Mona let the comment pass without comment. Instead, she turned her attention to the rehearsal.

"Six o'clock sharp," she said with the hint of an un-amused glare. "It starts at six o'clock. And you will be there long before that if you know what's good for you."

I nodded, hoping the conversation would move on to something else.

"And don't forget to bring the marriage license. We can't get married without it and Pastor Cheryl says she wants it in her hands at the rehearsal in case you're planning on forgetting to bring it to the wedding. No license—No marriage. Got it?"

For a split second, I couldn't remember where I had put the license. Somehow, I had been thinking that Mona had it. Then I remembered I had put it in the silverware drawer in my kitchen along with Mona's wedding ring and my passport.

"No sweat," I said in what I hoped came across as a reassuring tone.

"And Sunday morning," Mona continued, "Chia will do my hair and makeup and then Pam, Chia, Corinne and Brin and I will eat a light lunch and get to the church before 1:00 pm. That's when you are going to get there, too, right?"

"Right as rain," I said as I wondered what the phrase "right as rain" meant and what, if anything, it had to do with getting married.

"My Dad has the limo lined up to take us to the church and then to the reception at the *3 West Club*. Afterwards, the limo will take us to JFK. It's all so exciting," she said without a smile or any sign of excitement.

"I just wish there was more time to relax after the reception."

There was a long sigh followed by, "And that's it. Then we'll be off onto the next adventure. Any questions or last requests?"

"Just the usual blindfold and cigarette," I said.

"And the firing squad?"

"No firing squad," I replied. "The blindfold will help me pretend there aren't thirty-million of your friends and relatives crushing me with their 'Best wishes' and 'Congratulations,' and the cigarette smoke will guarantee they'll keep at least fifteen feet away from me at all times."

Mona ended the exchange by saying, "If you want the blindfold and cigarette you'll have to get them yourself, they're not on my list. Oh, look at the time! I've gotta go. Nice seeing you, Mike. Maybe we'll bump into each other again one of these days. Don't be a stranger."

"I'll see you at the rehearsal," I said, as we each leaned across the table and shared a kiss.

"And don't forget to pack your underwear," she added as she walked towards the door.

Honestly, I don't know how she knows these things.

Before I paid the bill and left the restaurant, it crossed my mind that somewhere in the boxes next to my studio wall there was, along with my socks and underwear, a pair of pajamas that needed to be packed.

Now that lunch was over, I wasn't sure what I was going to do next. Robert was going to head over to Long Island after work, have dinner with his parents and curl, or go curling, or do whatever it is that caused me enough back pain to put me in bed for two days last winter. So getting together with Robert was out.

Hanging out with Mona wasn't an option, either, and I had made up my mind not to go back to Mom, Frieda or Grandpa van Rijn; at least not until Mona and I stopped by to say "Good-bye" on our way to the airport after the wedding.

The thought suddenly occurred to me that this "visiting Mom" plan was not going to work. To begin with, we wouldn't have time to stop by the museum after the wedding and, second, the MoMA would be closed long before we would get there anyway. Knowing that there might not be another opportunity, I decided to go and say my final farewell to Mom before I headed back to my apartment.

Although it was a pleasant day and I had all the time in the world, I decided to take a cab to the MoMA. Robert was standing at the main entrance as usual and he looked at me as though I was from outer space, wandering lost in the abysmal labyrinth of Manhattan plaintively whispering, "E.T. phone home" to everyone who would listen.

"Mr. Maurison, what are you doing here?" Robert asked.

"Why not," I said. "I'm packed and ready to roll. All I need to do is pick up my tuxedo tomorrow. What about you?"

"Me, too," Robert replied. "The tuxedo, I mean."

I waited to see if there were any other words working their way up through Robert's verbal firewall. To my surprise, there were.

"I've written the toast for the reception."

"Is it a good one?" I asked.

"Chia thinks so. You'll have to decide for yourself."

I nodded, Robert winked, and that was that.

I took the lobby elevator to the Fifth Floor, walked into the gallery and sat down in front of Mom. I listened carefully to hear if she had anything to say. I sat there a long time but Mom didn't even say, "Hello."

I tried to break the ice by saying, "How are things? I thought I would stop by and say 'Good-bye' before the wedding on Sunday. We have to go straight from the reception to the airport so we won't be able to stop by afterwards."

There was no response. Either someone had set Mom on "mute" or she simply wasn't there anymore. My guess was that she was gone. Somehow, just as I had created her out of my lonely imagination as a child, I had now allowed Mona to supplant her as the love of my life.

William Blake once wrote, "If the sun and moon should doubt, they would both go out."

I had doubted . . . and Mom had gone out like a candle in the wind.

As I sat in front of *Les Demoiselles D'Avignon*, I was a child for one final time. My mother was gone and once again, I had not even had a chance to say, "Good-bye."

For the first time I could remember, I avoided Robert by sneaking out another exit from the museum. Without any particular plan in mind I walked west on 53rd and turned north on 7th Avenue. Carnegie Hall passed by on my left and I found myself crossing 59th, entering Central Park and heading towards Rat Rock.

As a child, I had taken the easy way up to the top of this large outcrop of bedrock Manhattan. As a teen, I had broken the law by climbing up where a slip could cost you a broken leg, a concussion or a citation. For some of us, it was a rite of passage to adulthood; a test of courage; a stick in the eye of authority and all the laws and rules that went along with it.

In recent years, the ground around the rock has been softened with wood bark and climbing the rock is now allowed. Today I took the easy way to the top and looked around at the ring of tall apartments that surround the park. The happy chatter of children, the self-imposed, defiant coolness of teenagers and the occasional young couple pursuing romance performed a *mélange* of Shakespeare and Jerry Seinfeld—bit players in a production of "Much Ado About Nothing." At least it was nothing to me.

There on Rat Rock, I was as alone as I had ever been in my life. At that moment there was no Dad, Mom, or Aunt Lucille. There was not even Mona. There was just me, Mike Maurison, Private Eye, swallowed up by the tragic sadness of life with nothing to do but wait for the fading sound of half-hearted applause and the descent of the final curtain.

This old production had had a good run but the time had come for it to close. A new show, with a new cast and a new plot had already begun rehearsing in preparation for its first performance. Tomorrow evening would be the final dress rehearsal. Opening night, complete with red carpet, musical fanfares, designer dresses, tuxedoes and celebrity guests, would premier the following afternoon.

Mona will be the leading lady, the headliner, the star; and like the male dancer who lifts the *prima ballerina* over his head to make her appear as beautiful and graceful as possible, I will be playing the supporting role. With my name below the title, dressed in non-descript black and white, I will serve the role of consort to the one whose name will be written in lights and in whose presence the knees of the *paparazzi* will quake and tremble.

I scrambled off the rock and *exuented* stage left, heading east to face my destiny. I had promises to keep and miles to go before I'd sleep. I had chosen the road less travelled; a road that would bring joy to my heart and a spring to my step because it would lead me to Mona and to worlds yet undreamed.

But first it was going to lead me to the underwear, socks, shoes, and pair of pajamas I needed to pack.

Chapter 13
Dress Rehearsal

Saturday, July 13

I woke on Saturday morning fully aware that in less than thirty-two hours I would be married to Mona. During the night I hadn't sweat a single bullet over the possibility of leaving my fly open during the wedding. On the other hand, there had been a dream.

In the dream, Mona and I were climbing into the limo after the wedding reception and heading off to the airport. Someone handed me an envelope. In it was a bill for $25,000: the cost of the wedding, including the church, the flowers, the limo, the rehearsal dinner at Rothmann's and the wedding reception at the *3 West Club*.

Whether the actual cost turned out to be more or less, the amount of money that Mona's parents were spending on our wedding had finally begun to sink in. It was enough money to pay the rent on our new apartment for an entire year. It was three times the cost of our honeymoon. It was, according to some quick calculations, enough money for Mona and me to take a two-month trip on a luxury cruise.

When I look in the mirror all I see is me, a poor *schlemiel* born into nothing and barely able to keep my head above water. I don't own a tuxedo and I don't own a yacht. The only time I go out of town is when I am on an expense account paid by a client. I don't own a car or a house. I am thirty-one years old, for god's sake. In all these years, I have been to exactly one curling club and have never set foot on a golf course. When it comes to relationships with my soon-to-be in-laws, I am Gilligan and Mona's parents are Mr. and Mrs. Thurston Howell III—except that Mona's parents aren't quite as snooty.

To their credit, I have never heard them say anything that would lead me to believe they are disappointed in their daughter's choice of a husband. I have been welcomed into their home without question, and they have never once asked me to take off my shoes before walking on their living room carpet.

Part of me wants to stay as far away from their money as possible. That's the proud and independent Mike, the one who wants to prove he can make it on his own without any help from anybody.

The other part of me is glad to be marrying into a family that knows the meaning of financial security. That's the poor and hungry Mike, the one who never had much of anything and who never argues when someone offers to pay for his dinner.

The real me is somewhere in between these two Mikes. It doesn't bother me that Mona's parents have dough, but it doesn't impress me all that much, either. None of it makes Mona any more or less attractive. That, I guess, is why her parents have accepted me. They know I am not marrying Mona for their money, but for Mona.

Like Mona's Dad told her, "Just be Mona. That's all Mike wants is for you to be yourself."

He was right about that, of course, and I love him for knowing it.

As far as the wedding extravaganza is concerned, I don't need opulence or glitz to feel good about things. A wedding on the beach at Coney Island followed by a Boardwalk reception catered by Nathan's Famous Hot Dogs would be enough for me . . . as long as we could share the fun with our families and friends.

Eating at Rothmann's and dancing at the *3 West Club* don't really matter, either. As long as Mona's parents are willing and able to pay for it and as long as nobody's nose is pointed too far towards the ceiling, I will be content. I will eat the food. I will enjoy the ambiance. I will dance, and I will be thankful for the family's generosity and love.

But when all is said and done, the only thing that will matter is Mona. The rest is gossamer.

At 8:30 a.m., my cell phone started chirping, buzzing, beeping and *Bolero*-ing. There was a text message, an email, a phone call and a voice message—all from Mona.

They all said the same thing: "Call me. Now."

So of course, I did.

When Mona answered the phone and sang, "Good morning to you!" I had the odd feeling she was so happy about something that she was probably jumping up and down in her bathrobe and slippers. As it turned out, I was wrong about the bathrobe and the slippers because she was already dressed and ready to greet the day, but I was dead right about the jumping up and down part.

"Mike, you gotta hear this," she said, with so much energy I decided I had better sit.

"You had better sit," she said. "It's gonna knock you right off your feet and out of your socks!"

"I'm already sitting," I assured her. "What's the news?"

"I got a job!" she shouted. "I mean, I already have a job, but now I have another one! I just checked my phone and there was a text message, an email and a voice message from yesterday afternoon and I don't know how but I must have missed all of them I mean I never noticed they were there until just a minute ago . . . ."

"Mona," I said as I cut her off. "Take a breath, slow down just a little and tell me what is going on."

I could hear Mona suck in enough oxygen to replace what she had expended on the previous sentence.

"Okay, I'm better now," she said. "But I am so excited! I got the librarian position at Hunter College! It's an assistant position but it means I get to be a librarian, a real librarian and get paid for it. And there is a benefit plan and . . . ."

"Slow down," I said again, followed by, "Mona, that's wonderful news."

"They want me to start as soon as I can, but no later than August 15th. The Fall term starts at the end of August and they want me to be all oriented before the students show up."

"And," I said, "they are actually going to pay you for this?"

"Yes," Mona replied, missing the sarcasm completely. "It will be a lot more than I'm getting now and I will have weekends off and holidays with pay and two weeks' vacation and personal sick days and maternity leave and I can't believe I got the job!"

It all sounded too good to be true, not only for Mona but for me, too. We could really use the extra income and maybe I could piggy-back onto her medical plan. On the other hand, it seemed to me Mona had sounded way too enthusiastic about the maternity leave angle, and yesterday at lunch she had said something about our children going to college, Where the heck are we going to squeeze four or five kids into a one-bedroom apartment? On the other hand, the thought crossed my mind that maybe our children could get a tuition break at Hunter because their mother is on staff and . . . .

As usual, my brain was leaping tall buildings with a single bound and zipping along faster than a speeding bullet. Even though Mona had been talking fast enough to set a new land speed record, I found myself crossing the finish line a good two laps ahead of her.

"It's all happening so fast and all at the same time!" Mona said. "I can't believe it's actually happening but all of it is good—so good! What a way to start my new life with you; our new life together."

There was silence for a moment. I figured Mona had pulled in for a pit stop to refuel and change her tires for the home stretch but I was wrong. She had said all she wanted to say and there were things she needed to do and places she needed to go.

"That's it," she said. "I just wanted you to be the first to know. We can talk about it later. Maybe on the plane or . . . well . . . I gotta go. Bye."

It did not surprise me that Mona got the job. After all, she had worked at the NJCU library for four years while she was earning her BA in English Lit, and she had worked part-time in the CUNY-Queens library during her graduate program in Library Science until she took her current job at *Books and Things*. Now it looked as though all that effort and networking were finally paying off.

Suddenly and unexpectedly one more thread had been woven into the tapestry of our lives. As a bonus, this particular thread was not only beautiful but convenient, too. The Hunter College Library is only four blocks south of *Books and Things* and just fourteen blocks from our new apartment on 81st. With my office nearby, we will still be able to have lunch together whenever we feel the need for a mid-day rendezvous.

This was one of those moments when I felt the urge to say "Thank you" to somebody. When Mona prays she says it to God all the time, but I'm not sure I can be so casual about it.

The only time I ever said "Thank you" to God was last November, after surviving a fractured skull inflicted by the foot of a not-very-friendly drug dealer. I still have trouble figuring out how God punches a button, or blows out the candles and makes a wish, and then Mona gets a job, but as silly as it sounds, it makes as much sense as chalking it up to "coincidence," "karma," "good luck," or "random chance."

In any case there wasn't much I could do about it except to be happy for Mona. I tucked the good news in my back pocket and high-tailed it over to the rental shop to pick up my tuxedo.

This particular experience made me feel like a high school kid getting dressed up for the Senior Prom. The tux guy made sure the jacket and pants fit me well enough to prevent folks from confusing me with Columbo. As some sort of gesture to make me feel as though I was getting a special deal, they threw in a cheap pair of black socks as a gift to go along with the patent leather rental shoes. I was suitably impressed and will be eternally grateful for their generosity.

The tux and shoes were put into a zippered plastic bag. I then signed a form where I promised to return everything in good condition by Tuesday morning or I would have to return the socks. Since I was in no hurry I took the bus back to my apartment with the bag draped over my arm, probably getting the tux crumpled after all our efforts to the contrary.

Once I was home, the tux came out of the bag and was unceremoniously hung in the closet. The shirt was pulled out of its plastic wrap, shaken out as best as possible and hung up next to the tux. The shoes, suspenders, cummerbund, and shirt studs found a place of honor on the kitchen counter and since I was going to wear the thistle cufflinks Robert had given to me, I dropped the rental ones back into the zip bag. The tux and shirt were the only things left hanging in the closet because the shirt and pants I had on were going to have to carry me through the evening rehearsal, lazing around on Sunday morning, and then get me to London on the plane after the wedding. Unless I spilled something all over my pants at the rehearsal dinner I figured that a generous wallop of deodorant would take care of the rest of it. This plan wasn't necessarily made by choice since, after stuffing the underwear, socks, pajamas and second pair of shoes into my suitcase, I didn't have room to pack another change of clothes anyway.

The weather was cloudless and hot, just as it had been the day before and the day before that. Since I had time on my hands, I walked over to Central Park, grabbed a corn dog and an iced coffee for a late lunch and strolled over to nearby Cedar Hill. I honestly don't know how it got its name. There are probably cedar trees on it but since I can't tell a cedar from a pine from a fir I just have to assume there are cedars somewhere nearby.

The Hill is essentially a grassy knoll that does not attract a great many people even on a Saturday afternoon. There were some folks lying in the sun and some kids climbing in the trees. There were sounds of laughter and the sound of music leaking out from someone's ear buds; someone who had apparently set the volume on their I-Phone to the decibels of a jet engine. Even so, it is one of the more peaceful corners of the Park.

At first, I sat down on the grass half in the sun and half in the shade. Soon I was lying on my back thinking about all the things that needed to be done before Mona and I exchanged the continent of North America for the continent of Europe.

After what seemed to be only a few minutes, my phone started ringing. It was Mona checking in to make sure I hadn't fallen asleep somewhere and lost track of the time.

"It's 5:15 and I'm almost ready to head for the church. How are things with you? Are you nervous yet?"

To be honest, I hadn't been nervous until that very moment. I had in fact fallen asleep and lost all track of the time. As I sat up my neck felt as crisp and dry as parchment paper. The shade had long ago moved over to somewhere else and my face, neck and arms were as red as Chinese lacquer.

"No worries," I said through clenched teeth, "I'm on my way. See you soon. Bye."

True to my word, I was immediately on my way, frantically heading back to my apartment at a full sprint. When I reached Fifth Avenue, I waved for a cab, forgetting I had left my wallet in the apartment and had only brought enough loose change to pay for my lunch.

The cabby delivered me to my door but did not seem pleased when I told him I didn't have a credit card, a debit card or any cash in my pockets. He also didn't look convinced when I told him to sit and wait for me to come back with the cash.

Other than call the cops, the poor guy didn't have any choice except to leave the meter running and hope, against all odds, that he would wind up with a big tip from the jerk who was obviously trying to stiff him.

I didn't have time to run up and down the stairs twice, so I grabbed everything I needed for the evening, came back downstairs and jumped in the cab.

"Take me to the church on time!" I commanded.

The cabby seemed to have lost his sense of humor.

Instead of laughing, he turned around and said, "I'm not going to take you anywhere until you hand over the money you already owe me along with an advance payment for where you want to go next. *Comprenez-vous*?"

"*Je comprende*," I replied, grateful to be reminded that Mona would be *sprechen sie française* when we landed in Paris.

After greasing the driver's palm with the required cash, we headed back to Fifth Avenue and turned south in the direction of the church. It was 6:00 when I jumped out of the cab and told the driver to keep the change.

The heat of the afternoon and the sprint back to my apartment reminded me that I had forgotten to apply the antiperspirant/deoderant.

The front doors to the church were locked and I had forgotten which of the side doors would be open on a Saturday afternoon. Half way down the street side of the church, I saw a sign that said, "Church Office." It was unlocked, and I entered the chapel in as casual a way as I could, considering my skin was burning and my lungs were sucking air like a greyhound after a long, futile attempt to catch a mechanical rabbit.

"Hey, gang," I said cheerfully. "Is everyone here yet?"

Mona looked at me as though I was Freddy Kruger strolling into her boudoir. Her eyes moved from my face, to my feet, to my arms and back to my face again. Her mouth opened for a moment, but then closed without making a sound.

Chia, ever the good cop, bad cop, filled in the blanks by saying what everyone else was thinking, "What the hell happened to you?"

"I took a nice stroll through the park," I sort of lied, "and I guess I forgot to put on the sunscreen."

"Duh," I heard Corinne say under her breath while Brin added the more prosaic, "No kidding."

Mona walked over and laid her cool, comforting hand on the back of my neck.

"Nice going, Mike," she said. "I knew I could count on you. Glad you could make it."

Everyone who was supposed to be there was there except for Pastor Cheryl, who had scurried over to her office to get something just before I walked in. When she returned she was so distracted by the business-at-hand that she failed to notice the little drama that was still unfolding in front of her.

The late afternoon sun touched the stained glass windows and scattered the colors of the rainbow across the chapel. Even in my discomfort, I could not help but marvel at the beauty of the place.

Pastor Cheryl brought the house to order and started to explain the choreography to everyone who had anything to do during the service. She shuttled Daniel, Robert and me off to stage right while showing the ladies where they were supposed to stand stage left. After asking who was coming in first, second, third and fourth she lined the women's team up against the starting blocks in the back and sent them one by one down the straightaway, pointed towards the finish line.

"Don't walk too fast," she said. "This is your time in the spotlight so don't rush it. Take your time and enjoy the moment."

When the girls were locked and loaded Pastor Cheryl nodded to the organist, who had just come over from practicing on the big organ in the main sanctuary. The chapel organ would have been considered a large one in any normal size church but here it was dwarfed by the monstrous pipes clinging to the walls of the larger sanctuary next door. Even so, when the sound of Rossini's *William Tell Overture* kicked in I could tell that the smaller instrument was perfectly capable of holding its own.

Mona's frown disappeared as she joined the rest of the wedding party in cracking up as the absurdity of the choice of music hit home.

"Whose idea was that?" she demanded after the theme from *The Lone Ranger* abruptly stopped in mid-measure.

The bridal party and the groomsmen all pointed at each other and the laughter started up all over again.

Pastor Cheryl, who had been laughing along with everyone else, put her arms up in the air saying, "Okay, it's good to laugh but I hear there is a dinner waiting for us down the street and I would hate to have the entrees get cold. Let's see, where were we?"

The organ started up again, but this time the chapel was filled with the dulcet tones of Bach's *Air on a G-String*.

Brin started off the parade followed by Corinne on her crutches and then Chia and Pam taking up the rear. Each of them held what appeared to be red ribbons and bows snatched from the remnants of old Christmas wrapping. As far as I could tell, they did the procession perfectly and the pastor seemed to feel the same way.

"Well done," she said. "That's a wrap. Do it that way tomorrow and you'll have everyone standing up by the time you're finished!"

That was, of course meant to be a joke, because everyone stands up at that point anyway to honor the bride when she first pokes her head through the back door.

Next, to the strains of "Here Comes the Bride," Mona came floating down the aisle like an angel riding on the clouds of heaven. Her ribbons were white, of course, and her smile outshone the prismatic sunlight that had turned the chapel into a spectacular kaleidoscope. Mona's smile looked, in fact, as though it was about to go completely out of control. It got bigger and bigger to the point where the corners of her mouth began to twitch. Before she got all the way down to the front she had to put her hand over her mouth to calm it down.

Mona's other arm had been locked onto the arm of her father. When the time came for him to hand his daughter over to her new partner in life, he got his first close-up view of my face and tried so hard not to laugh that he completely forgot to give Mona the traditional kiss on her cheek.

With Mona now latched onto my arm I became painfully aware my scorched arm could not tolerate the touch of a single finger, let alone the clasp of an entire arm. Fighting back the tears, I joined Mona in turning to face Pastor Cheryl up close and personal for the first time.

Cheryl began by saying the traditional words, "Dearly beloved, we are gathered here in the presence of . . . ." but she never finished the sentence.

She had, at last, noticed my fire-engine-red face and begun cracking up all over again.

When she had brought herself back under control, she looked at me, and then Mona, then back at me, and said, "What the . . . ."

Then she paused as though she had suddenly remembered where she was.

After the pause she said, "What in the world happened to you?"

Robert started laughing so hard he had to sit down on the front pew. Daniel looked around as though he had wandered into the wrong saloon and everyone else tried to pretend everything was perfectly normal, as if they were a flock of ostriches.

The rest of the rehearsal went as well as could be expected.

Mona's parents said, "We do!" when the pastor asked if our families were giving their blessing to our marriage.

To my surprise, Aunt Lucille mysteriously appeared in the back of the chapel and shot off an antiphonal echo by shouting out, "I do" to the same question.

Aunt Lucille was my prodigal mother's sister. She and her two children were the only family I had left. I had expected her to attend the wedding but I was caught off-guard by having her show up for the rehearsal. But as they say, the show must go on.

While Chia was reading some excerpts from 1 Corinthians 13, Mona looked at me, let go of my arm, put her hand up to pinch her nose and said, "PU. Did you know you stink?"

After a few well-focused sniffs, I had to agree my cachet was on the verge of extinction.

After Pastor Cheryl had gotten my attention with a few well-placed "ahems," I began repeating her words as I said my vows to Mona. After Mona had done the same she pointed out the vows chosen by the pastor did not include the phrase, "to have and to hold." Mona asked if the words could be slipped in somewhere and the pastor said she would take care of it.

We then exchanged phantom rings and knelt down on a fancy little bench that is formally and pretentiously called a *prie dieu*. After pretending to endure a long prayer of blessing, we stood back up and the pastor explained this was when she would pronounce us husband and wife.

She then put our hands together and said, “Who God has joined together let no one put asunder.”

After sharing one final blessing, Pastor Cheryl, with a grin on her face, said, “Go ahead, Mike. Practice makes perfect. You may kiss the bride.”

I gave it my best shot and while everyone else applauded, I realized my lips had been burned to a crisp along with everything else. Through the fog of discomfort, I felt the pastor turn us around so we faced the pews and heard her introduce us as Mr. and Mrs. Mike and Mona Maurison.

Arm in arm we went through the motions of rewinding the processional as the organist kicked off the opening chords of the “Wedding March” from Mendelssohn’s *Midsummer Night’s Dream*, the title being a perfect description of the time of year and time of day we were listening to it.

The next bit was the one thing Mona had asked me to choreograph; namely, how to get the four women in the bridal party to walk out gracefully with only two men from the groom’s side. As it turned out, the aisle was as wide as I had remembered it to be, so Robert offered one arm each to Pam and Chia and, with one on each side, walked them out with Danny doing the same with Corinne and Brin.

The rehearsal had turned out to be such a big success that Pastor Cheryl closed it out with a prayer. As a token gesture of compassion, no one said another word about my suntan for the rest of the evening. As we left the chapel and headed one block over to Rothmann’s Steakhouse for the rehearsal dinner, I couldn’t help but notice that the organist began to play “The Funeral March of a Marionette” by Gounod. No doubt it was meant as a sly wink at what would be the groom’s final night of unwedded bliss.

On the way to Rothmans's Mona reached into her purse, pulled out a small bottle of roll-on deodorant and handed it to me.

"Keep it," she said. "I don't want it back."

Later, during dinner, Chia let me borrow her "Blush Nude" lipstick to ease the pain of food touching my lips.

"Keep it," she said. "I don't want it back."

The dinner of course, was a big success. The steaks were cooked to order, there were four pasta dishes and three salads to choose from and folks were free to order whatever wine or beer suited their fancy--which is another phrase that makes absolutely no sense to me.

It turned out Mona had invited my Aunt Lucille to come to the rehearsal because she didn't think it was fair for so many of her family to be there without any of mine. It was sweet of her to be so considerate but I would have enjoyed my dinner more if we had been seated with Robert and Chia instead of directly across from Aunt Lucille.

The dinner and conversation provided a nice distraction from my sunburn. It was only at the end, when everyone was giving me a hug, slapping me on the back or poking me on the arm I realized I needed to go home and do something about it, pronto. Pam and Danny had driven over from Bayswater in Pam's car so they were gracious enough to drop me off at my place on their way home.

There was nothing in my apartment to put on my skin and all the local stores had closed up for the night. I worried that taking a shower would dry out my skin even more so I did my best to wash under my armpits using one of the old, unmatched socks I found lying on the bathroom floor. It was more than obvious that the clothes I had been wearing were no longer eligible to be worn anywhere ever again until they had been put through the "heavy duty" cycle in a washing machine at least twice.

Eventually I took two ibuprofen, laid my back down on the sofa, gritted my teeth and, after spending an hour writhing around trying to get comfortable, I finally fell asleep with tears in my red and swollen eyes.

Chapter 14
To Have & To Hold

Sunday, July 14

I knew I needed to get some help with my sunburn but I didn't want to fork out a week's pay by going to a hospital emergency room. The only thing I could find nearby was a walk-in clinic a few blocks north that opened on Sunday mornings at 10:00 a.m. Since I hadn't slept very well anyway, I got up early, dug though one of my storage boxes, put on some clean, loose-fitting clothes that smelled good, and headed over to the Laundromat with the ones that smelled bad. Because I was in a hurry, I didn't have time for two long wash cycles so I had to hope one short cycle would be enough.

Normally, I would have walked over to the clinic but, because the clock was ticking faster than usual, I took a cab. Taking the cab also gave me the opportunity to drop off my suitcase and carry-on bag at Mona's place so the girls could put it in the limo when it came to pick them up. I also had a small backpack I kept with me to hold all the things I would need during the day.

Brin met me outside their apartment and reminded me that I wasn't allowed inside because I might see Mona and that would be bad luck. To this day I cannot think of a single reason why looking at Mona would bring anyone bad luck at any time or in any place. I suppose the idea came from the same person who made it mandatory for every bride to wear something old, something new, something borrowed, something blue, and a six-pence in her shoe.

It was also, no doubt, the same person who dreamed up the idea that at certain times of the year, a boy can't kiss his girl unless they are both standing under what *Wikipedia* describes as an "obligate hemi-parasitic plant in the order *Santalales*." Yet traditions have their place, and even though my family didn't make much of an effort to practice them, if even one of them makes Mona happy then I'm all for it.

At 10:00 a.m. sharp, I walked into the clinic and was handed a bunch of forms I needed to fill out before I could see anyone. I scribbled on them as fast as I could so other people wouldn't get in line ahead of me. At 10:15, I was the first person called in to see a doctor. After the usual routine of weight, temperature and blood pressure the doc came in and had me take off my shirt. She looked me over and told me that as far as sunburns go mine was not too bad, just an average 1st degree. She said the pain should ease up after a couple of days and that the itching would stop a few days later when the dead skin began to peel off.

"Keep taking the ibuprofen," she said, adding some other suggestions that might make me more comfortable including taking a cool shower with as little soap as possible.

I hurried back to my apartment where I took a shower, smeared on some moisturizer cream with *aloe vera* in it, put on the clothes I had rewashed at the laundromat, and finished it all up with a large dose of antiperspirant/deodorant.

My friend Sid had offered to pick me up in his car at 12:30 a.m. and get me to the church early so Mona wouldn't worry about whether I was actually going to show up or not.

I looked at my watch and noticed it was already 11:35. Since I was going to change into my tux at the church I figured I had enough time to run down the street and pick up something to hold me over until the reception. Missing breakfast had been a bad idea but missing both breakfast and lunch would have been an even worse idea. I made sure my tux and backpack were by the door, ready to go and hurried down the street to pick up a sandwich.

I walked past Juan's corner store and opted for a lox and bagel at the deli two blocks away. Time was running out so I ate the bagel on my way back to the apartment, walking at a pace fast enough to keep me on schedule but not so fast that I might break into a sweat.

Things had been so hectic and confused that I hadn't noticed the sky was no longer bright and cheery as it had been all week. It was, in fact, cloudy and dark enough to qualify as being ominous. Before I got back to my apartment, it started to rain and by the time I was inside, it had started to pour. I didn't have a jacket with me, a hat or even an umbrella. My watch said 12:20, so I drank some tap water out of the palm of my hand, grabbed my gear and hustled down to the ground floor to wait for Sid.

When he pulled up to the curb his wipers were going so fast they were throwing water clear across the sidewalk. Holding all my stuff as tightly as possible, I slogged through the downpour, wishing the cats and dogs had chosen to go somewhere else.

In the time it took to throw my gear into the back of the car and scramble into the front seat next to Sid I was soaked. My loose-fitting clothes were sticking to my body and rubbing against my skin like wet sandpaper. The thought of strapping a seat belt across my chest made me cringe. I urged Sid to get me to the church so I could change into my dry tuxedo as soon as possible.

Because of the morning worship services, the front doors to the church were still wide open when we pulled up, but I had Sid drop me off at the Church Office.

"Thanks, pal," I said with sincere gratitude for the favor.

Noticing the rain was still pouring down, I added, "I'll see you inside."

If such a thing is possible, I got even wetter as I ran over two pedestrians on my way to the door.

Inside the door, there were puddles everywhere from all the people who had been coming and going since the rain had started falling. I made my way to the "Groom's Room" adjacent to one of the Men's bathrooms and immediately got out of my clothes. Even my underwear was wet, which was a problem since they were the only pair I had, but I slipped my rental trousers on anyway.

The tuxedo shirt was thoroughly starched, and it scratched my skin like haircloth. Fortunately, Robert showed up already dressed and, being completely dry, he was able to help me put my studs and cufflinks on. Buttoning my collar was too painful to tolerate, so I left the collar and the bow tie for later. Because of the sunburn and the stiff clothes, I asked Robert to help me put on my spiffy black socks and dress shoes. It crossed my mind for the hundredth time that sitting all night in a cramped seat on a crowded airplane for five hours was not going to be a particularly pleasant way to begin a honeymoon trip to Europe.

Danny poked his head in and told Robert he had to help him usher people to their seats.

"See you later, Mr. Maurison," Robert said as he waved and walked out the door.

"Hey, Robert," I yelled to him through the door. "Let Mona know I'm here, okay?"

When Robert replied with his signature, "Sure," I knew the message had been received and would be delivered.

Meanwhile my street clothes were hanging up trying to dry. It was now 1:20 p.m. and since there were still 4 ½ hours to go before we would leave the reception, I was fairly sure they be wearable by then.

As I sat and looked around the room with nothing to do, I recalled that I had always wondered what the groom thinks about just before his wedding. Now I knew and to tell the truth it isn't particularly breathtaking.

There was a knock on the door so I said, "Come in."

Pastor Cheryl's head appeared.

"How's it going?"

To my surprise, she actually asked this in a way that sounded as though she was looking for an honest answer.

"Everything's good, except for my sunburn," I replied.

"Sit tight," she added. "I'll be sending your buddies back to the room after Robert seats your aunt, and Danny seats his mother. I'll come back with them and have a short prayer. Then I'll go back to the bridal room and have a prayer with them, too. By the way, they're all ready to go"

There was a pause as if she were hesitating to say something.

The pause ended as she added, "Then, after they get lined up, I'll come and get you so the four of us can go out and take our positions. That will be the cue for the organist to start the processional. Any questions?"

All I could think of to say was, "No."

It's been said, "What you don't know can't hurt you," so I suppose it was a good thing I didn't know about the chaos that had broken out in the bridal suite.

At 12:45 when Mona was getting out of the car to come into the church, the limo driver, who was holding up an umbrella to keep her dry, tripped over the curb and went down in a heap. Mona suddenly found herself taking an unplanned shower.

Before she could scamper through the church door, her wedding dress, her face, and her hair got a good hosing down. As soon as they got into to the Bride's Room, Chia got busy trying to repair the damage. For some reason Chia had brought a blow dryer which they put to work drying Mona's hair so Chia could put it back together. When the hair was dry enough, Brin took on the chore of trying to dry out the dress.

Mona's face had also taken a hit. Chia hadn't thought ahead enough to use water-proof mascara and as a result of the rain Mona was looking like Alice Cooper on a bad day. Corinne put down one of her crutches, grabbed a handful of tissues and leaned over to wipe off Mona's face before the mascara ran onto her dress.

"Too many cooks spoil the broth," goes one saying; and "three's a crowd" goes another.

In this particular case, both sayings were as true as blue but sadly Corinne was number three. As she stepped forward, she tripped and tried to keep her balance by jamming her second crutch into the floor in front of her. Unfortunately, Mona and her wedding dress happened to be in the exact same spot. The crutch caught on Mona's dress halfway down the back, pulling Mona backwards and ripping out 20-inches of the waist seam. Mona managed to keep herself from falling but the sudden move caused Chia's fingers to pull through Mona's hair like an afro pick, leaving a tangled mess in its wake.

All this, ironically, was taking place at the very moment that Pastor Cheryl was saying, "They're all ready to go."

Corinne was so upset with herself that she burst into tears. Chia, Brin and Mona were too preoccupied to do anything to help her feel better so Pam sat down with Corinne and tried to keep her tears from staining both of their dresses.

Mona's mother was there, too, of course, and she ran in and around and out of the room frantically looking for a needle and thread or a dozen safety pins.

To her eternal credit, Mona remained cool and calm about the whole thing. That of course, is what her friends would like everyone to believe.

Closer to the truth is that when the dress ripped, Mona started laughing so hard that tears began running down her face, making the mascara problem even worse. She continued to laugh, almost hysterically at times, until her hair had been reassembled, her face had been repainted, her dress had been dried and the seam of her dress had been pulled tight and held together with several long pieces of duct tape that Mona's mother found in a nearby custodial closet.

Pastor Cheryl entered the room just as the final repairs were being polished off.

Oblivious of what had happened, she turned to Mona's mother and said, "It's time for the mother of the bride to be escorted to her seat by her grandson."

Mona was so tired from laughing that she sat down on a chair, not caring whether the back of her dress got wrinkled or not.

Her mother planted a soft kiss on her cheek and whispered the words that only she could have spoken.

"Mona, on the day you were born there was some tearing during your delivery but you came out just fine—everything turned out just fine. So don't let a little tearing get you down. Today is no different from then. Once again you will come out fine. Everything will be just fine if you let it be fine."

Her mother smiled, stepped back and said "I love you, my darling princess."

Then she left to be the last person seated before the wedding began.

Robert and Danny came back to my room, smiling and poking me on the arm because they couldn't think of anything else to do. The pain this caused to my arm reminded me that I hadn't buttoned up my collar or put my bow-tie on.

Somehow, my neck had swollen two sizes larger while I had been waiting. There was no chance of getting that little button through the little buttonhole without cutting off the blood supply to my brain. Seeing the need for Plan B, Robert put the bow tie around my neck and under the collar, cinching it closed as gently as possible.

Danny noticed a small box sitting a small table at the back of the room. Curious, he looked inside and found a small, white rosebud that was supposed to have been pinned on my lapel. As Danny did his best to keep from sticking the boutonniere pin into my chest, the door opened and Pastor Cheryl came in.

"I've already had my prayer with the women," she said, "and let me tell you, they really needed to have a prayer."

There was a pause, as if she was waiting for some sort of question or comment about what she had just said.

Seeing that nobody was paying a whole lot of attention to her she said, "Well, let's pray before we walk in."

I have no memory of what the pastor said when she prayed. The only thing I remember is the last thing she said to me before we walked into the church.

"I hope you remembered to bring the wedding license today. You never gave it to me last night."

So it came to pass that as I stepped out into the chapel with seventy-five people staring at me and with Mona and her entourage ready to march through the back door, I realized the wedding license, my passport and Mona's wedding ring were still sitting in the silverware drawer in my kitchen.

Mona, of course, had been going through a crisis of her own. Now however, as the sounds of Bach began wafting through the chapel there was nothing either of us could do except to restrain ourselves from the impulse to run out of the place screaming.

The four women came down the aisle as slowly as they could without standing completely still. All were beautiful in their own way, wearing full-length orchid-color taffeta gowns tied at the waist with thin, dark pink satin ribbons. Complementing the dresses were orchid-flower bouquets tied with the same dark pink satin ribbons.

When Mona made her appearance on the arm of her father, all thoughts of rings, licenses and passports were erased from my mind like a full reformat on a disk drive.

What I didn't know at the time was when Mona saw me, all the stress and worry of the previous hour evaporated from her mind as well. The time had come for us to be joined together in holy matrimony and nothing else mattered to either of us.

It was the time of our lives. It was an end and a beginning. It was a pure joy and a perfect peace, and for perhaps the first time in my life, I was full to overflowing with the very love that

Pastor Cheryl had spent an entire evening trying to describe to us.

Just like the previous day, Mona floated down the aisle like an angel on a cloud. Once again, her father was invisible until he turned to Mona, kissed her on the cheek and placed her hand in mine.

Although I have never told Mona, I did not even notice her wedding dress until after the service was over and the photographs were being taken. During the service, all I could see was Mona's face: A face that radiated beauty, love, passion, intelligence and everything else I had never dared hope I would find in someone—someone who I would love—someone who would love me for as long as we both should live.

It didn't matter to either of us that Mona walked down the aisle so slowly that the organist, not seeing her in his mirror, decided she must have already made it to the front and stopped playing while she was still twenty feet from finishing her processional.

It didn't matter to either of us when Pastor Cheryl inserted a Spoonerism by giving our names as Moke and Myrna.

It didn't matter to either of us when Chia dropped her bouquet and then her Bible when she was stepping forward to read the scripture.

It did however, matter to Mona when after saying our vows I placed an invisible ring on her finger. For the rest of the service she kept looking at her finger, looking up at me, and looking back at her finger again, not sure whether she should ask me what was going on or give me the now-traditional kick on the shin.

While we were kneeling during the closing prayer, Mona reached over, pulled my left hand closer to her and began to play with the ring she had just placed on my finger. She twisted it around for a while and then gently, at first, and then with a little more steam, tugged on it as if she was trying to pull it off. Whether she did this teasingly; seriously with malicious intent; or simply as an attempt to pass along some sort of telepathic message, I have never discovered. Mona has never said anything about it and I have never asked.

The service wound down as Pastor Cheryl pronounced us husband and wife, joined our hands together, and asked God to grant us a blessing "both now and in the many busy, happy years to come."

After we had kissed, she introduced us to the crowd. We smiled, and walked down the aisle fast enough to get to the back of the church before the organist stopped playing.

Soon Robert and Daniel returned from the Western front alive and with a beautiful woman on each arm, Robert then showed his romantic side by being the second person to kiss Mona as a married woman. As long as it was on her cheek, I saw no reason to complain. Mona, however, seemed to enjoy it enough to kiss him back.

Mona then reached up and straightened my tie, which had been hanging loose and crooked throughout the service. As the *coup de grace*, Robert whispered in my ear that my fly had been open the entire time.

Except for the ring, and maybe even because of it, the whole shindig turned out to be perfect. Everyone said they enjoyed it and Pastor Cheryl ended up with enough bloopers to share at wedding rehearsals for the rest of her career.

While everyone was milling around waiting for the photographer to start taking pictures, I spotted Thor's nephew Zach. I waved him over and asked if he would be willing to drive to my apartment and bring back the three things I had left sitting in my silverware drawer.

To his credit, Zach said, "Sure."

Not to his credit was when he asked if the three things happened to be gold, frankincense and myrrh.

After playfully glaring at him for a satisfying moment, I gave him the key and off he went to save the day . . . along with my neck.

Fortunately, Pastor Cheryl was planning to attend our reception. This would make it easier for everyone to sign the marriage certificate before we headed off to Europe.

Even though we would be legally married when we boarded the plane, none of Mona's ID's including her passport, drivers license, credit or debit cards, will list her as Mona Maurison. We will, however, bring along a photocopy of our Marriage Certificate—if, that is, we can cajole the Club into making a copy after we've signed it.

The photographer was a friend of Mona's family and he was very good at what he did. He took charge of the ritual, bringing all the likely suspects together in every possible combination so that: 1. Everyone felt they had been treated with the proper respect; 2. Everyone felt as though they would be immortalized in our wedding album, and 3. The photographer could make as much money off of the reprints as possible.

The final picture taken was one of Mona and me posing with Aunt Lucille and her two grown children. I have no doubt Aunt Lucille will treasure that photo much more than we ever will.

The reception took place in the "Solarium Room" at the *3 West Club,* within walking distance of the church. The option to stroll down 5th Avenue had been undercut by the continuing outpouring of celestial water, accompanied by the occasional sound of thunder echoing between the nearby skyscrapers.

Cabs were in short supply as everyone tried to get from the church to the club at the same time.

Mona and I had nothing to worry about since the limo had been placed at our disposal. Since there was enough room in it for the entire wedding party, we invited them all to ride with us in abject luxury. Everyone chose to join us except Pam and Danny who opted to bring my not-yet-dry clothes along in a cab.

The Solarium is a nice room that can seat about as many people as had shown up for the wedding. Its most distinctive feature is an exterior wall made entirely of glass, overlooking a large outdoor terrace with views of the surrounding buildings. Although an awning had been pulled out to provide some protection from the rain, the terrace didn't see a lot of traffic during the party.

The reception was more or less a catered buffet with lots of exotic nibbles and a few more hearty dishes to satisfy folks like Thor who, as he already confessed, had come for the food. An area had been cleared for a dance floor and a small combo consisting of four men with trumpet, guitar, bass and drums provided the music. The music quietly, randomly and unobtrusively morphed from classical to swing to jazz and on to an eclectic plethora of golden oldies. I suppose they could have thrown in some rap, too, but seeing how it isn't easy to do rap without someone actually using words, it was probably best they didn't try.

The table for the wedding party was set on a little platform two feet higher than the rest of the room. We were all sitting around, eating, talking, posing for pictures and smiling until our jaws locked.

Mona's friends from the bookstore oversaw the guest book and made sure everyone received one of the favors Mona and her roommates had worked so hard to make. It was fun to see Sam and Susan, Aunt Lucille's toddler grandchildren, sneaking around using their magnifying glasses to inspect everything; including the floor, the curtains, Mona's dress and, of course, the salt and pepper shakers on top of the wedding cake.

We hadn't been there long when Zach bounced into the room carrying a small plastic shopping bag.

He walked up to the wedding table and put the bag down in front of me saying, "Sorry, Mike, the other two Wise Men had previous commitments this afternoon. They send their love and congratulations."

I said, "I'll take the bag, but if you're looking for a manger you're in the wrong place."

I knew he wouldn't take a tip even if I tried to force one down his throat so I just said, "Thanks, Zach. You just helped a dead man feel alive again."

Zach made a small, obsequious bow and headed over to the buffet.

While the photographer snapped a few more pictures Mona, Pam, Robert, Pastor Cheryl and I signed the Marriage Certificate in all the right places. While Cheryl headed off to make some photocopies, I handed my passport to Mona so she could put in her purse. Without saying anything, she looked at the velvet wedding ring box I was holding in my hand and then looked up at me with a questioning eye.

"Later," I said, "but soon."

Mona shrugged her shoulders, gave me a very small smile and an even smaller kiss and the band played on.

At around 4:30 p.m. someone shouted, "Toast!" This was followed by someone else shouting, "Toast!" This continued, with more and more voices chiming in until Robert, who was sitting next to me, stood up.

When the two-foot elevation of the platform was added to his already considerable stature, he loomed eight feet three inches over the rest of the room, dominating it like Hagrid at Hogwarts.

"Quiet," he said rather quietly.

To my surprise, the room quieted down immediately. Once again, I was seeing a side of Robert I had never seen before. There he was, one of the shyest, least-spoken men I have ever known, reeling in a rowdy audience like Frank Sinatra and Elvis used to do in Vegas.

Robert looked around for his glass of Champagne but since one of the waiters had just picked it up to bring him a refill he opted for his water glass instead.

"I have a toast," he said. "Because I'm the Best Man, I have a toast."

He paused as though trying to decide whether to *ad lib* something or stick with the script he had written. For some reason or other, he defied the Second Law of Thermodynamics by choosing to say a few words without benefit of a teleprompter.

"Mike asked me to be his Best Man. Two months ago, he was mine. Mike is a good man . . . an honorable man. I am lucky to be his friend."

He reached into a pocket and pulled out a piece of paper.

After opening it, he raised his glass and said, "I have a toast. Here it is:

"Mike, this afternoon you got married to Mona. Before Mona came along you were a nice guy but a lonely one, just like I was before I met Chia. But now you have Mona and Mona has you. I can't say that you are stuck with each other, but I think I can say that you are stuck *on* each other! Stay stuck, my friend.

"Stay stuck on Mona like feathers stuck on a bird enable it to fly. I want the two of you to fly like a bird and soar like an eagle because you are inseparably stuck on each other.

"Like skin that is stuck on your body, keep each other safe and secure.

"Like paint that is stuck on a canvass, bring color, shape and form to your life together.

"Like musical notes that are stuck on a piece of paper, bring melody and harmony into the world, making it a better place for those around you.

"Mike: with Mona you are bigger, stronger and more beautiful than you were before. Live your life so you will be for Mona what she has become for you.

"Now, here's the toast.

"To Mike: May you and Mona be stuck on each other in such a way that when people look at you they will see God's smile joined with your own."

"To Mike! . . . and to Mona!"

The glasses clinked and everyone who was paying attention to what was going on took at least one sip of whatever they had in the glass they had just lifted up.

There were other toasts after Robert's. There was one from Mona's father and one from Pam. Even I worked up the nerve to offer one to Mona and she giggled her way through the one she had for me.

While we were chewing on the last of the Buffalo wings, Thor came over to our table and handed me a slip of paper.

"My brother lives in London near the Charing Cross railroad station. He's got a store. If you're in the neighborhood stop by and say 'Hi' to him for me."

I stuffed the address in my wallet and immediately forgot about it.

As we stood up to cut the cake, most people stopped talking to watch.

Taking advantage of the lull, I announced that I had an important announcement to make.

"Some of you have asked Mona if you could look at her ring. Some of you may have noticed that she didn't have one. Well, if you haven't already figured it out I left the ring at home and didn't have it to give to her during the service. But now, thanks to Zach, I have it and I would like to place it on her finger as a sign and seal of my love for her 'til death do us part."

Just as I had done at Robert and Chia's wedding reception, I got down on one knee, took Mona's hand in mine, placed the ring on her finger and said, "Mona, with this ring I give myself to you. Wear it as a reminder of the promises we made today. I love you and I will love you forever."

As I stood up someone shouted, "Kiss the Bride. Kiss her again!"

People started clinking their forks against their glasses so we had no choice but to do what we were told. Later, we both agreed that kissing is something we should do more often and not just when pressured by the hue and cry of popular demand.

Next, as Mona waved her left hand in the air flashing her ring for all to see, we cut the cake and smushed small pieces of it into each other's mouth.

After the cake had been served Mona and I danced and everyone stood watching as the band played an old love song, "I Only Have Eyes for You."

Mona danced with her father and I danced with her mother. Then I danced with Aunt Lucille and soon everyone was dancing with everyone else. It was a good way to end the evening and a good time for Mona and I to slip out and change into our travel clothes.

As I was dancing my final dance with Chia, I asked her about Robert's speech.

"Where in the world did that come from? Did you write it or help him write it? Where did all those words come from and how did he say it all so well? Help me out here; I don't get it."

"Mike," Chia said, "Didn't Robert ever tell you? During his senior year of high school, he won Third Place in the New York State High School Speech Competition.

"When he sits around and talks, he talks like Robert. When he speaks from a written speech, he sounds like Abraham Lincoln or Dr. King. He spent a long time on the speech he gave today. It doesn't really come easily for him like it does for some people, but when he takes the time to prepare a speech he pours everything he has into it. Just like he did today. And Mike . . . he did it for you."

Appropriate to the context I was left speechless. Robert had once again brought out a new surprise and handed it to me on a platter. With some people, what you see is what you get. With Robert, what you get is all too often something you had never seen before.

When I first met Robert years ago, I knew right away there was something beautiful buried deep inside his otherwise stoic exterior and I liked him for it.

Today, in a new and unexpected way, I was shown just how deep and profound that beauty is . . . and I love him for it.

After a brief final turn on the dance floor with Mona, we performed our disappearing act. A few minutes later, after Mona applied a new layer of *aloe vera* on my sunburn, we magically reappeared, transformed into our plain-Jane ordinary selves.

I threw Mona's garter over my head into the hands of Chia's brother, Miggy, and Mona threw her bouquet into the eager arms of her roommate, Corrine. The rain stopped long enough for everyone to crowd out onto the sidewalk and see us drive away in the limo. As we pushed our way through family and friends, we were softly and gently pelted by handfuls of popcorn that had been handed out in sandwich baggies. The popcorn was not only biodegradable but until it dissolved in the rain or was swept up by someone with a broom, it would provide a nice meal for the pigeons. For Mona and me the popcorn provided a symbolic way for those who had touched our lives to shower their love and blessings on us as we embarked on our new life together.

For a fleeting moment, I wished that I had some popcorn to throw back at them, but once we were in the back of the limo, I was distracted by Mona showing how much she loved me.

Compared to that, the popcorn didn't stand a chance.

- -

I have always prided myself on being independent and completely free from the burden of having to rely on anyone else for anything. To her credit, Mona has been working overtime to show me the error of my ways.

Take this wedding thing for example. I was happy to step back and let her be in charge.

The trip to Europe is in the same category. If it had been up to me, I would have taken care of the whole pilgrimage by booking a flight to London and getting off the plane. Then I would have found a tourist map and figured out where to go from there. That's how I do things and it works for me.

Now that I'm part of a team I'm discovering that the things that work for me don't always work for Mona. I am also learning that with two romantically inclined people there is never such a thing as a tie vote. If one person votes, "No," the matter has been decided . . . the "Nays" have it. On those occasions when we don't agree on something Mona generally seems to feel more strongly about it than I do so if it doesn't involve my job or what I do when Mona goes to church I'm usually willing to break the tie by compromising in her favor.

Some people might consider me to be a wimp or a push-over because of this but the way I see it is why fight over something that doesn't really matter all that much? The old bumper sticker said, "Make love, not war." When it comes to Mona, I really, really prefer the love.

What I'm leading up to is this: After the limo dropped us off at the airport and after we had checked our luggage and gotten our tickets printed out, I was so confident in Mona's judgment that I fell asleep in the waiting area. Maybe it had something to do with the champagne at the reception. Maybe it was because my sunburn had kept me awake for most of the previous night. Maybe it had something to do with the motion-sickness medication I took when we walked into the ticketing area.

Whatever it was, it put me into such a deep sleep that it took every trick in Mona's psychological warfare manual to convince me to stand up and stagger onto the plane and into my seat. I vaguely remember asking Mona if there was going to be a movie during the flight but, other than that, the next thing I remember was the Pilot announcing we were beginning our descent to Heathrow.

As I said, I used to value my independence. Now I realize that "letting go and letting Mona" is usually the better road to take. After all, Mona was the only thing that saved me from waking up in the JFK waiting room and discovering that my plane had already landed in London.

Chapter 15
Trafalgar

Monday, July 15

As the plane began its descent, I told Mona I was sorry I had been such a bore during the flight. Mona said that except for the times when I crushed her against the bulkhead, snoring and slobbering, I had been as much of a husband as she had bargained for.

When I asked if I had missed anything she said, "Not much. The only interesting things were the two times you sleepwalked over to the bathroom. Passengers were actually taking bets on whether you would find your way back to your seat on the first try or not."

I didn't bother to ask how the bookies made out.

Since it was nearly 10:30 a.m. British time, the sun was up and the green countryside of England gleamed where the sun was able to squeeze its way through the clouds. As we flew closer to Heathrow the fields began to disappear beneath houses and towns, roads and freeways, railroad lines and sprawling factories. It was clear we were approaching the city of London, spreading and oozing its way across the landscape like a gigantic puddle of spilled molasses.

The way I see it, New York doesn't exactly sprawl; it just sort of sits where it is; as if God made it in one piece and then dropped it out of the sky. In contrast, my first impression of London was that it was something more organic, like a tree with its life-blood moving outward towards its edges rather than flowing inward like New York City does towards its beating heart: Manhattan.

As soon as we touched down, I noticed my sunburn did not hurt as badly as it had the day before. Adding that to a trans-Atlantic nap, I practically bounded off the plane with my carry-on bag in one hand and Mona's in the other.

After picking up our luggage, we went through customs as easy-as-you-please with maybe one exception: When I reached for my passport and couldn't find it I felt like Mel Brooks in *High Anxiety* until Mona gently reminded me that I had given it to her to put in her purse for safekeeping.

Once we emerged from customs as legal visitors to the United Kingdom, Mona pointed the way towards the train that would take us to Paddington Station. We were wheeling our luggage along on a cart until we came to an escalator that went straight down and deep below ground level. Mona was so excited she stepped on the escalator and descended into Hades leaving me behind with the luggage.

There were signs everywhere that warned, "Do not leave luggage unattended at any time." Ignoring the sign and not knowing what else to do, I put the three suitcases on the escalator one at a time and sent them down to Mona. Either no one noticed or no one cared that we had bent the rules just a little. When we reunited at the bottom of the escalator and headed towards the train, Mona noticed we could have skipped the escalator by taking an elevator.

The train zipped us along just like the ones back in New York, passing through deep cuts where most of the scenery was masonry walls and nondescript buildings, along with the usual assorted trees and bushes. Eventually we arrived at Paddington where we withdrew some local currency from an ATM, walked over to the nearest Underground station and took the Bakerloo Line straight to Trafalgar Square. If I had closed my eyes during the ride, I would have thought I was back in New York, riding the subway home on the #6 train under Lexington Avenue.

I can honestly say that both our honeymoon and our new life as husband and wife began the moment we emerged from the Charing Cross Underground Station and stepped into the sights and sounds of Trafalgar Square. In front of us loomed the Lord Nelson Column with the Admiral taking in the view from the top. Across the square to our right stood the National Gallery and next to it stood the iconic steeple of Christopher Wren's Church of St. Martin's-In-the-Fields. The sight was exotic, of course, but also so familiar it seemed as though we were coming home for the first time.

Mona's parents had booked us into *The Grand at Trafalgar Square*, a large hotel just half a block behind us on Northumberland Avenue. According to the minute-by-minute schedule they had prepared for us, we were supposed to arrive at the hotel at 1:10 pm. They must have done their homework because the time showing on my cell phone was 1:14 pm. In five minutes, we were checking into the hotel and five minutes later, we were sprawled on our bed exhausted.

Mona started it all off by trying not to let her smile get away from her. The excitement finally got the best of her and she started laughing. For the first time since our wedding we were alone, relaxed and with time on our hands. Mona's parents had scheduled us to eat lunch at 1:30 pm but we never got around to it. Instead, we laughed, and cuddled, and spent the rest of the afternoon discovering what it feels like to be a husband and a wife. As far as we cared, it didn't matter that we were in London at all. We would have had just as much fun that afternoon if we had been in Hackensack.

If my sunburn hurt, I never noticed.

At 5:00 pm, it dawned on us we had not only missed lunch but also the bus tour of London Mona's parents had scheduled for us. This got Mona laughing all over again when she finally realized it was going to be our honeymoon after all and not her parents'.

The afternoon had been so good that we seriously considered ordering dinner from room service and spending the next two days in bed seeing if practice, practice, practice, could get us to Carnegie Hall without having to fly our way back over the Atlantic. In the end, we decided we should stretch our legs and check out the neighborhood before it got completely dark.

The hotel Concierge suggested we might enjoy walking down to the Thames and then stopping for dinner at a pub on Whitehall before looping back to the hotel by way of Trafalgar Square.

We walked down to the river side by side but when we came to the Victoria Embankment, we walked hand in hand. Several evening dinner cruises drifted past in front of the giant Ferris wheel that Londoner's have dubbed "The Eye." Up the river, we could see the Westminster Bridge leading to Big Ben and the houses of Parliament on our side of the river.

In spite of the traffic zooming along next to us, it was more romantic than I had imagined when I dreamed about the Thames while walking along the East River Esplanade.

Following the Concierge's directions, we turned up Whitehall Avenue. As we neared Trafalgar Square, we saw several pubs and chose one on our side of the street. Inside it could have passed for a Hollywood cliché of what Jolly Old England should look like. Deeply moved and inspired by the setting, we ordered Fish and Chips along with two English ales and dined like a king and a queen enjoying a banquet in the presence of a host of loyal subjects.

When we finished eating, we walked up the street and took in the beautiful lights that illuminated the buildings around Trafalgar Square. After a romantic kiss or two, we decided it was time to head back to the hotel and start practicing again.

Chapter 16

Trash or Treasure?

Tuesday, July 16

Breakfast in bed.

Well maybe not exactly in bed, but Room Service was kind enough to deliver our request for an old-fashioned, traditional English breakfast: rashers and bangers, grease-fried eggs, a broiled tomato, small boiled potatoes, a butter-saturated slice of toast and a pot of marmalade. All of it washed down with tea and milk poured into a cup at the same time from two different containers one being a teapot wrapped in a hand-knitted cozy.

There are so many fat calories in this meal that you can watch your waist begin to enlarge before you eat the toast. With healthy eating being a high priority these days, we had to put in a special order since this particular breakfast no longer appears on the menu.

Mona announced she didn't plan to wear her wedding dress again anytime soon; so she led the *Charge of the Light Brigade* through the sodden feast until, in the end, the food defeated us.

The clock said 8:00 a.m. and, according to our schedule, we were thirty minutes ahead with plenty of time on our hands before the National Gallery opened at 10:00 a.m.

As we straightened up the breakfast dishes, Mona picked up a crumpled piece of paper from the floor to add to the pile of culinary debris.

For some reason she un-crumpled it and asked, "Mike, what's this? It says, 'Huàng Than Du,' with a phone number and an address on 'Chandos Place near Charing Cross.'"

It took a moment for this to register in my brain but when it did I said, "Oh, that must be the note Thor gave me at the reception. I stuck it in my wallet and forgot about it. It must have fallen out when I tipped the guy who brought breakfast."

"Who's Huàng Than Du?" Mona asked.

"Thor said it's his brother. Did you say Charing Cross? That's where we are now, isn't it? or are we in Westminster? or Trafalgar? I'm so confused. But Charing Cross is the name of the Underground station where we got off the subway so Chandos Street, or Place, or whatever, must be around here someplace."

Mona got a look in her eyes that said, *Hey, do you want to have an adventure before we have our adventure?*

Her lips backed up her eyes by saying, "Hey, we've got over an hour to kill. Let's look him up and see if he runs a pawn shop or something. Let's do it for our good friend Thor. I'm ready to go!"

So off we went, down to the Concierge to find out how to get to Than Du's address. It turned out to be easy. We turned right at St. Martin's Church and then slipped into an alley in the back that turned into Chandros Place. Less than a block further on we found a newsagent shop that matched the address. The place was already open for business.

Inside was a man who looked exactly like Thor, only older and heavier.

"Are you Mr. Du?" Mona asked.

"Yes," the man said, "I am Du. In fact with this belly of mine some people say that I am 'over-Du.' Get it?"

Mona and I both groaned. Thor couldn't have delivered the line any better.

"Well," Du continued. "What can I do for you? Need a paper? Or a lotto ticket? How about a *Twirl* for breakfast?" he added, holding up a Cadbury chocolate bar.

"No thanks," I said. "We just stopped by to pass on a 'Hello' to you from Thor."

"Văn? . . . Văn Tong?" Du looked surprised. "Do you know Văn?"

"If he goes by the name of Thor, then I suppose we do," Mona answered.

"He's a friend," I added. "His pawn shop is just down the street from where I live in Manhattan. In fact, he was at our wedding on Sunday and told us to say, 'Hello' to you if we got the chance."

Not knowing what else to say, I gave a small wave and said, "So . . . 'Hi!'"

Du got all excited and called for his wife to come out from the back to meet us.

"This is my wife, Thị Yen. Maybe you know our son, Zach? He lives with Văn and works as a private eye. We talk on Skype every Friday night."

"Sure I know Zach, and I'm the private eye he's worked with a couple of times. He's a good kid and he's helped me get out of a few scrapes. It was nice to meet you. We're glad you were in."

"What?" he said, with a worried look on his face. "You're not leaving? You just got here! No, wait."

He tuned to his wife.

"*Me*, you watch the store. I'm going to show our friends around."

Without bothering to ask, Du handed each of us a *Twirl*, grabbed me by the arm and dragged us into the back room and up a flight of stairs to their bedroom apartment on the second floor. We didn't know it at the time but thanks to Du our honeymoon plans were about to enter a detour.

A quick glance at my cell phone told me it was 8:50 a.m. so I figured we could engage in a little small talk before heading over to the National Gallery. While Du talked, I flashed an "okay" sign to Mona and she nodded back.

What Du was talking about had to do with a painting he found in a trash bin in the street behind his shop. The painting appeared to have been removed from a frame, rolled up, placed inside a cardboard tube and sealed with packing tape.

"I'm not sure what it is," Du said. "I talked with Văn about it and I guess that's why he gave you my address—to help me out with some advice. Would you be willing to look at the painting and let me know what you think?"

The speech was followed by a long silence as Mona and I stared at each other like Medusas turning each other into stone.

I broke the silence by saying, "Do you mind if I talk this over with Mona for a moment by ourselves?"

"Sure," Du said, "I'll get some tea while you talk."

I moved across the room and sat next to Mona.

"What do you think? Do you want to look at the painting? We still have time to get to the museum by 10:00 am. I say let's take a peek."

Mona nodded but before I could even say anything to Du, he brought in a tray with tea while balancing a cardboard tube underneath.

"Here's some tea and here's the painting. I knew you would want to see it."

The tea sat untouched while Du carefully pulled a rolled canvas from the tube. Gently he unrolled it onto the dining table.

It was a dark figure, a face and torso, shimmering with glints of golden-yellow highlights, set against a lighter, un-detailed background. In Du's apartment, sunlight from a nearby window reflected on the varnish making it hard to see clearly. Du noticed this too and closed the blinds.

As my eyes adjusted to the light, I saw the face of my Grandpa Van Rijn staring back at me. It wasn't the same face as the one I knew so well from the Met Museum in New York but there was no doubt it was the same person although much, much younger.

Like the painting in the Met, the man's eyes looked straight out of the canvass with his head turned slightly to the side. He was wearing what appeared to be a brown furred robe over a dark gray shirt with the hint of a crimson red satin sash around his waist at the bottom of the painting. On his head was a square, off-white, brimless Dutch-style cap tilted at an angle I could only describe as jaunty. In the lower right corner of the painting were the initials "RL" connected by a line, and the date 1631. The "R" had a distinctive loop in the middle.

"I know what you're thinking, "Du said. "I looked up some things on the internet.

"Did you know that between 1800 and 1850 over 9,000 Rembrandts were imported to the United States? A few years later, there was a list of 15,000 Rembrandts in public and private collections. Today the number of authenticated Rembrandts is around 450. It seems there was a real trade in forgeries and in adding fake signatures to old paintings. One source said there are over 100 Rembrandts that have been stolen or are otherwise unaccounted for."

"How come you know so much about art?" Mona asked.

"I don't know anything except what I read on the internet and that's why I want your opinion. According to Văn, you both know a lot about art and one of you is a private eye. That seemed to be a good combination for the advice I need."

There was a pause and then Du asked, "Well?"

It crossed my mind that both Rembrandt and Thor had the same middle name but I let the thought go, looked at the painting again and offered a shoot-from-the-hip opinion.

"Since the painting has been taken out of a frame and hidden in a cheap cardboard tube, it would suggest that it's probably a forgery that embarrassed someone so much that they kept the frame and threw out the painting as inconspicuously as they could.

"But that doesn't really make any sense. Even if it was a forgery, the painting is good enough to fetch at least some money at auction, especially if was painted by a 17th century contemporary of Rembrandt who could be identified.

"The only other explanation I can think of is that it is a real Rembrandt, stolen and placed in the trash bin to be picked up by someone as part of some black market transaction. The plan was probably going smoothly until you messed it up by finding the painting before the other guy showed up.

"Mona," I added, "What do you think?"

"I think you're probably right about the black market thing," she said, "but it's got to be a fake. The odds are so much against it being an original."

"Du," I asked, "can I borrow your computer for a minute?"

"Sure," he replied, pointing to a table in the corner of the room, "It's right there, ready to go."

I sat down and *Googled*: "Rembrandt stolen paintings."

Not much showed up, but there had been a very similar Rembrandt *Self Portrait* dated 1630 that had been stolen from the National Museum of Stockholm in 2000 and recovered five years later.

"Du," I said. "I don't know what to say. All I can suggest is that you take it over to the National Gallery and have one of the curators take a look at it. If it's been stolen it should be returned. If it's not, then you either own a valuable painting, an interesting forgery, or you are in big trouble with a very angry criminal network."

Du thought about it for a moment before replying, "I was afraid you were going to say that but of course, you're right. Stay here while I make a phone call."

When Du came back, I asked if I could borrow his phone and download an app I thought might come in handy sometime. Du shrugged his shoulders and handed me his phone.

"Here," he said, handing me a second phone. "If it's such a good thing you might as well do Thị Yen's phone, too."

Ten minutes later, we trotted over to the National Gallery. It was 9:50 a.m. so the public entrance hadn't opened yet. Because Du had called ahead, the guard let us into the administrative offices. After waiting for twenty minutes, we were greeted by the Assistant Curator for Conservation. After the painting had been ceremoniously unrolled and inspected the curator's preliminary verdict was inconclusive.

"I have never seen or heard of this painting before but we'll have to contact Interpol to see if it has been stolen. Then we'll run it by our specialized staff for analysis. If you're willing to leave it with us I'll see that you receive a receipt."

Du said "Yes."

Without asking, Du put my name down as co-owner of the painting.

When the curator asked me to sign, I asked Du, "What the heck are you thinking?"

Du said, "Maybe I won't be able to pick it up when they're done. Maybe I'll be dead. Who knows? You're here standing around apparently with nothing else to do so why not? Be sure to put down your address and phone number."

I couldn't argue with his logic so I added the info and signed the receipt just to make him happy. Since we were now partners in this whole thing, I added the phone numbers for Du and his wife to my cell phone's "Contacts" list, both listed under "Du."

The curator said, "Is there anything else I can do for you?"

Du said, "No, I've got to get back to my store."

Mona said, "How about a private tour of the museum?"

I said, "Mona! Don't . . ."

The curator said, "I can arrange it if you don't mind waiting for a few minutes."

We shook hands with Du. We said "Ta ta" and "Good luck," and five minutes later we were being escorted into the museum by a postgraduate intern from Oxford.

It was 10:45 a.m.

We knew exactly what we wanted to see and where to find it. Having the intern along for the ride made the whole thing more fun than either of us could have dreamed. We not only had the chance to see the amazing collections close up and personal, but we also got to see some of the areas otherwise not open to the public.

Inside the staff entrance, for example, is a bust of Wellington, originally carved to fit into the center of the empty wreath held by the two figures over the main entrance to the museum. The bust and figures were supposed to be part of what is now known as the Marble Arch.

The arch, commemorating the British victory over Napoleon, had originally been part of the newly built Buckingham Palace. When the palace was remodeled and enlarged the arch was relocated to the northeast corner of Hyde Park where it stands in the middle of a traffic island. Only members of the royal family and the Kings Group, Royal Artillery can parade through it.

The information was useless trivia, but to us of course, it was pure gold!

After a quick lunch in the museum café, we took a cab through Admiralty Arch and up the Mall to Buckingham Palace.

We spent a few minutes staring at the man in the sentry box with the rifle, the red jacket and the bearskin hat. He was standing as immobile as the traffic around Turtle Bay when the U.N. is in session. Who would have guessed London could be so boring.

So we took another cab over to the Tate Britain Gallery a mile or so up-river from Parliament.

The Tate houses the national collection of British art, which means that Rembrandt and O'Keefe can't get in even if they purchase a ticket. It's not that the London curators are snobs, or anything but if you're not British enough you are shuffled off to the National Gallery or the Tate Modern with the rest of the foreigners.

If you are a fan of Turner, Blake or Constable then by all means, buy a plane ticket to London right away before global warming puts downtown London under water.

If you like trivia, the Tate has over 70,000 works of art and the second most-viewed item on-line is Marcel Duchamp's *Fountain*, a ceramic urinal with writing on it. Go figure. It is so popular they have a whole row of reproductions attached to the wall of the Men's Room down the hall.

Mona and I discussed why a French urinal created by a French artist was hanging on the wall of a museum called the "Tate Britain." We decided that, in some convoluted way, it probably made sense in a country where people live in places with names like Flushing, Looe, and Crapstone.

After spending two hours trying our best to appreciate everything there was to see, we sat on a bench and stared at each other with glazed eyes. For some reason the European art scene was not turning out to be as exciting or inspiring as we had hoped. Maybe there *can* be too much of a good thing. Maybe our heads were in London but our hearts were still back with our friends at the Met and the MoMA in New York. Here in the Tate, we felt as though we had crashed someone else's party and found ourselves surrounded by someone else's friends.

We stood up and left.

As soon as we stepped outside the museum, my phone rang.

It was a high-pitched woman's voice speaking so fast and with such a thick accent I couldn't understand a word she was saying.

So of course, I handed the phone to Mona.

Mona stood quietly with the phone stuck in her ear listening. Every so often she said something like, "Yes," or "Could you repeat that," or "Are you sure?"

Finally, she said, "We'll be right there," and handed me the phone.

"What do you mean, 'We'll be right there?' Where? What's going on?"

"That was Thị Yen. She sounded hysterical. I could hardly understand anything she said, but I think she was trying to say that someone broke into their house and tore it all up. Du's not home so she phoned you. I don't know why she phoned you but she wants us to come over right away. I said we'd be right there."

It was 3:45 pm when, for the second time that day we headed over to Chandros Place.

Mona's parents had given us plenty of spare change to throw around so we paid for another cab and were standing in front of Du's store in ten minutes.

Thị Yen met us at the door but stopped and carefully looked up and down the street before letting us inside. She locked the door behind us and silently led the way upstairs to their apartment.

"Here it is," she said. "The mess! Oh, what a mess!"

Personally, I have been in plenty of messy apartments and compared to those I would have only scored this one a 2 out of 10. There were, however, a few things clearly out of place, especially around Du's computer table and desk.

"Tell us what happened," Mona asked.

"Please," Thị Yen said, "sit down. I am sorry I did not prepare tea. I am so upset."

"Go ahead," I said. "We can skip the tea."

"It's that painting," she wailed. "It's that terrible painting. The moment he brought it home, I said to him, 'Throw it away! It's trash! It will bring us back luck! I don't want it in my house!'

"But Du wouldn't listen to me. He phoned Văn and after they talked, he kept the painting. He looked at it every day and spent hours on the computer looking at pictures. Already that *thing* was taking over our house and our lives. 'Get rid of it,' I begged him.

"Then you came this morning and he took it to the big museum and when he came back he did not have it anymore. I was so happy."

She smiled at the memory but her face quickly became serious and almost distraught.

"Du left at Noon to go to Battersy to get a part for our furnace and to talk to our banker about our loan. He must have turned his cell phone off because I phone him and he doesn't answer.

"I close the store early so I can buy food for dinner and when I come back the front door is closed but not locked. I carry the food upstairs and put it away in the kitchen and when I come out, I see papers on the floor. Du's computer is on and the things on his desk are moved around. Du is so neat. He never leaves anything out of place. Ever.

"I am afraid so I call Du and when he doesn't answer, I call you because you are a private eye like my son, Zach, okay? I don't know what to do. I am so upset."

Mona and I sat there not knowing what to say or do, either.

"When is Du coming home?" I asked, trying to break the silence.

"Soon, I think. Maybe 4:30, I think."

"And what was taken," I asked.

"I don't know. Everything that I have is here. I don't know what Du has. It's so fearful. I am so afraid because someone is in my house. What should I do?"

"Don't you have family or friends you could call?" Mona asked.

"No, just Zach and Văn and Du's aunt. They all live in New York. Everyone else stay in Vietnam or, well, they're gone. We have friends, but you are smart man who knows about things like this. So I call you."

Mona suggested that Thị Yen call the police but she said, "No."

She wanted to wait until Du came home, since he is the one who makes those sorts of decisions.

"It's that terrible painting," she wailed again. "I told him it would be bad luck!"

Mona and I had reservations for a dinner cruise on the Thames that evening but as the Scottish Poet Robert Burns once put it, "The best-laid schemes o' mice an' men gang aft agley."

We sat and stared at the walls while Thị Yen made tea. Then we sat and smiled at each other while we drank the tea. By the time the tea started to get too cold to swallow Du showed up.

Thị Yen said, "Du, I phone you all afternoon. Why you not answer?"

"Because," Du said, "I left my phone on my desk. I forgot it. Why? . . . What were you calling me about and why are Mike and Mona here?"

As he said this Du shook our hands and since we had stood when he walked in he made us sit again.

"Because," Thi Yen answered, "we were robbed . . . I think I mean . . . I think *you* were robbed."

She pointed over to his desk in the corner.

Du slowly walked over and stood looking at the desk, the shuffled papers and the computer. He opened the drawers to his desk and looked inside. He checked a few files on his computer and then turned around with a puzzled look on his face.

"My phone is missing. It's gone. I can't tell if anything else is missing. I'll have to think about it and sort through all the papers before I can be sure."

"Why would someone break into your place just to steal your phone?" I asked. "That makes no sense to me at all."

"Maybe they want my pictures? Or my address book? I don't know."

"It seems odd to me," I replied, "they didn't touch anything else. It looks as though they were looking for only one thing and because they left such a small mess they must have found it right away."

I waited for a moment in case Du wanted to say anything. He didn't so I did.

"Du, I don't think they broke in to steal your phone."

"Maybe you should call the police and give them a report?" Mona asked for the second time.

"No," said Du. "Maybe later, but not now.

"When I was growing up in Vietnam I . . . well . . . the police weren't very nice to my family so . . . I try to keep away from them. . . . even here . . . where we have lived for twenty-five years . . . .

"No, I think we will not call the police," he continued. "I'll just get a new phone and see what happens. I think it was kids. They saw the phone, took it, got scared and ran away.

"Thank you for coming over but now you must go and enjoy your honeymoon. Go on, scoot!"

We said our goodbyes. We said "Thank you for the tea." We said, "We hope it all turns out," and we left.

We managed to get to our cruise boat in time and ate dinner while we watched the sun set like a brown ball sifting through the thick haze. As it turned out, the view of London from the Thames was less romantic than I had hoped. Sort of like the East River.

It had been a long day. When we got back to the hotel, we went straight to bed and slept like Rip van Winkle.

My last thought before fading out, was to ponder why so many parents give their kids the middle name, "Van."

Chapter 17
Famous Dead People

Wednesday, July 17

Today Mona's parents had penciled us in for the Tower of London. They had even purchased advance tickets so we could avoid the long lines. Neither of us had ever been to a real castle before so we felt like the Connecticut Yankee dropping into King Arthur's Court but without the eclipse.

There were Beefeaters guarding the place. They were carrying spears and wearing red uniforms inspired by "Alice in Wonderland" with Mary Poppins hats on their heads. It was all very English.

We skipped the tour and tripped along the cobblestones by ourselves to see where Raleigh and Bolyn were subdivided, where the two young princes were murdered and where the cruel and bloodthirsty monarchs worshiped on Sundays.

The highlight, of course, was the display of the Crown Jewels. Because of the crowds, and to prevent anyone from trying to engage in impulse buying they herd everyone through the display at around two miles an hour. This gave us such a brief glimpse of the diamond-encrusted scepter and headgear that we had to fork over a small fortune to buy a book with pictures so we could see what they actually looked like.

There is a tradition that says the castle will never fall to an enemy as long as there are ravens walking around so the Beefeaters make sure the ravens stay put by clipping one of their wings and feeding them so much birdseed they would be too fat to fly anyway.

It is, apparently, a matter of national security

Our grand tour continued with a stop at the Tate Modern Gallery, a cavernous space located in a remodeled power station alongside the Thames. We were getting tired of museums but we both wanted to the see Monet's *Water Lilies*. It was bigger than we had imagined and our necks ached from staring up at it. In art books it has always looked drab green and fuzzy but in person, it shimmered with color and texture. I won't say it is worth a trip to England to see it but it was worth the time we took for our pit-stop visit to the museum.

On our way out, we paid our regards to a few Picassos, Mondrians, Modiglianis and Braques, which along with the Monet had somehow escaped exile to the National Gallery for not being British.

"Why are we doing this?" Mona asked as we gulped down a Ploughman's Lunch at a nearby pub. "We're supposed to be on a honeymoon and we're spending all our time standing in lines, rushing around and getting too tired to enjoy anything."

"But Mona," I said as I chewed on a pickled onion, "we leave for Paris tomorrow and we still have Parliament and Westminster Abby this afternoon and the *Taming of the Shrew* at the Globe Theatre tonight. If that's too much what do you want to leave out? And what would you rather do for the rest of the day?"

Her answer humbled me.

"I just want to be with you."

We skipped Parliament and spent the extra time strolling slowly through Westminster Abbey. We took time to sit in a couple of chairs and soak in the gothic splendor of the place; musty and fusty with history. Under my chair was a flagstone with the words "O Rare Ben Johnson" carved in it. There is a story that Johnson asked King Charles I for eighteen-inches of ground in Westminster Abbey so when he died the king had him buried standing up.

Of course, I apologized for sitting on his head.

What a place!

There were famous dead people buried everywhere we looked and after a while the abbey began to seem more like a cemetery than a church. But that all changed when someone started playing a Bach Toccata and Fugue on the great organ.

As Mona put it, "Now the place seems more like a place to worship."

While Mona bowed her head and prayed, I couldn't help but think this was a place where God probably feels comfortable kicking back and simply being awesome from time to time. The atmosphere was so holy that I added a short prayer of my own.

"Thank you God, for giving me Mona and for giving us this trip to such a beautiful place."

It wasn't much of a prayer but as I learned months ago it's sort of nice to have someone to say "Thank you" to when I'm feeling . . . well . . . thankful for something.

We spent the rest of the afternoon strolling around, walking in and out of stores and shops, listening to people with funny accents, and nibbling on crumpets and treacle washed down with shandy; which by the way, doesn't go very well with treacle.

We held hands, took time to kiss, went back to the hotel, ate a leisurely dinner in a nice restaurant and traded Shakespeare for an early bedtime.

London can be a very romantic place—but only if you slow down and take the time to stop and smell a few of those fragrant, red, English roses.

Mona, of course, is the most beautiful rose of them all.

Chapter 18
City of Lights
Thursday, June 18

Our flight to Paris didn't leave until Noon so we slept in and had a late breakfast before checking out of the hotel and dragging our luggage back to the Charing Cross tube station.

Off we went, back to Heathrow for the mid-day commuter flight to Paris. It seems strange to think that flying from London to Paris is a commuter flight; only a few miles further than New York City to Boston. The flight took us an hour and fifteen minutes. If you live in England or France it isn't such a big deal, but for Mona and me it was a massive leap from one world to another.

Unlike London where everyone speaks English, in Paris everyone speaks French. I know this seems obvious but until you actually get off the plane at De Gaulle International Airport for the first time, the reality of the language difference is hard to fathom.

Since everyone in London speaks English, Britain was like being in America but with an accent. In France, we felt like strangers in a strange land.

Back in New York, everywhere you look there are immigrants and tourists from all over the world. Until we landed in France, I had never really considered how hard it must be to set up shop in a place where you can't read the signs, carry on a conversation or even ask directions without feeling like calling it quits and curling up on the sidewalk for a good cry.

Unlike our friend Robert, we didn't do any curling . . . or any crying for that matter. That was because Mona had armed herself with a step-by-step list of where to go, what train to catch and what taxis to take to where we were going to stay. In our case, it was a small room in a small hotel in the Latin Quarter a few blocks up from the Seine near the Cathedral of Notre Dame.

In Manhattan, the Latin Quarter is called Spanish Harlem but in Paris, the Latin Quarter got its name from all the students at the Sorbonne who spoke Latin back when the Cathedral was still new. Hearing this ended what little hope I had that my smattering of Spanish would be of any use.

"Well, here we are," Mona announced as we dropped our luggage onto the floor of our room and threw ourselves on the bed exhausted.

What Mona said was, of course, an all-purpose phrase equally valid anywhere you might choose to say it. That may be, but as usual, Mona got it right. We were here. We were in Paris, faced with one of the only blank spaces on our itinerary. Mona's parents had helpfully marked out the rest of the afternoon and evening as "Free Play." I was so tired I had a hard time choosing between recess or taking a nap on a flannel blankie.

After a short rest, we chose recess and headed outside for a walk around the neighborhood. Since we had to choose between walking uphill or downhill, we chose the easier of the two and headed towards the Seine.

The Left Bank is famous because of all the literary figures who wandered around there in the old days. Hemingway, Gertrude Stein and Fitzgerald used to hang out together, drinking wine and sharing *bon mots* for their own entertainment. None of them was particularly famous back then so no one paid any attention to them. Later, of course, they got older and more famous, and then they died.

Their spirits live on in the booths along the riverbank where beret-wearing vendors sell watercolors, used books, sheet music, and prints cut out of old books. There are also booths selling the usual t-shirts and souvenir teaspoons with a miniature Arc de Triumph or Notre Dame on the top instead of a Tower Bridge or Big Ben like in London.

"I'm hungry," I said.

I spoke loudly so my voice wouldn't be drowned out by the growling of my stomach.

"Where do you want to eat?" I added.

"Right here would be nice," Mona said.

We sat down at a sidewalk café and ordered crepes and two glasses of red wine. Neither of us is a snob or a *sommelier* so we couldn't tell whether it was a Beaujolais, a Pinot Noir or a generic Claret, but we were hungry and thirsty and it was all just marvelous.

Even though it wasn't on our itinerary until Saturday we walked two blocks and crossed the bridge that took us to the *Île de la Cité* and the Cathedral of Notre Dame.

"Where do they keep the hunchbacks?" I asked and Mona replied by giving me an elbow to the ribs.

When we came close enough to look at the carvings on the three enormous doorways in the West Portico, all Mona could say was, "Wow!"

Over the central doorway was a massive scene of Judgment Day. There were dead people rising from their coffins and an angel and a devil in the center of the action holding a scale that was giving everyone either a thumbs up or thumbs down. The winners piously look up at Jesus who is sitting impassively over the whole scene with his hand raised in blessing. The losers, bound together with a long chain, stand as though they are in a queue waiting for the bus to arrive that will take them to hell. With their luck, the bus will come early and be an express.

I suppose the carving was put there in the Middle Ages to scare people into being good, decent and totally dependent on the Church's corner on the salvation market. Personally, I found the whole thing to be too grim for my taste.

Months ago after talking it over with Mona I decided if God is good and loving and if Jesus did all the dirty work for me then I don't have to worry about anything. If on the other hand God wears a black hat and robs banks for a living then I don't have to worry about anything either because we're all sunk no matter how you look at it.

The church was bigger than Westminster Abby but darker and with fewer tombs and monuments. There were plenty of candles. People buy and then light them as prayers to some saint or to Mary or maybe even to Jesus if they feel brave enough to go straight to the top. The candles shimmered and shone like fireflies dancing in the darker corners of the nave

Every so often, a loud voice came over a loudspeaker and said something that sounded like, "Shut up and behave yourselves. This is a church, not a football stadium." That is, of course, a rather loose paraphrase but it captures the general intention of the announcement fair enough.

Things got better when the organ started playing something that sounded soft, muffled and soothing. The whole place echoed like the Grand Canyon and it seemed as though the organ was like a wind, slowly blowing itself into a gale all around us. When the music suddenly crescendo-ed into a roar sounding like an approaching cyclone I yelled to Mona that it was time for me to go outside and climb into a storm cellar.

We were too far away to walk to the Eiffel Tower, the Louvre or the Arc de Triumph that evening so we went back to our room to write a few postcards while the afternoon commute left town and headed for the suburbs.

When we went back outside the sun was setting. Traffic had stopped buzzing on all but the larger avenues. Patrons of restaurants, cafes and bistros were spilling out onto the sidewalks and sometimes even into the streets as the sound of music, laughter and love began creeping through the alleys and boulevards on little cat feet.

We walked uphill to a plaza next to the Pantheon and picked out an empty table that was half on the sidewalk and half in the street. Mona's French came in handy as she looked over the menu and ordered for both of us.

"What did you order?" I asked.

"I have no idea," she said. "I just looked for the highest price, moved down the Euro scale a notch or two, pointed to one line that said *boeuf* and one that said *poulet* and let the dice roll."

The meal came with a small, unlabeled bottle of wine. Whatever it was that we ate was wonderful. As the darkness fell and the lights of the city began to shine and twinkle, the phrase "love is in the air" became as tangible as the big neon advertising sign in Times Square.

Hand in hand, we walked four blocks down to the Seine. Notre Dame was to our left, lit up like the lead actress in a play. The lights were reflected in the water, doubling their effect and creating the illusion the entire world had turned into sky, with stars gleaming from every direction.

Our hands separated and wrapped themselves around our waists drawing us as close to one another as possible as we walked. We joined the parade of lovers down the *Quai de la Tournelle* before crossing to the *Il Saint-Louis* on the *Pont de Sully*.

There we saw jugglers and men selling flowers on the sidewalks. Musicians were playing simply for the sheer beauty of it without any thought of receiving a donation—their instrument cases lying closed at their feet.

The lights became hypnotic, drawing us into a dream of our own creation.

As we turned to face one another, our hands moved yet again, drawing us even closer in embrace. Our lips touched. We breathed warmth and passion into each other's hearts and our souls joined the music of the night in a song of love.

Such is Paris after dark. The City of Lights. The City of Love.

In London we had practiced.

In Paris we performed.

Chapter 19
Almost Giverny

Friday, July 19

My phone rang at seven o'clock the next morning.

With my eyes still closed, I reached over to the nightstand, picked it up and said, "Yeah, well, who are you and why are you calling me . . . ?"

I didn't get a chance to finish my sentence because I recognized the voice of Du saying, "Mike? Mr. Maurison?"

"Hi, Du. What's going on? Tell me. I'm all ears, like a rabbit."

Du didn't laugh and my guess was he wasn't smiling, either.

"Mike, there is something missing from my desk besides my phone. It's my copy of the Museum receipt for the painting. As far as I can tell it's the only thing I can't account for. Thị Yen told me the painting was going to bring bad luck and now I think maybe she was right. What should I do?"

Mona was now sitting up in bed, somehow managing to groan, stretch and yawn all at the same time.

"What's going on? Who's on the phone?" she asked.

I waved at her to be quiet and punched the speakerphone button so she could hear the conversation.

"Why would someone want the receipt?" I asked, "They can't just go over to the Museum and claim the painting like it was in a Lost and Found booth. They can't check it out like it's a library book. Whoever he is . . . or whoever they are . . . they couldn't get the painting without an ID. Besides, the curator met us and I doubt he would release the painting to anyone that didn't look like us.

"Have you decided to call the police yet?" I asked, hoping he would say 'Yes.'"

"Not yet," he said. "Something's going on but I don't want to get the police involved until I know what it is."

Mona started waving her arms at me so I gave her the phone.

"Du, whatever you do don't take the painting back from the museum. Leave it where it is. If you bring it home it might get stolen and you and Thị Yen could get hurt."

"Sure thing, boss," he said. "I was thinking the same thing.

"By the way," he asked, "are you going to be back in London before you fly home?"

I took the phone back from Mona and said, "Sorry, Du, but 'No.' We'll be taking a direct flight home from Rome next Friday."

"Oh," was all that Du said, the word oozing with profound disappointment.

"But keep in touch," I said.

"Let us know if we can be any help," Mona shouted into the phone from three feet away.

"Sure, boss," he said. "Whatever you say. But I've got to tell you I'm feeing nervous about this whole thing, mostly for Thị Yen but also for me."

That was the end of the conversation but it wasn't the last time I got a call from Du's phone.

A "light continental breakfast" came with the room so we took the old, creaky elevator down to the basement to drink some coffee and chew on croissants.

Today we were joining a bus tour that would take us to Monet's studio and home in Giverny and then, after stopping for lunch, head over to the Palace of Versailles to see where the rich and powerful fawned, preened and ate cake before they lost their heads in the French Revolution.

We spent an uneventful hour driving through the countryside before pulling into a parking lot. We got off the bus and walked down a gravel path alongside a gravel road that took us to where Monet spent the last years of his life painting water lilies.

The house was on our left and just past it was his studio, with barn-sized doors large enough to carry large canvases in and out. Across the road to our right was the garden he planted and built in a Japanese style.

The centerpiece of the garden is a large pond filled with water lilies and spanned by the low arch of a Japanese Bridge, a scene painted many times by Monet over the years. It was an inspiration to stand there and see where nature and artist had met and produced offspring possessing the spirit and flesh of both.

The sound of Ravel's *Bolero* began blaring across the silence of that inspired place. I would not have been more embarrassed if I had been standing in Notre Dame during Mass.

After flipping the switch on my phone to "silent," I glanced at it and saw the name, "Du," staring back at me.

"It's Du," I whispered to Mona.

"What's up with that?" she whispered back. "Doesn't he know that we're on our honeymoon?"

"Hold on for a second," I whispered into the phone.

I walked down the path and ducked into a gated maintenance path that went through the hedge surrounding the garden—all the time wondering why my cell phone reception was better here than it was in central Paris.

Once I was out of earshot from everyone else, I put the phone back to my ear and said, "Okay, Du. I hope this is important because . . . ."

I never finished the sentence because the ranting voice of Thị Yen completely overwhelmed me. It may be hard to believe, but she was sounding even more hysterical than the last time she had called.

Mona was still back with the crowd rhapsodizing over the scenery so I had to figure out what Du's wife was saying all by myself. It wasn't easy, but after listening for a minute or so I began to put some of the pieces together.

"Du is gone . . . message on phone . . . no call police . . . scared . . . painting bad luck . . . told to wait . . . not do anything . . . closed store . . . sitting upstairs . . .not know what I should do . . . help me . . . can you help me?"

Whatever it was she was trying to tell me, it didn't sound good.

The one thing that confused me was her comment about the painting. Was she saying it was bad luck, like a black cat? Or was it about the things that actually happen when you have bad luck; in this case, something bad happening to Du?

Based on what I had seen and heard I was deathly afraid that somebody wanted the painting and was willing to do anything to get it.

"Thị Yen," I said. "Try to relax. Everything will be okay. I'm glad you phoned. I'll call you back in a few minutes. Drink some tea."

As the tour group walked over to the large garden that Monet planted next to his house, I pulled Mona aside and told her about the phone call.

"Damn!" she said.

I had never heard Mona swear before but they say you never really know someone until you've been married to them for a week.

"What are you going to do?" she asked.

"Don't you mean, 'What are *we* going to do?'" I asked back at her.

Mona thought about it for a moment before saying, "You're right. 'Wither thou goest I will go.' So what do we do?"

I wasn't sure about the 'wither' place but whatever it meant I was glad Mona had agreed we would be going there together.

Thinking aloud, I said, "Whatever Thị Yen's talking about doesn't sound like something that can be handled by phone. Maybe we need to go back?"

"Maybe," Mona chimed in, "you should phone Văn—I mean Thor—and ask him what he thinks about all this."

"Damn it," I added to the mix. "Can't we finish the tour first? I mean it won't take us very long to go through the house and . . . ."

"Go ahead," Mona said. "But give me the phone and I'll make the call. This is more important than Monet and you know it."

As always she was right and I knew it. But Monet!

Mona found an old stone bench, probably one that Monet had sat on while painting something and started dialing Thor.

With crushed resignation I sat next to her with a sigh that was probably heard inside the house two hundred feet away.

It was 5:30 am in New York and whether Thor was awake or not when the phone rang he was awake when he answered it.

"A very happy morning to you, Mike," he said, more awake than I would have thought possible. "How's the honeymoon?"

Mona had put the call on speakerphone so I was able to cut in and say, "It's good for us but I'm not sure things are going well with your brother in London."

Thor asked what was going on and it took so long to bring him up to speed that by the time he got it straight some of the people in our tour group were already heading back to the bus.

"I'll phone Thị Yen right away and see if I need to fly over. I could leave this afternoon if I have to . . . ."

My phone started buzzing and vibrating with a second call. Mona told Thor to hold for a moment and then she punched the same secret buttons that Robert pushed when we had been shopping for Mona's ring in Manhattan.

"Here," she said, handing me the phone. "It says 'Du.' It's probably for you."

"Hello?" I asked, not knowing if there was going to be more bad news on the other end.

Unfortunately, there was more bad news at the other end.

"Is this Maurison?" a muffled voice asked. "Mike Maurison?"

"Who's asking?" I asked.

"A friend of Huàng Than Du. I think you know him."

"Maybe, maybe not," I said. "What's your point?"

"Mr. Du is tied up at the moment and asked me to give you a message. He wonders if you would be so kind as to do him a favor."

"Who is Du, and why should I do him a favor?" I asked, hoping for something that might give me a hint or a clue about who this friend of Du's was.

"Du and I are both collectors of fine art," the voice explained. "Du would like to loan me the painting he recently acquired but like I said, he is tied up and can't do it himself. He would like it very much if you could go to the museum and bring him the picture."

"And where would he like me to bring the picture?" I asked, still hoping for a slip of some kind from the scumbag on the other end of the phone.

"Don't worry about that. Du will let you know when you need to know. Just do him the favor and get the painting, and please don't ask any more unimportant questions. Du will be very hurt if you keep asking questions.

"Oh, by the way," added the Muffler Man, "I almost forgot: Du wants me to tell you he does not want the police to be involved in any way. He doesn't like the police and if he finds out you talked to them he would begin to feel very uncomfortable."

The phone went dead so I handed it back to Mona so I could reconnect with Thor.

"Thor," I asked. "Are you still there?"

"Yes, but as soon as you hang up I'll be able to phone Thi Yen. Is there anything else you want me to know?"

With Mona listening, I told him about the phone call I had just had with the Muffler Man.

"What are you going to do?" Thor asked.

"I need to talk this over with Mona, but I think we will be making a detour back to London. I've got something up my sleeve but I need to be there to see if it gives me a winning hand or not. You talk to Thị Yen and I'll talk to Mona and let's text what we decide. It's cheaper."

"Sure thing, boss," he said, sounding just like his brother.

"What do you mean, 'it's cheaper?'" Mona scowled, "This could be a life or death thing and you want to save a few cents on a phone call? You're pathetic."

I always hate it when Mona is right, and at the moment, I was hating it . . . again.

"We've got to go back and let the police know what's going on," Mona insisted.

"No," I said. "Not yet. There are at least two things these people don't know . . . at least I don't think they know.

"The first is you. They have Du's cell phone, and now, apparently, Thị Yen's, too. They also have the museum receipt for the painting. It has my name and contact information on it but not yours. No doubt they also found my name and phone number on Du's phone and his wife's phone and decided that I'm the go-to guy to get their painting back."

"Is that the first thing?" Mona asked. "If it is, I don't get it."

"The first thing is that they don't know about you. Your name isn't on anything and even if it was your last name hasn't been changed to Maurison, yet. Wherever I go, you can follow along and no one will be the wiser for it.

"The second thing is that I downloaded an app onto both phones that will give me their exact location on a map."

I punched a few of my own secret buttons and brought up a map with three arrows on it. One arrow was pointed just north-west of Paris. When I zoomed in it pointed just outside Giverny, within a few hundred feet of what the map said was the "Monet House."

The second arrow pointed at Du's store and the third arrow pointed into the exact center of Trafalgar Square.

"That's where the phone call came from," I said.

I would have patted myself on the back if my arms had been long enough.

"If I check the app every so often I can see where Du's phone goes, and when the phone comes to a stop, that is probably where Du is."

Mona chimed in, "If this painting is such a big deal and worth all this trouble they may be tracking you, too. From now on I think we should have a trial separation so we aren't seen all paired up."

As usual Mona simply skipped the big question of whether we should fly to London or not and got straight into the details of how to get there.

As for now, we were stuck on a tour headed to a long lunch followed by a long layover at Versailles.

The bad guys in London didn't know we were in France and would be expecting me to show up and do something right away.

So I shot off a text message saying, "I am in France will return to London tomorrow a.m. keep in touch."

"Why tip them off to when we're flying in?"

"I didn't. We'll be there before dinner tonight."

We stayed with the tour, ate lunch outdoors by an old mill with a waterwheel, got to Versailles, skipped the palace, took a taxi to the train station, caught the next train to Paris, transferred to the Metro and were back at our hotel by 3:00 pm. A text message from Thor said he would be arriving at Heathrow at 7:30 am tomorrow morning and, when I checked the map Du's phone was still near Trafalgar Square.

At 5:30 p.m., we boarded a plane at De Gaulle International and by 7:00 p.m., we were back in England headed to a hotel room near Trafalgar Square where Mona had booked two rooms online during lunch. By the time we checked in, Du's phone had come to rest in Holland Park just south of Notting Hill and Thị Yen's phone was still at the store on Chandos Place.

My plan was to notify the police and have them raid both Du's place and the address in Holland Park at the same time but first I sent Mona over to check out Du's store.

"Nothing," she said when she got back. "The store was locked and nobody answered when I rang the bell. The downstairs was dark and the curtains were closed upstairs."

Next, I phoned Thị Yen and to my surprise, after a few rings she answered.

"Mike Maurison," she shouted into the phone. "Help me, please!"

The muffled voice of a man took over the conversation by saying, "Yes, Mr. Maurison. Du is eagerly awaiting your arrival. He will send someone to meet you at the airport when you arrive. Just phone this number when you get off the plane and Du will feel much better than he does now. Do you understand? His condition will be much improved if you would tell us when and where your plane will arrive."

In the background, I could hear a muffled cry of pain. I couldn't tell if it was Du or Thị Yen. The sound didn't make a lick of sense. I couldn't think of any reason why they would want to hurt Thị Yen when all their threats had been directed at Du and it didn't make any sense that it was Du. Why would he be at home when just a few hours ago Thị Yen had said he was missing?

Regardless, there was a question needing an answer, so I made one up.

"I'll be on a British Airways flight arriving at Heathrow between 11:00 am and Noon tomorrow morning. I don't want

Du to feel badly about any of this so if it will make him feel better tell him I'll phone you when I walk off the plane."

"Du will be pleased to hear it. Ta ta."

"Nice save, darling," Mona said. "Now you have to hope you were lucky enough to come up with an actual flight arrival. If you didn't . . . ."

I finished her sentence by saying, " . . . I'll be getting another phone call in a few minutes."

"What do we do next?" Mona asked.

I was already dialing Du's number.

There was no answer but several minutes later a text arrived that said, "See you soon." So at least I knew someone was still holding the phone in Holland Park.

It was time to go to the police.

Not knowing what else to do we collared the first Bobbie we saw and asked for advice. Within ten minutes, we were in a police car on our way to New Scotland Yard one mile and four minutes away.

After telling our story to the receiving officer, we were ushered into an office with a very civilian-looking woman sitting behind a desk.

"I understand you have a concern," she understated.

In a few minutes she was joined by two men.

It took thirty minutes to spill all the beans and it was probably going to take a lot longer than that to pick them up again. It was nearly 10:00 pm and we hadn't eaten since Noon. The officers must have heard our stomachs complaining because someone brought in a tray with tea and sandwiches on it. For a few minutes, at least, England felt jolly again.

The police asked me to phone both numbers on the pretense of giving the bad guys an update on my arrival.

With everyone listening in and with the full technology of the London Police tracing the call I called Thị Yen. Her phone was answered by Muffler Man #1.

"This is Mike," I said, knowing full well he knew it was me before he answered the phone. "I'm catching an earlier plane and will be getting in to Heathrow at 7:30 tomorrow morning. Is Du okay?"

"Yes, of course," came the reply. "But he's chewing on something at the moment and can't talk or come to the phone. I'll let him know you called."

Next, I called Du, and like before, there was no answer and the arrow that had been pointing at Holland Park disappeared from my phone.

"The battery probably died," said one of the officers. "Those apps chew up a lot of power. But no matter, we've got a lock on the location through the GPS."

Officers were dispatched to both locations within minutes. Thirty minutes later two SWAT teams the British call "SFO units" were preparing to surround the buildings—armed officers fully prepared to approach and storm the buildings if necessary. Since there was no apparent sign of imminent danger, they scheduled the confrontation for 6:00 a.m., about an hour after sunrise and an hour and a half before I was scheduled to arrive at the airport.

Chapter 20
He's Dead! He's Dead!

Saturday, July 20

Mona and I were stuck at the police station all night but we played our part in what was going on outside.

At 5:40 a.m., a man slipped out the front door of Du's store to get some take-out coffee and crumpets. He was picked up like a sack of potatoes.

At 5:59 a.m. I phoned both numbers at the same time to act as a distraction. There was still no answer at Holland Park but the Muffler Man at the store said, "Where are you? You should be in the air right now!"

In the background, I could hear the sound of a bullhorn, "This is the London police. Come out with your hands up. Your building is surrounded and there is no way of escape."

Three officers had already entered the building and were waiting at the bottom of the stairs leading to the apartment.

In a matter of minutes, a lone man descended the stairs and was cradled into their arms like a newborn baby.

Apparently, he hadn't bothered to hang up the phone because we could clearly hear the question, "Is there anyone else upstairs?"

"Only the lady," was the response, this time coming from a voice no longer muffled.

They found Thị Yen gagged and tied to a chair. Later, we were told that when she was untied she went into another of her patented, hysterical rants; a rant that didn't stop until one of the officers brought her a cup of hot tea from the kitchen.

At Holland Park, the bullhorn brought no response at all.

When officers entered the flat, they found Du slumped in a chair untied, un-gagged, and barely breathing. An ambulance, waiting outside "just in case," took him to the nearest hospital.

Courtesy of a police car, Mona and I arrived at the hospital fifteen minutes after Du.

Du had apparently suffered a heart attack while being held and the kidnapper had no doubt panicked and abandoned him to die even while the sting operation continued to run from Du's place above the store.

The last communication I had received from Holland Park was the text message from Du's phone at 8:30 p.m. the previous evening. By 10:00 p.m. either the phone battery had gone dead or the perps had been scared away. Du could have had the heart attack as much as nine or ten hours before he was found. None of it looked good for Du.

I left a message on Thor's phone telling him what had happened.

"Don't mess around," I shouted into Thor's voice mail. "Grab a cab as soon as your plane touches the ground and get to the hospital ASAP!"

Thị Yen arrived at the hospital and we sat for a long time waiting to hear if Du was going to make it or not. After watching the second hand tick around the clock a hundred times, one of the ER doctors walked in and said that Du was still unconscious but "stable." When we asked about a long-term prognosis, the Doctor wouldn't guess what condition Du would be in if or when he opened his eyes and started looking around.

"He might make it or he might . . . ." the doctor said as tactfully and sensitively as he could. "We will do everything we can to bring him back."

The doctor said we could go in and see him if we wanted and of course all three of us did.

After we saw Du and walked back to the waiting room Thị Yen broke into hysterical wailing again, screaming, "It's the painting . . . that terrible painting! It has killed my husband. I warned him but he wouldn't listen. And now he's dead. He's dead!"

Mona and I, as we had done more than once during the past week, held each other in an embrace; but this time the embrace was not from passion but for comfort.

A short time later Thor and Zach arrived from the airport and we all went back into Du's room. Zach had joined Thor at the last minute and now found himself not only dealing with the shock of seeing his father but with the responsibility of comforting his mother. Thor simply stood unmoving, shaking his head back and forth as though unable to accept that the whole thing was actually happening.

With too many people surrounding Du the nurse shooed us back to the waiting room.

For Mona and me our honeymoon—with its tightly scheduled and high-intensity visits to monuments and museums—suddenly seemed trivial. We were confident we were where we were supposed to be and knew we had done what we could, but now as we sat with nothing else to do but wait we were feeling both helpless and useless.

"Psst . . . Mona," I whispered. "I've thought of something we should do."

We excused ourselves and caught a cab to the National Gallery.

It was thirty minutes before opening but when we explained why we were there, someone ushered us in without question.

Even before we had time to sit, our favorite curator walked up and said, "I've been trying to reach Du since yesterday. Someone answered the phone but no one would say anything. What's going on?"

"Why were you phoning Du?"

"Yesterday just after lunch a man stopped by my office. He had the receipt for the painting and a typed and signed letter from Du authorizing him to pick it up. I told him I wouldn't allow it until I had talked to Du personally. He insisted that I give him the painting and when I refused a second time, he threatened to get a court order.

"I said, 'go ahead, but I'm not giving you the painting.'

"None of it seemed right, and when Du didn't answer his phone I decided to wait until this morning and try again; and then phone you if Du didn't answer."

"Thanks for holding down the fort," I said.

Mona added, "We didn't come for the painting. We just wanted to know if it was still here and warn you that someone might come by and try to get it."

After we explained what had happened, the curator said, "I believe they have a good reason to want that painting. We've done some visual examination and our specialists have decided they can't find a single thing that would preclude the painting from being a genuine Rembrandt.

"No one is saying it *is* a Rembrandt, but we have never seen a forged painting that looked anywhere near as authentic as this one."

Mona and I looked at each other, stunned.

"I can't say for sure, but if it turns out to be a Rembrandt it would possibly sell at auction for $25-35 million. The record was $33.2 million back in 2009 but the novelty of your painting and its exquisite composition would probably lead a bidder to go even higher."

There was a brief pause before he continued.

"By the way, the National Gallery would be honored to put the painting on display if it turns out to be genuine."

Even in the shock of the moment, I couldn't help but smile at the curator's less-than-subtle bid to get the painting for the museum. The very idea the painting might one day hang in the National Gallery as a genuine Rembrandt was beyond what my imagination could handle.

"But where did the painting come from?" Mona asked. "It had to come from somewhere. Someone must own it and these crooks clearly stole it from somebody."

"Good question," the curator said. "I'd like to know the answer myself but like I said, that will be up to the police and Interpol to figure out. I suspect when the news of this painting hits the papers there will be dozens, if not hundreds of people who will come forward to claim the painting is theirs, handed down from generation to generation and hidden from the world for over 400 years.

"I'm glad I don't have to be the one who separates the sheep from the goats," he said, laughing at his own good humor.

"I guess Du could be a wealthy man if he pulls through," Mona said. "Maybe the painting will turn out to be good luck after all."

I felt doubtful about Mona's optimism but I was grateful she had made the effort to put a positive spin on what had so far been a tragedy.

I had told Thor to give me a call if there was any news about Du so there was no real reason for us to go back to the hospital. Mona and I were free to wander around London and either do something, do nothing or, as Mona suggested, we could just stand on a sidewalk and watch the traffic drive by on the wrong side of the road.

What we did was walk across the street to the Church of Saint Martin's-in-the-Fields where Mona sat down in a pew and prayed.

I didn't join her in the prayer thing.

I wanted Du to get well, of course, but I figured that God already knew what I was thinking whether I got down on my knees and closed my eyes like Mona or not.

To each their own.

That at least is how I felt about it, but as I walked around the inside of the church reading the plaques, I cheated.

I found myself thinking, "God, help Du get better. Please!"

The whole thing was so subconscious I heard myself starting to tack the words, "Pretty please" onto the end. I tried to hit the delete button before the message was sent but since God already knew what I was thinking it didn't matter either way.

When Mona stands up after praying she's usually smiling for some reason. Today was no exception.

"How come you look so happy all of a sudden?"

"Because I'm with you and neither of us is in a hospital bed fighting for our life."

"I can run with that. What do you want to do now?"

"I don't know. There are more museums."

"Yes," I said. "There are always more museums. In fact, if we spent the rest of our lives in Europe I suppose we would die of old age before we saw half of them."

"Does that mean you never want to see another museum again? Or does it mean we'd better get started right away or we're going to miss out on one of them?"

"It means the same thing you said to me the other day."

"And what was that?"

"It means I'd rather be with you than go to a museum--or not go to a museum for that matter. Maybe we could go back to the hotel for awhile?"

"No," Mona said. "Not that I don't want to do that, but since we're here in London and we may never be here again let's go do something or go somewhere . . . I don't care what or where. Let's just get on the Tube without looking at a map and pop up someplace that has a funny name or something and then just walk around without any of the tourist stuff. What do you say?

"Hey!" Mona called out as I started walking away. "Where are you going?"

"Come along little dogie," I said over my shoulder. "We're off to join the unwashed masses where they live."

"I'm not a dogie," Mona replied as she hurried to catch up. "My mother is still very much alive as you well know."

We disappeared into the Charing Cross Tube entrance like Alice falling into the rabbit hole except neither of us happened to be late for a date; important or otherwise.

There was only one rail line to choose from so Mona pulled a ten-pence coin out of her purse, flipped it in the air and said, "Heads."

It was tails.

"Oh, darn! "she said. "I guess we'll have to take the Bakerloo Line."

"Which way, Mrs. Greeley?" I asked. "Shall we go west, young lady?"

"Into the sunset," she replied. "And let's get off at Piccadilly Circus. We've gone through the station four times already and each time I wanted to get off and see it. There's this cute little statue of Eros, the Greek God of love . . . ."

Mona would make a good tour guide. If she didn't know the answer to somebody's question she would just make one up and the person wouldn't know because, if they did know, they wouldn't have asked the question in the first place.

In the tourist guide business lying and fudging are almost always "win-win." As a bonus, the smarter you pretend to be the more tips you get; which would make it more like "win-win-win." In Mona's case, the lie is that the statue isn't of Eros at all, but of someone who just sort of looks like him. Like any good husband, however, I knew it was not in my best interest to interrupt my tour guide while she was on a roll.

" . . . who was called Cupid in Roman mythology . . . "

I was okay with Mona rambling on about Bullfinch but later when she started quoting Virgil, I drew the line. Lucky for me the train came to a halt.

"Hallelujah! Piccadilly! We're here!" I said, cutting her off in mid-sentence.

"Last one up is a rotten egg," she said.

Up the escalator we ran, like foxes trying to outrun horses ridden by people wearing tight little red coats and little black hats with little visors that don't actually serve any purpose except to look funny.

As we emerged into the late morning light, the roar of congested traffic and the smell of carbon monoxide hit us like a tonne of briquettes.

Cars were everywhere, driving wildly alongside a gold-plated Eros who was standing on one foot, which was very bad form for an archer about to loose an arrow into some lover's behind. The thought crossed my mind as to what might happen if he missed low . . . .

"Look," Mona said with the enthusiasm of a puppy. "It's like Broadway!"

Behind Eros was the Criterion Theater featuring a blockbuster show. Two blocks away *The Phantom of the Opera* was plastered on a marquee. We were in the center of theatergoers' heaven.

"Maybe we can get tickets for a show tonight?" Mona panted, still playing the part of a puppy.

"Maybe Du will die tonight," I said grimly.

"That wasn't very subtle," Mona said glaringly.

"Sorry," I said. "I guess I don't feel particularly trivial at the moment."

Without saying a word, we dropped back down the Tube, stuck a finger randomly on the map and got on the next train to St. Paul's with a transfer at Holborn.

When we came up the stairs from the station, we had no idea where we were. After taking a few steps toward the street Mona turned around and said, "There it is!"

Behind us, soaring above the roofs of the buildings that crowded around us, was the cross that tops off the third largest domed church in the world. only St. Peter's in Rome and some really, really, big church in Africa are bigger. After a quick stroll down a narrow walkway we stood, awed and overwhelmed by the size of the building.

The inside of the church was even more humbling as we entered a space seemingly large enough to fly an airplane. Monuments that towered over us when we were close to them, appeared almost small when viewed from a distance; their glory diminished by the immensity of the building's interior.

"Look at that!" said Mona, pointing at a towering monument to the Duke of Wellington. "Let's go over and . . . ."

My phone started humming and buzzing in my pocket so I stopped listening to the tour guide and punched the word, "Answer." It was Thor.

"Good news, Mike. Du's awake. Come on over. He wants to tell you something. No need to hurry though, his heart could give out any second."

Because you can never tell with Thor, we high-tailed it back to the hospital realizing we had completely forgotten about lunch . . . and breakfast . . . and, except for the late night sandwiches at Scotland Yard . . . yesterday's dinner.

Back home I can go all day on caffeine or on one of Juan's burritos. This was, however, the first time I had gone without food for so long on adrenaline alone.

Du lifted his IV-attached hand and gave us a wave and a smile as we entered his room.

"Everyone else out," he said even though there was nothing he could do about it if everyone chose to stay.

The room cleared out anyway so Mona and I sat next to his bed.

"What happened to the painting?" he asked. "I can't talk about it with Thị Yen in the room or she would put a pillow over my face. That painting is why all this happened so tell me, what's up with it?"

"It's still at the National Gallery," I said. "One of the bad guys tried to withdraw it like money from a bank but the curator wouldn't honor your receipt and threw them out. The real news is that the museum is beginning to think it's a real Rembrandt."

Mona added, "I don't want you to have another heart attack, but the curator said it could be worth $25-35 million."

While Du let the information sink in I noticed that the little jiggly line on his heart monitor didn't skip a beat or even show a blip.

"That's what I thought all along," he said with a sigh. "And Thị Yen is right about it being bad luck. I'm not sure what to do with it. I can't hang it on my wall and I probably wouldn't live long enough to spend all that money even if I got it; not to mention that Thị Yen has told me she'll have nothing to do with any part of it.

"Personally, I'd just like to pretend the whole thing didn't happen and go back to running my store."

"Why not?" Mona said, cutting to the chase as usual. "You can do whatever you want. It's your life after all."

"Thank you," Du said with tears in his eyes. "Thank you, both of you. I'd probably be dead if it wasn't for you, and those crooks would have gotten away with it, too.

"You've done enough. My family is here. So go back to whatever it was you were doing before all this happened and enjoy your honeymoon.

"Live and love while you can," he added, "before you wind up like me!"

He smiled and gave us a wink.

"Now get out of here. I don't want to see you again . . . at least not until the next time you're in London. When you come, stop by the store and Thị Yen will fix you some tea."

Du closed his eyes, rolled over and turned his back on us so we left.

After saying good-bye to Thor, Zach and Thị Yen, we headed to our hotel. On the way, we ordered hamburgers and fries to hold us over. Then we grabbed our bags, checked out, headed to the airport, flew to Paris and checked back into our place on the Left Bank.

We were too tired to eat dinner so we each swallowed two croissants and fell asleep.

After only 25 ½ hours and one lifetime away, we were back in France—with one day left in Paris.

Chapter 21
Mona Lisa Smile
Sunday, July 21

We slept until Noon, got dressed and walked outside, shielding our eyes from the bright sunlight filtering through the tree-lined streets. We sat at a café, consumed our fill of bread, cheese and wine, and went to visit the Louvre.

"How many more museums can we handle," Mona asked.

"I don't know," I said. "But this is one we have to see."

"Why? What would happen to us if we skipped it and went home?"

"We would . . . we would . . . ." I was at a loss for words.

"We would," said Mona, "regret it for the rest of our lives."

How I can love Mona more each day than I did the day before is a mystery I will never solve. Since I met Mona I have learned that "impossible" is not necessarily the opposite of "possible." Mona says it is a God thing. To be honest, I have given up trying to find an explanation that makes any more sense than hers.

The Louvre, of course, is huge. It is so full of famous things that even Sister Wendy has probably never seen all of it. It is so easy to get lost, they give you a map that not only shows you where things are but also shows you how to get back to where you started. Otherwise, like one of those hedge mazes, you might get to the center but never find your way out again. I thought I had memorized the place but we had only taken a few twists and turns before I had to look at the map.

I hadn't bothered to take my camera out of the case since we left New York and Mona hadn't taken any pictures either, but Mona insisted we take some non-flash photos in the museum. She posed in front of the *Venus de Milo* with her arms behind her back and had me stand beneath the *Winged Victory* with my arms outstretched like I was about to fly off somewhere like Icarus. Mona posed in front of *Liberty Leading the People* with her right arm upraised but her chest covered.

Then, with the *Mona Lisa* in the background, surrounded by people shoving and pushing to get to the front, Mona posed in front of her namesake with a smile that was not only enigmatic, but twitching like the smile she had at our wedding rehearsal.

We spent more time taking silly pictures than we did looking at the paintings, with the exception of the Rembrandts. Of interest to us was a *Self Portrait* dated 1633 with the full signature "Rembrandt" instead of the monogram that was typical on his earlier paintings.

Grandpa van Rijn had grown a mustache and the painting had become significantly darker than the one Du had pulled out of the trash. The face was a bit older and worn, as though the previous two years had been hard on him for some reason.

After seeing the Rembrandts we left the museum, ate lunch, walked across the Seine to the D'Orsay to see the great French masters of Impressionism and then back across the river to the L'Orangerie to take in more impressionists and post-impressionists. No doubt, the artists would have been pleased because their paintings left a good post-impression on us. From L'Orangerie it was only a short walk to the Place de la Concord. There we stood and looked up the Champs Elise towards the Arc de Triumph looming in the distance.

We were then officially done with Paris. There was nothing left to do but stroll back to our hotel and eat a leisurely dinner. By evening, we were too tired to do anything but sleep.

The sleep was good.

Chapter 22
Michelangelo Slept Here
Monday, July 22

Travelling to De Gaulle International Airport had become so routine that getting there again was a snap. Our flight to Florence took a detour to Basel for a one-hour layover. We managed to get seats on the right side of the plane so we could see as much of the Alps as possible. With the morning sun to our backs, the view was clear and beautiful. Using a map, we could guess we were looking at the Jungfrau, the Matterhorn, and in the far distance Mt. Blanc. As we entered Italy, we could see Lake Maggiore and a few minutes later, somewhere over Milan, we began our descent into Florence.

The countryside of Tuscany seemed close enough to touch. There were geometric squares of vineyards and scattered hilltop villages that had once prospered until falling under the rule of the mighty Medici family.

Driving into Florence from the airport was not particularly inspiring. Modern suburban blight and several construction cranes led us into the old city with its mix of once-stately Renaissance palaces alongside more recent, retro-styled structures built long after the city's heyday back in the late Middle Ages. Because all the buildings have the same stone or stucco exteriors it's hard to tell if any particular building is old enough have a "Michelangelo Slept Here" plaque or not. All of this is part of the city's beauty, charm and romance.

Our hotel was north of Old Florence, not too far from the *Duomo*, or Cathedral. Since we had some time left in the day we walked over to the church and looked around. There wasn't a line to get into the Cathedral but there was a line to climb up to the famous dome. We were in no hurry so we chose the line and climbed up to the top.

The dome is the largest masonry dome ever built and the crowd of people climbing the narrow stairway to the top sometimes came to a complete stop due to even slower climbers ahead of us. Half way up there was a gallery where we could look down at the people in the cathedral swarming about like ants when you stir up their nest. As we entered the upper levels, the stairway twisted and turned through some of the four million red bricks that make up the bulk of the dome. Occasionally there was a little window where we could catch a small glimpse of Florence spread out below.

The finale, of course, was the thrill of stepping outside onto the lantern at the top of the dome. There is nothing in Florence that comes close to the height of the dome so the view is unobstructed across a vast sea of red-tiled roofs stretching out in all directions. For us Florence was never more beautiful than it was that afternoon from the top of the cathedral dome.

Back on the ground, we decided we didn't need to go inside the church because we had already seen it from the balcony. Instead, without having to stand in line or pay an entry fee we admired the "Gates of Paradise" by Ghiberti, a massive set of two doors leading into the cathedral Baptistry on the opposite side of the Piazza.

Twenty gilded bronze sculpted panels depict the life of Christ with eight bonus panels at the bottom representing the four writers of the Gospels and four saints of particular interest to Italians. The doors got their fancy nickname from Michelangelo.

I suppose the endorsement would have been a useful reference on Ghiberti's portfolio except for the fact that Ghiberti died twenty years before Michelangelo was born.

Looking at the doors doesn't cost anything partly because they face a public street but mostly because they are only copies. The original door panels are on display somewhere else where you *do* have to pay something if you want to see them. Except for the inside of churches and the outside of buildings, you have to fork out a lot of dough if you want to see anything really old or famous in Florence.

Mona, with her literary bent was excited to discover that Dante was baptized in the building nearly 200 years before the doors were installed in1452. For the rest of the afternoon I had to endure Mona's anecdotes about the local Florentines who Dante described in various states of torment in his *Inferno*. The whole thing sounded like the *Last Judgment* at Notre Dame except with recognizable features superimposed on the faces of the doomed and the damned.

Although Old Florence appears to exist solely to shuffle tens of thousands of tourists through its streets and alleys every day it is actually, like London and Paris, a place where history and contemporary life live side by side. In Florence, however, the crowds are crammed into very small and narrow spaces like subway stations during rush hour in Manhattan. After plowing our way through the pressing logjams of humanity, we were glad to find refuge in a quiet backstreet near our hotel.

In the alley, we found a small café that had not yet been completely inundated by the camera-toting hoards. We found a table and rested our feet until a waiter came over and took our order.

Mona, showing no creativity at all ordered spaghetti because as she put it, "I always wanted to see what real Italian spaghetti tastes like."

The waiter fortunately spoke enough English for me to ask, "Bring me whatever you would order if you wanted to eat dinner with your girlfriend."

In the best English he had, the waiter corrected me by saying that he had a boyfriend. Even so, he assured me he understood what I meant and would do his best to fill my order.

Mona was inspired to say she was relieved to know there was at least one man in Italy who would probably not want to pinch her on the behind. As it turned out no one tried to pinch Mona's behind the whole time we were in Italy. Whether she was disappointed in this or not I have no idea.

Que sera.

After dinner, as darkness fell upon the city we strolled down to the Arno to see the city at its romantic best. During the day, the Arno is a fairly wide stretch of brown, slow-moving water that makes the East River look like one of the three that flowed out of the Garden of Eden. At night however, the Arno was as lovely as could be. Mona was inspired enough to kiss me each time we stopped to look at the view. Although neither of us complained about it, the kissing caused us to cancel our stroll earlier than we had planned.

We returned to our hotel like homing pigeons.

Chapter 23
Separation Anxiety

Tuesday, July 23

One thing Florence has going for it is that everything is within walking distance. This is fortunate because there is no way to get around the old sections of Florence without joining the rest of the lemmings wandering around the narrow streets looking for a cliff to fall over.

In Italy if a menu or sign is in English it is safe to assume it represents something that is overpriced and not likely to be consumed by a native Italian. There are, however, bakeries, corner groceries, *trattorias* and *osterias* scattered around in local neighborhoods and they are usually worth a visit. It's possible, I suppose, that Florentines prefer to go out and do their shopping at suburban malls or the Italian equivalent of WalMart when they get the chance. People, after all, are people wherever you find them.

Mona and I also finally figured out that the phrase "light continental breakfast" is redundant. All continental breakfasts are by definition, "light." If you put your average continental breakfast on one side of a scale and one *Venti* cup of Starbucks coffee on the other, Starbucks would win hands down . . . every time . . . and that would include the weight of the Italian coffee that comes with the breakfast. I suppose that is why Mediterranean folks are able to eat pasta every evening and still look so fit and trim.

One more day of Italian breakfasts and Mona said she would be able to fit into her wedding dress again—finally offsetting the old-fashioned English breakfast we had on our first morning in London.

The Arno, the Ponte Vecchio and the Uffizi Gallery all intersect at about the same place and the walk from our hotel was less than a mile. Mona's parents had gotten us advance tickets to the Uffizi just as they had with the Tower of London and the Louvre. Once again, this turned out to be a good thing because even before the museum opened the line of wanna-be Uffizianos was nearly a block long.

When the doors opened at 8:15 a.m. we were among the first to go in. I had the entire place memorized and was able to guide Mona on a tour of the things both of us wanted to see.

The key word to remember when you visit the Uffizi is the word "Renaissance." The Renaissance was when the Gothic arch and flying buttresses became passé. It was a time when Italy experienced both the creation of a middle class and a lucrative trade with worldwide markets—markets opened up by Italians like Marco Polo and Christopher Columbus. In Italy, "city states" grew and consolidated with noble families competing with one another and the Papacy for power and prestige.

In Florence, the noble family was the Medici who, to our eternal debt, threw a lot of their money into affirming their social status by patronizing the arts of music, sculpture, painting, poetry and architecture. Michelangelo, da Vinci, and

Cellini all made big bucks being commissioned to decorate Florence with beautiful things; and the writer Machiavelli, with his book *The Prince*, made sure the Medici understood how to keep their *glutei* firmly ensconced in the seats of power.

The Uffizi has more paintings, sculptures and table service by Renaissance artists than any other museum in the world. Perhaps the most famous painting is *The Birth of Venus* by Botticelli. Painters were men in those days and most of them could not resist the opportunity to paint women in the nude. The Greeks and Romans set the precedent for this with their sculpture and more than anything else the Renaissance fashioned itself as a rebirth of the sort of art that made Rome famous back in the day.

As a result, Botticelli was given a free cultural pass to take a scene from Roman mythology and paint what was at that time in history the most celebrated nude ever put on canvas.

It is still a good painting—not particularly erotic, but captivating and challenging in its own way—complete with eyes that launched a thousand PhDs.

As a serious student of art Mona found a bench in the gallery and spent quite a while studying the painting.

When she had finished cogitating, she stood up and said, "She could really use a good hairdresser."

As they say, "Art is in the eye of the beholder."

We spent most of the morning bantering a lighthearted, running commentary on the famous and not-so-famous pictures hanging on the wall. The two exceptions to our laughter were da Vinci's *Annunciation* and the two Rembrandts. But even van Rijn was snarked a little.

The better of the two Rembrandts was snarked because it had once been thought to be a self-portrait but it isn't . . . it never was . . . and people should have known better because anyone who has ever seen a real Rembrandt self portrait would immediately know that the person in this painting is someone else.

It's still a nice painting, though, and much, much better than the other Rembrandt which ironically *is* a genuine *Self Portrait*. Sadly—and this is the snark—the condition of this painting and its lack of detail would have condemned it to storage if it had been painted by anyone else besides Rembrandt.

To be fair, both snarks are mere quibbles since Rembrandt is really a post-Renaissance painter anyway and is not, so far as anyone has ever suggested, Italian. The fact he is hanging in the Uffizi at all is perhaps the most impressive testimony to his greatness.

If you really, really like art and architecture a lot then Florence is worth a day on your itinerary, but by the time we were done with the Uffizi Mona and I were more or less done with Florence.

After walking across the *Ponte Veccio* and looking at the Pitti Palace from the outside, we walked back across the river to the *Piazza del Signoria*, the large square that stands behind the Uffizi and in front of the *Palazzo Vecchio*.

The palazzo was the home of the Medici family. This massive structure, capped by a towering campanile, is second-to-none as a witness to the Medici's power, prestige and sheer *chutzpa*. The blue-starred tiles with the Medici lions over the front door and the little balcony on which they periodically emerged to wave at the *paparazzi* verge on the pretentious.

As we found out, part of the fun of Florence is seeing the monuments built by people who were once feared and considered great—people who have now gone to dust—with their greatest legacy being the work of artists who centuries later proved to have been greater than their patrons.

On our way back to the hotel we decided to stop by the Medici Chapels and see the two tombs designed and sculpted by Michelangelo. Much of the work was never finished on these tombs and the haunting, faceless eyes of the unfinished figure representing *Day* on the tomb of Giuliano de' Medici is perhaps more memorable than if it had been finished and all polished up like the image of *Night* that reclines next to it.

Next on our final pilgrimage through Florence, was a stop at the *Galeria dell'Academia* to see Michelangelo's statue of David.

If David had entered his sculptures in a race at Churchill Downs, he would have won the trifecta with *David, Moses* and *The Pieta*. People might argue over which statue was the win, place or show but all would agree that each is a derby champion in its own right.

There are other statues by Michelangelo in the *Galeria* and some of the most memorable are unfinished like *Day* in the Medici Chapels. The star of them all however, is *David*. Like so many works of great art, *David* turned out to be far more impressive and inspiring in person than in books or reproductions. The statue itself is 17' tall and stands on a 6' pedestal. If you do the math as I did you might conclude that 23' is a long way up for a statue to go. Its weight, by the way, is over nine tons, which would make it one heck of a doorstop.

If it ever fell over, somebody would have to fetch the Salvation Army movers who took away my furniture and pay them to stand it back up. It's *that* heavy!

Time was flying by and a train trip to Rome was on tap for the morning. We stepped out into the late afternoon sun and walked ten steps over to the *Piazza San Marco* looking for a gelato before heading back to our hotel. Because the Piazza is outside the traffic-free zone on the north edge of the Old City, busses, cars and vans were scooting around as they circled the small square.

As we perused a menu at a *ristorante* there was a screech and a crash. A blue van with *FedZeta* written on the side had been struck sideways on the front passenger side by an old Range Rover. Everybody in the neighborhood ran around to see the damage at the front of the vehicle except for me and Mona.

Over the years, I have noticed that when something happens everybody looks at the same spot. I have always wondered why I should follow suit. After all, there may be something even more interesting going on somewhere else that no one else is paying any attention to. Even if there didn't turn out to be anything else of interest there would still be plenty of time to rubberneck along with everyone else afterwards.

I think of it like being a referee at a football game. While the 90,000 folks in the stands and the main TV camera all focus on the guy with the football most of the referees are looking other places and seeing things that are probably missed by everyone else. What they see are the infractions, the violations and the fouls. It then becomes their job to make sure the player who commits the crime gets busted.

That is why I didn't run up to the front like everyone else and why I stayed standing where I was holding up the rear. It turned out to be a good decision.

From where we stood, it quickly became clear that something was in fact happening in the backfield—something that looked suspiciously like a rule infraction.

Before the truck had come to a full stop two nondescript men stepped out of the crowd with a crowbar and a bolt cutter.

As soon as I noticed it I told Mona to start taking pictures of them and, if she could get close enough, of the guy who had been driving the Range Rover. To her credit, Mona did exactly as I told her, even managing to click the camera into video mode to catch all the action.

Mona probably figured I had gone out of my mind, but I knew in a moment, this whole accident had been a set-up from the get-go. From the look of things, it was obvious there was something inside the van that the two men—who were clearly in cahoots with the other guy—wanted very much.

It only took a few seconds for them to wrench open the back doors of the truck. One climbed in and a few seconds later, he handed a wooden box the size of a small carry-on suitcase to his accomplice.

Something heroic stirred inside me and for some reason I have not been able to understand since, I leapt into the fray and tackled the guy with the box. I suppose it would be more accurate to say that I *tried* to tackle him. When he didn't go down the two of us started a tug-of-war over the box. Since everybody else was standing at the other end of the truck, no one stepped in to help me out.

As Mona continued to film the fiasco the other guy jumped down from the van and pushed both of us, still holding the box, across the street and through the side sliding door of a white mini-van. The door was shut behind us, the second guy climbed into the front passenger seat and the man who had driven the SUV left the scene of the accident and hopped into the driver's seat.

At that point, all Mona could do was to wave *arrivederci* as I drove down the street with my new friends.

With a little help from the man in the front, the guy with the box managed to push me off the middle seat and down into the small space between the middle and the two front seats. As a nice touch he put the wooden box on top of my legs and sat on it. I was pinned to the floor like a dead butterfly on a display board.

Someone threw their jacket over my head and from then on there was nothing left to do but count off the seconds and try to make a mental note of every turn we made in order to keep track of the general direction the mini-van was going. My guess was that we first headed northeast and then made a sharp turn heading southwest at a much faster pace. After five minutes or so, we slowed and made a right turn. This meant we were probably heading northwest. My mental map of Florence clicked into gear and told me that if my calculations were correct we were heading in the general direction of the Florence airport.

From what I could gather from the sound of the men's voices they were very pleased with whatever it was they had done. However their collective enthusiasm seemed to wane somewhat when they started poking at me like a shopper might poke at a tomato to see if it was ripe.

Having a thirty-something-year-old American citizen with glasses lying in the middle of their get-away car was probably not part of their Plan A so they were going to have to figure out a plan B that had me in it.

Plan A didn't worry me much but Plan B was actually quite frightening. Plan B could involve tossing me out of the car at a high speed, or it could involve being knocked unconscious and waking up with three or four feet of dirt on top of me, or I could become a pawn in some sort of international hostage drama that would lead off the Ten O'clock news broadcast in Rome.

Plan B began when the mini-van came to a stop and someone pulled me out of the van onto what felt like concrete. The jacket was still over my head and I was blindly led a short distance before being prodded up a few small steps and told to lie down flat on the floor. I was hoping it was not an airplane for several reasons.

First of all I didn't want to be kidnapped into oblivion and second, if I didn't take some Dramamine right away I was doomed to throw up whatever bits of croissant were still hanging around in my stomach.

The sound of engines starting up and propellers whirling were clues suggesting this was probably going to end up being one of my most unsatisfying days ever.

In a matter of minutes, we were taxiing, speeding up and taking off into parts unknown. By noticing that the late afternoon sun was filtering in from the left side of the plane I guessed we were headed north towards Milan or beyond into Switzerland.

All I could think about was Mona and what a lousy honeymoon this had turned out to be.

My hope was that the images Mona had caught on video would help the cops ID both the thugs and the car I was in when they drove away.

When it became clear that there wasn't much I could do about being a hostage in a plane flying ten or twenty thousand feet in the air, I shifted gears and began wondering what was so special about that all-important box. All I knew was that the box had been stowed away in the back of a truck—a truck with the name *FedZeta* written on it. It hadn't felt very heavy and nothing rattled around when I was fighting over it. The images of precious jewelry, heroin or a Faberge egg came and went as I sorted out the possibilities.

It was all a waste of time, of course, because knowing what was in the box wasn't going to have anything to do with what would happen to me in the next few hours. Trying to imagine what was in the box was only a way to pass the time, but with my head covered and my stomach turning inside out and squeezing up into my throat I was hoping the time would pass as quickly as possible.

After about twenty or thirty dry heaves I felt the plane begin to descend. I was so green in the gills that I lost all track of time, having no idea whether we were still in Italy or about to land in Denmark. All I remember about the landing was hitting my head against something when the plane bounced on touchdown.

My agony of defeat came to a fitting conclusion as I experienced the traditional fraternity ritual of having my pants and shoes removed, followed by being tied up and left lying in a small clump of bushes alongside a makeshift runway. One of the kidnappers must have wanted his jacket back because he pulled it from my head just before I disappeared into the foliage.

My last and only glimpse of my surroundings showed a single-prop, red and white Piper Cherokee with the registration number "HB-RNx" on the side—the "x" being a letter or number I didn't have time enough to read.

As I was lying on my back staring at the sky through the leaves, I heard the plane roar away on takeoff. After less than a minute, the sound of the airplane disappeared completely. It was gone. Whether everybody and the box took off with the plane or whether someone or the box stayed behind I had no idea. In fact, I honestly did not know for sure if the box had ever found its way onto the plane. For all I knew it was sitting in someone's garage back in Florence.

After a short time, I managed to roll out of the bushes, sit up and look around. The plane had landed in a pasture, and there was nothing else to see in the twilight except for pine trees and the silhouette of what looked like a granite ridge to the south. Fortunately, my hands and feet had only been secured with duct tape.

With a little effort, I was able to tear the tape on my ankles apart bit by bit with my fingernails until I had loosened my feet from its grip. A short way off I found a dead tree and after rubbing the tape on my wrists back and forth, I was able to free my hands, too.

The stars were beginning to shine and in the chill of the late evening mountain air, I could see a light or at least the glow of a light through the trees on the far side of the meadow. It didn't take me long to start heading in that direction. The meadow was soft on my bare feet but when I hit the line of trees there were needles, cones and broken branches covering the ground. This slowed me down considerably.

It turned out the light came from a calendar-perfect Swiss chalet, small and white, clean and bright; complete with a balcony. Although I couldn't tell for sure in the dark, I imagined there were baskets full of red geraniums hanging over the railing.

If I had been properly dressed and not quite so desperate, I might have considered yodeling for attention. Instead, I knocked on the door and almost started bawling with relief when someone actually opened it and took me in.

"Thank you, thank you," I said over, and over.

"It's all right." The response came in perfectly good English. "I mean, *we're* all right—but are *you* all right?"

"No," I said with all sincerity, "I'm not all right at all."

In a moment, I found myself holding a cup of hot coffee and covered by a warm blanket. Dinner was already prepared and ready to eat and I found myself invited to share the food and spend the night in a guest room.

The chalet turned out to be owned by a German couple named Herb and Gerta who used it as a vacation retreat during the summer when it wasn't under thirty feet of snow. After listening to my story, they said the house was halfway up a mountain in the Swiss Alps where there was no internet, cell phone coverage or even a landline for them to connect with the outside world. They didn't even have electricity.

They did however have an old-fashioned hand-cranked wireless radio connected to an antenna that ran to the top of a nearby tree.

"It's no use trying to climb down the hill tonight," Herb said, "but we'll try and ring up someone in the village and walk down first thing in the morning."

"While Herb's doing that I'll heat up some water so you can wash up before dinner. I'm sure he'll have a pair of jeans that will fit you."

Both Herb and Gerta left to do what they had to do. In the meantime, I sat in a warm, candlelit room, inside a chalet high in the Swiss Alps, enjoying a comfortable chair with a blanket on my lap and a hot cup of coffee in my hands waiting to take a hot bath followed by a home-cooked dinner.

Under the circumstances, I figured I had to be the luckiest person in the world.

Chapter 24
I Need a Hug
Wednesday, July 24

It took about thirty minutes to walk to the village the next morning. It might have taken less if I had been wearing shoes and pants that actually fit. But you won't find me complaining about the generosity of Herb and Gerta—two people who quite possibly saved my life.

The local police had already contacted the police in Florence and Interpol was already involved because the theft and kidnapping had involved travel across international borders. The fact I had been found alive meant that all the energy could be put into finding the bad guys instead of looking for me.

"HB," the first two letters on the tail of the plane indicated the plane was registered in Switzerland. Whether any of this was helping with the search, I had no idea. To be honest, I really didn't care. All I wanted to do was to get back to Mona in Florence.

The first thing I did when I got to a phone was call Mona.

"Hey, Babe!" I said.

"Don't call me 'Babe,'" Mona said tersely, followed by, "Florence has been a total bore without you. I love you so much and I've missed you and I've been so worried and now I'm so happy that you're alive and . . . and . . . I'll never forgive you for sticking your nose into other people's business and leaving me standing all by myself in a foreign country holding a camera in my hand while you get shoved into a car and driven away and wind up in Switzerland of all places. I am so angry at you I could spit and . . . and it's so good to hear your voice again."

"I love you too," I said.

"Come back soon," Mona added, after she had caught her breath. "I really need a hug."

"I've got one in my pocket just for you and when I get back to Florence, or Rome, or wherever you are, I'll give it to you forever."

"Mike, just come back, okay? Just come back and be my honeymoon husband again."

One of the local police officers tapped me on the shoulder and said there was a phone call for me and it sounded important. As far as I was concerned there was no phone call in the world as important as the one I was having with Mona, but I knew I would never get back to Florence until I had done my duty and answered the millions of questions the authorities wanted to ask me.

So I said, "I gotta go. My public needs me. Love you lots. Bye," and Mona said the same.

The phone call was from Interpol. They offered me an all-expense-paid trip to Geneva so I could meet with them personally. The helicopter that would take me there was already on its way to pick me up. I didn't really want to go to Geneva but, given where I was, it was probably the fastest way to get back to Florence anyway.

It was around 12 Noon when we landed next to a large building in Geneva. Somehow, somebody had gotten my exact physical measurements because there was a pair of shoes and the clothes to go with them waiting for me when I stepped out of the helicopter. They fit perfectly.

Before the grilling began, I was ushered into a small room and offered lunch, which I inhaled as if it was helium squeezed out of a birthday party balloon. My voice didn't change pitch, but a few minutes later I was told to start talking. I did what I was told, and talked and answered questions for over an hour.

I was shown pictures of different men but I couldn't identify any of them. They showed me a picture of a minivan and I said it looked like the one that had driven away with me in it.

I was shown a picture of a small airplane and I said, "Yes, sir. That's the plane I saw."

Last, but not least I was shown a picture of a small wooden box about the size of a carry-on bag.

Once again my answer was, "Yes, that looks like what I saw."

When the interview was over, I had to sign a dozen documents before they were willing to drive me to the airport to catch a flight to Florence. It turned out to be the same airline that Mona and I had taken two days earlier. I had to pay for the tickets out of my own pockets, which, as you might guess, were empty. Because Mona was able to charge the tickets over the phone, I was able to board the plane before it took off without me.

I arrived in Florence less than twenty-four hours after I had been spirited away. For the first time it sank in how small Europe really is.

Today was the day we should have taken the train to Rome. Tomorrow, we were to see Rome and the day after we were supposed to fly back to New York.

"I'm tired, "I said. "I want to go home."

With Mona at my side, we climbed into a local police car and drove to police headquarters for more interviews. While I was there, I learned the stolen box contained two unique and priceless commemorative coins designed by Benvenuto Cellini. The bad guys were suspected to be members of a terrorist cell who had planned the heist as a fundraiser for a big project they were working on.

When I finally walked out of the police station, the sun had set and I was dead on my feet. Mona ordered room service at the hotel but I fell asleep on the bed with my clothes on before the food got there.

Whatever else needed to be said would have to wait until tomorrow.

Chapter 25
Rome In a Day
Thursday, July 25

Hanging around thugs and crooks is part of what I do as a private eye. I do this because people pay me to do it. It's what I do for a living.

Thugs and crooks understand this and seem to enjoy the challenge of doing all they can to keep out of sight, at least when I am being paid to look for them.

What I haven't figured out is why thugs and crooks seem to gravitate to me when I am not looking for them. It's like trying to find an auto parts store. When you need one you can't find one but when you don't need one there seems to be one on every corner.

When I am on vacation and no one is paying me anything I would like the thugs and crooks to stay as far away from me as possible. This includes honeymoons.

I would think the thugs and crooks would want to cooperate with me on this; that they would want to stay away from me all of the time and not just when money is involved.

This trip to Europe with Mona has taught me that life does not always make a whole lot of sense. Maybe it is because thugs and crooks are not as smart as they ought to be. Maybe it is because there are so many thugs and crooks in the world you can't avoid them. Maybe it is because I am just really, really, unlucky.

When I woke up, Mona was sitting in a chair next to the bed staring at me. She didn't stop staring even after I woke up and started staring back at her. Eventually she blinked first and started laughing. She stood up and twirled around like a little girl wearing her first ballet dress. When she had finished twirling, she sat on the chair and started staring at me again. This time there was a big smile on her face.

"What's going on?" I asked. "What's the deal with the staring and the twirling and stuff?"

"Because," she said.

"Because what?" I asked. "Is it because you love me so much that you can't take your eyes off of me? Or is it because you can't believe what a complete idiot you married?"

"Yes," she said.

She crawled onto the bed and kissed me with one of the longest and most disgusting kisses I had ever received. I returned the favor and of course, we ended up missing breakfast again.

We were enjoying the bliss of married life until my phone rang. It was Thor.

"Mike," he said, "Have you filed for divorce yet?"

"What's up?" I asked, ignoring his question.

"Can you fly through London on your way home tomorrow and maybe stay over an extra day. There are some loose ends to tie up and we can't do it without you."

"What sort of things," I asked, somewhat distracted by Mona nibbling on my ear.

"Things that have to do with Du and the police and things like that. Legal things. It won't take long but you need to be here, otherwise, you'll probably have to fly all the way back from New York. I'm being a pal, trying to save you both a few bucks and a bite out of your calendar."

I knew we had a day or two to spare and Mona's folks would probably pick up all the ticket changes that would be involved so I said, "Sure, why not; nothing else has gone the way we planned so what else is new? When I find out the details I'll let you know when we'll be coming in."

"Thanks," Thor said. "You're a dear."

I hung up before he did.

"Oh, boy," Mona said. "Just what I need . . . another adventure."

Mona started mumbling about how nice it will be to spend the rest of her life sitting in the quiet, cloistered solitude of a University library showing undergraduate students how to find books in the computer catalogue.

As she mumbled, my thoughts began to ramble along the lines of how sweet it would be if I had a newer, larger office and was able to hire someone like Zach to do some of the grunt work that takes up so much of my time.

When the mumbling and rambling were finished I was ready to pick up where we had left off when the phone rang, but Mona was ready to move on to other things.

"So," she said. "What do we do now?"

It was clear she didn't care what I thought because she went on to answer her own question before I had a chance to cut in.

"I already canceled last night's hotel reservation in Rome," she said, "so all we have to do is rearrange our return flights and then, when we get that all straightened out you'll call Pam and tell her she'll be picking us up at JFK on Saturday instead of tomorrow. We can buy our train tickets to Rome at the station."

With Mona doing all the thinking my brain could have left for a vacation in the Bahamas and been gone a week before I even noticed it was missing.

After we rescheduled everything, we headed off to the train station, paid extra for First Class seats and pulled into Rome ninety minutes later. We took a cab to our hotel for an early check-in and ate brunch at a nearby café. It wasn't even Noon yet and we had free play for the rest of the day.

"What's the one thing you want to see or do in Rome," I asked.

"I'd like to see the Coliseum and the Forum," she said. "How about you?"

"I'd like to see St. Peter's, the Vatican Museum, and the Sistine Chapel but that would take up more time than we have."

"Not if we paid cab-fare for the whole thing. Let's give it our best shot. Let's do it all!"

"Hi-yo, Silver!" I shouted as the café patrons started whispering about how crazy Americans are.

"Beam me up, Scottie!" Mona shouted back.

We were off to the races.

We decided we'd be able to see the Coliseum and the Forum after dark if necessary so our first stop was the Vatican. Because we expected long lines, we headed for the Vatican Museums and the Sistine Chapel first. Fortunately, because the line was so short, we were inside in less than thirty minutes.

With Mona in the lead, we headed straight to the Pinacoteca Gallery to see da Vinci's *St. Jerome* and Caravaggio's *Deposition from the Cross*. Then, with Mona still in the lead, we dashed through the manuscript hall to see the 4th century biblical *Codex Vaticanus*. Upstairs were the Raphael rooms which include his incredibly large and detailed painting, *The School of Athens*. Next, and without breaking stride, we arrived at the Sistine Chapel without a tour group in sight. There were, in fact, hardly any people in sight at all. For some strange and inexplicable reason we had the Chapel almost completely to ourselves.

We slowed our stride and did our best to break our necks looking straight up. We saw Adam almost touching God, we saw lots of Sibyls and, of course, we saw another *Last Judgment,* all painted by Charlton Heston.

To save time we went directly into St. Peter's through a door in the back of the chapel. On our way, we passed a long line of people waiting to climb to the top of the church dome.

As we burst into the Basilica, our feet stopped moving for the first time in two and a half hours. From where we stood, the sight, the space, the splendor, the sound and even the air combined and conspired to overwhelm every one of our senses except taste. We stood as still and as numb as the statues that stand in a line on top of the building's façade.

I had a strong suspicion that the whole of St. Paul's in London could be dropped inside St. Peter's and there would still be room to move around.

"What hath God wrought?" Mona exclaimed, probably quoting from someone I had never heard of before.

When we got our breath back, we walked over to see the *Pieta*. From there we hurried over to the center of the church to get a close-up look at the 95-foot bronze altar canopy built by Bernini. For some reason it is called a *baldaccino.* I suspect there must be people who know why it is called a *baldaccino,* but if there are such people, I have never met any of them.

Next to the altar is the chair the Pope sits in and somewhere underneath is an ancient Roman crypt where St. Peter is buried . . . probably . . . maybe.

As we exited the front of the church we were again overwhelmed, but this time by the size of St. Peter's square which is large enough to hold over 300,000 worshippers, which would not be a bad turnout for a Sunday morning congregational meeting.

We ran through the square and hopped into a cab so quickly that I completely forgot to admire the Dome of domes, the largest and the most amazingly beautiful dome in the world. I had read about its beauty all my life and now I will have to take someone else's word for it because I forgot to look.

Because the Coliseum was the next destination to close, we headed there next. The tickets we purchased got us into the Roman Forum, too. The Coliseum is big . . . very big. The floor is gone, so we could see all the tunnels and rooms once covered over by wood and dirt.

There is evidence to suggest the Coliseum was built using the loot stolen from the Jerusalem Temple by Titus. His triumphal arch is nearby where it depicts some of those treasures carried into Rome during his victory parade.

A quick dash around the Coliseum took us past the enormous Arch of Constantine and then to the *Via Sacre*, Palatine Hill and the Roman Forum. Back when Julius Caesar was stabbed to death the Forum was downtown Rome in the sense that the Capitol Mall is downtown Washington D.C.

Ruins are everywhere but some are intact enough to give a feel for how magnificent they must have been when they were new. The Arch of Titus was the one thing Mona really wanted to see because it had such a strong connection with Jerusalem and Jesus. It seems Jesus died about 40 years before Titus burned Jerusalem and its temple to the ground.

Mona wouldn't put it that way. She would say that Jerusalem burned 40 years after Jesus rose from the dead. She might be right about that but either way the dating comes out the same.

Because we skipped the Capitoline Museum, we were done with the Forum so quickly we were able to add the Pantheon to our list. For over 2,000 years, the Pantheon has held the record for having the largest unreinforced concrete dome in the world. No other building from the days of ancient Rome has remained as well preserved as this temple. The Pantheon was built to honor every god the Romans could dream up which explains why it is so large and why it is called the Pantheon: a word that means, "All of the gods, all of the time," or something like it.

My cell phone said 5:48 p.m. when we emerged into the early evening light. We had somehow managed to see most of Rome in less than six hours. After a few high fives, we realized how hungry we were. There were cafés all around the Pantheon and not one of them was crowded because it was too early for most people to be eating dinner. Mona and I are not like most people, of course, so we found an empty table and ordered one four course Italian meal with enough food to feed us both.

Neither of us talked while we ate. Actually, we hadn't talked much all day. We had been too busy.

When we finished our gelato, and dinner was *completare*, Mona said, "Mike, do you think there is any romance left in us—I mean, after all we've been through the last two weeks?"

“Yes,” I said. “I’ve got lots of romance left in me, but it’s buried so far down it will take a mining consortium to dig it out and bring it back to the surface. How about you?”

“Since I didn’t take a detour to Switzerland like you did I probably have a little more left in the tank. If you can handle it let’s take a walk along the Tiber before we go back to the hotel.”

There isn’t much to say about walking along the Tiber in central Rome. In many ways, it is like the Arno, olive drab and slow moving, but larger and wider. It’s not that the Tiber is a bad looking river but, like Paris and London, there are no places to walk along it without cars zipping past at high speed. There is an enormous footbridge crossing the Tiber directly in front of the *Castel Sant’Angelo* and from the bridge, there are some nice views of St. Peter’s off in the distance. As we stood in the middle of the bridge over the Tiber in the center of Rome in the fading light of early evening, I was hoping for a romantic moment that would stoke the fires of love and lust in both of us. But the moment never showed up. Maybe it was because we were too exhausted.

On our way back to the hotel, we stopped to buy a second round of gelato. At the hotel, we each took a shower, packed our suitcases for the morning flight to London and fell asleep in each other’s arms.

Chapter 26
Not Dead Yet
Friday, July 26

Our first and last morning in Rome began, of course, with a light continental breakfast.

The news media in Florence had finally tracked me down and as we made our way to the airport my phone started playing *Bolero* so often that people who were old enough to remember kept looking around to see if Torvill and Dean had skated onto the ice.

Our first and last morning in Rome ended when we boarded our plane to London. It was an overcast day so there was nothing to see out of the windows as we followed Hannibal across the Alps in reverse.

We had long since given up on the word "thrift" so we took a long and expensive cab ride from Heathrow to see Du at the hospital.

Du was quite cheerful when we walked in.

"Hi there," he said with a smile. "I'm not dead yet."

"Thanks for pointing that out," I said.

Thor and Zach were there but Thị Yen wasn't.

As if on cue, Thor picked up the conversation.

"Before I begin I would like to congratulate the "Cellini Captive" who survived the "Terror in Tuscany" and escaped from the "Florentine Filchers" by "leaping from the plane" as it passed over a "remote, boulder-strewn pasture in the Swiss Alps."

"What," Mona asked, "are you talking about?"

"It's all over the papers," Zach said. "You're famous."

He held up a copy of a local tabloid with pictures of me plastered all over the front page.

"Please tell me this is *not* why you told us we had to come to London," I moaned.

My phone started vibrating again so this time I switched it to airplane mode.

"No," said Thor. "The celebrity thing is just a bonus, like the icing on a cake."

"Oh shut up," Du said. "Stop prattling and get to the point."

Thor started laughing so Zach stepped up and threw the first pitch.

"The museum called yesterday. They are submitting Du's painting to an authentication process that will take about two to three months before they get all the results. An expert on Rembrandt's technique and use of paint thinks it could be genuine. A visual examination of the canvas material found it to be virtually identical to canvass Rembrandt used during the early 1630s.

"The curator said that because the National Gallery has a vested interest in whether the painting is genuine or not, he asked Du if he would approve its transfer to an independent lab that specializes in checking into these things. Du signed it over yesterday afternoon."

“That is so exciting,” Mona said, as she bounced up and down on her toes.

Thor had collected himself enough to add, “But that’s not why you’re here, Mike. Du doesn’t want the painting and doesn’t care whether it is real or not. Yesterday he signed a notarized document that names you as its sole owner. Congratulations.”

Du was smiling. Thor was biting his lip and Zach was staring past me at the wall.

Mona was looking down at her feet and I had a fleeting vision of myself sitting on a yacht alongside an isolated white-sand island in the Caribbean sipping a colorful adult beverage with a little umbrella sticking out of the glass.

“Oh,” I said.

“It’s all yours, Mike, “said Du. “My life and my marriage are better off without it. Have a nice life.”

There was a pause and his smile disappeared.

“I’d like you to talk to Zach and Van before you decide what to do with it.”

‘Sure thing, boss,” I said with a wink.

Du smiled again and as he had done before when he was through talking he rolled over onto his side with his back to us.

“Let’s take a walk,” I said as we stepped out of the room together. “Let’s say the painting is real and we sell it for $30 million. What do you think we should do with it?”

“That’s up to you, isn’t it?” said Thor.

“No,” I said. “My name might be on the pink slip but as far as I’m concerned it belongs to all of us, including Du.”

I looked at Mona and she nodded her agreement.

After a lengthy confab we decided that if the painting turned out to be a genuine Rembrandt we would offer it to the New York Metropolitan Museum of Art for first right of purchase. If they could find a reasonable amount of money to pay for it we would sell it to them. Otherwise, we would put it up for auction with conditions that it be made available for public viewing, preferably at the Met. Terms of the sale would also give the National Gallery in London the right to display it for the first two years on the condition that they cover the costs of its full restoration.

Money from the sale would be divided into shares with 40% going to Zach, 20% to Thor, 20% to me and 20% to a trust managed by Zach for the benefit of Du and Thi Yen as circumstances might require.

As Du's son, Zach would be named executor and unless someone reneged with a lawsuit, our handshake and a few signatures would be as good as gold. The one caveat was that if Du ever changed his mind whatever was left of the dough would go back to him with no questions asked.

Thor said he knew a lawyer in New York who could do the paperwork so that was that.

Mona and I wanted to get back to the airport as soon as possible so we told Du what we had discussed and wished him a good recovery.

Du seemed pleased.

"See you soon," Thor said as we walked out the door.

"Oh, by the way," I said to Du as I stuck my head back through the door. "If none of this works out we can always pawn the bloody thing to Thor. I think it would look nice in his front window next to my Samurai sword."

The trip to the airport was uneventful except for when we were standing at the curb waving for a taxi in front of the hospital. From down the street we heard a women yell, "Thief! Thief! He's stolen my purse!"

A man came running down the sidewalk with a purse in his hand, pushing and shoving people out of the way. As he ran past, Mona swung her own handbag and caught the guy full-on in the face. He went down in a heap with Mona standing over him like a linebacker who has just sacked the quarterback.

People started crowding around and all I could think of was, *Oh, no! Not again*!

I grabbed Mona by the hand and shoved her into the cab before someone took her picture and called her a hero. There had been enough of that already and it was time to go home.

We boarded our plane and took off. Except for my staying awake the whole time and actually enjoying the movie, the flight home was as unmemorable as it could be.

It was 11:00 p.m. when Pam met us at the curb just outside the baggage claim at JFK. Since it was so late, and since it was only fifteen minutes to her house in Bayswater, she took us to her place for the night.

On the way, she asked how our honeymoon had been.

Mona said, "Not what I expected."

What I said was, "I'm glad we're home."

Chapter 27
I Muv Moo Doo

Saturday, July 27

We woke up at 12:30 in the afternoon Italian time but the clock next to our bed said 6:30 a.m. Pam was already up and it didn't take long before we had finished a heavy American breakfast that would have easily tipped the scales against a *Venti*. After putting the dishes in the sink, Pam offered to drive us in to Manhattan,

"No thanks," I said. "We've gotten used to travelling on our own so just drop us off at the Far Rockaway station and we'll take the "A" train into town.

Because of our luggage, we kept it simple and made just one transfer in South Manhattan to the #6 line, which took us to within a few blocks of Mona's apartment in the Upper East Side. To save walking with the luggage we took the final taxi ride of our honeymoon trip.

Mona's roommates were out so we had the place to ourselves. We sat on the sofa and leaned against each other as though we had not seen one another for a very long time.

"That was fun," Mona said. "Next time let's take a cruise."

"I'd probably fall overboard . . . ," I replied.

". . . and you'd have your picture on the front page of the newspapers again."

Mona stood up and began unpacking her bags. After piling up all the things that needed to be washed there wasn't much left in her suitcase except her toiletry bag and some brochures.

"What do I do with *my* stuff?" I asked. "Should I unpack it here or go back and do it at my place?"

"Tell you what, Mona suggested. "Let's go over to your place so you can get yourself straightened out. Then we'll bring back what you need to stay here until we move. We'll probably be going back and forth a lot in the next few days anyway."

What I didn't know was that Mona was setting me up for a surprise.

After the long flight from London, it felt good to breathe in the familiar ozone of Manhattan and to stretch our legs as we walked to my apartment.

When I opened the door to my flat, I had to face the shock of seeing my apartment all cleaned up. I had completely forgotten how nice it looked when we left on our trip. It even smelled clean.

There was another pleasant smell mixed into the rest. It wasn't exactly a clean smell; it was more of a new smell.

Mona motioned for me to go in first. I lugged my honeymoon luggage through the door and went over to sit on the sofa.

"What happened to my sofa?" I yelled pointing at the fresh, new sofa that was sitting where mine had been. "And where did this one come from?"

"I hope you like it," Mona said with a smile. "It's yours, actually. And now it's ours."

It slowly started to sink in that it really was my sofa.

"Did you have something to do with this?"

"Guilty as charged. I throw myself onto the mercy of the court!"

"*Te absolvo*," I replied with a smile of my own. "I really do love you more and more every day."

I walked over to Mona, put my arms around her and laid one of our patented sloppy kisses on her ear.

"You are," I whispered into her now-soggy ear, "more full of surprises than Robert. And that is very high praise!"

Mona pulled her ear away from my mouth and stuck her lips onto mine with super glue.

"I muv moo doo," she said with a muffle.

Mona explained she knew how much I wanted to keep the sofa but it had been way too disgusting to be allowed into our new apartment.

"We needed a sofa, so I figured if yours was sterilized and reupholstered it would split the difference and make us both happy!"

She arranged the whole thing with Zach and loaned him the key I had given her to my apartment. She even managed to match the original material perfectly.

"Let's see if it works," I winked as I pulled her down on top of me.

The good news was . . . it worked.

We woke up a short time later when our new landlord called and said our apartment was clean and ready for us to move in early if we wanted. It was already 11:30 a.m so we took a cab and picked up the keys before heading back to Mona's to grab a light Manhattan-style continental lunch. When we arrived, Brin greeted us with two large take-out pizzas.

As we ate, we talked about our trip, leaving out the part about Du and the painting because the money angle would have taken the conversation in a direction we didn't really want it to go.

"How did the pizza in Italy compare to this?" Brin asked with her mouth full of crust.

"I don't know," Mona said. "We didn't eat any."

After only one pizza, Mona set off to do her laundry and I tried to fight my jetlag by walking to my office to see what had stacked up on my answering machine.

The phone I used on our trip was a European smart phone I had rented while we were there. Only my closest friends had known the number for that phone. My own phone had stayed behind in New York. Now I had to check the phone messages on that, too.

At the office, there were at least thirty-five messages. Ten of them were from the same person begging me to call back because he was going to jump off the Brooklyn Bridge or—depending on which message I listened to—the Empire State Building, the Verrazano Bridge or the Statue of Liberty. He was going to do one of these things unless I called him immediately.

"I'm desperate," he said over and over.

His first call was recorded the day I left town and his last message was recorded the day I got back. I figured if he hadn't jumped off something by now he probably wouldn't jump off anything until I called him on Monday.

The rest of the calls were from people offering to pay me to repossess something or to serve a warrant on somebody . . . things like that.

My cell phone messages turned out to be more interesting.

One call that particularly caught my ear concerned a man who said someone had stolen three of his hats from the hat stand in his home. The funniest part was that they were not all stolen at the same time. There had been three hats, each stolen from inside the house on three different days. He said the whole business was driving him crazy. As a result, he was going to pay big bucks to have a security system installed in his home.

It sounded like easy money to me so I phoned him on the spot and set up an appointment for early Monday morning. There would be plenty of time in the afternoon for Mona and me to do whatever else we needed to do that day.

Another call that sounded interesting was from a female voice saying that without asking, her boyfriend had used her credit card to buy a $2,000, 60" flat screen TV for her apartment. When she saw it, she threw a fit and threw him out. Later that afternoon she let him in and left him alone to clear out his stuff. When she came back, the boyfriend was gone, his stuff was gone and her TV was gone.

She phoned him up and asked what was going on and he told her he had pawned it because "you said you didn't want it so I took it. Good luck and good-bye."

When he hung up, she immediately and irrevocably downgraded him to the status of ex-boyfriend.

"Help me find my TV," the voice said on the message, "and help me get my money back from that (*person with a disgusting name that I hope will have something disgusting done to him by a disgusting person*)." Her words were so salty that I had to rewrite some of them and then delete the message from my voice mail before it melted my phone into a lump of plastic.

I tossed her info onto the top of my "Think About It But Probably Not" file. Compared to hers the rest of the messages were boring, unchallenging, and probably not worth the time or the trouble.

Less than a year ago I would have fainted dead away if I had gotten that many jobs offered to me at one time. Back then, I had so little dough that I would have taken every one of them just to pay my back rent. Lately, however, I've been doing well enough to enjoy the luxury of being more selective in which jobs I take and which ones I turn down.

For example: I'd rather take one job that uses up a lot of time but pays well, than take on six or seven little ones that pay out in small change. Call me jaded, picky, or fatheaded, but . . . well . . . just go ahead and call me those things because I'm probably all of them.

Just ask Mona.

As I sleepwalked back to Mona's place I was thinking I should call the rental van people and reserve something to help haul our furniture over to our new apartment tomorrow afternoon. The rental part would be easy. The hard part would be finding someone strong enough to help me carry the stuff down to the truck and then carry it up the three flights of stairs to our new home.

"Hey you!" I shouted playfully as I walked through the door of Mona's apartment, "Do you think Robert would come over tomorrow afternoon and help us move the furniture?"

"I'm probably not the one to ask," Brin replied from the kitchen. "Maybe you should ask Mona. She's in the basement doing another load of laundry and I have an errand to run."

"Hi there sweetie," Mona said as she bounced through the door.

"Please don't call me sweetie," Brin replied as she passed Mona on her way out. "You know I don't like it when you call me that."

"Then I'll just have to recycle the sweetie thing for someone else."

Mona walked over to the dining table where I was sitting, eating an apple.

"Hi sweetie," she said as she bent over and gave me a kiss. "I gave Danny a call this morning. He still drives my brother's . . . his dad's pickup truck. He'll meet us here tomorrow at 12:30 p.m. We should have everything moved out and into our apartment by 3:00. It should only take two trips with the furniture. The clothes and other things can be tossed on top of the furniture and he can do a third trip if we need it."

Once again, Mona had finished her to-do list and was already starting in on mine.

"So how's the Private Investigator business?" she asked with breath bated.

"There's a man who keeps losing his hats and wants me to find out how and why. I'm seeing him on Monday morning. Why don't you come along? We can be a team again!"

"What kind of hats?" she asked.

"Does it make any difference?"

"Yes," she said. "It does."

My phone rang, which rescued me from a conversation that was going nowhere fast.

"Hey, hey, my friend! Toodleloo, Cheerio and Ta-Ta!"

It was Thor.

"Thor," I said. "You're more backwards than I thought."

"I've got good news," he said. "Du is out of the hospital. The doctors say he didn't suffer any serious heart damage and his arteries aren't going to close up and go home after work, either. If he loses thirty pounds and reduces his stress, he should be good for another ten years or more.

"Du is glad he isn't going to die yet." Thor continued. "He says there are some bills he needs to pay and some inventory to replace in his shop. When he's finished with that he says he'll be ready to die."

"That's good news, thanks," I said. "I'll send him a bereavement card so he'll know what he missed."

"That's not the good news," Thor said. "I mean it's good news but it's not the good news I phoned about. They caught the guy who kidnapped Du and was after the painting."

"Go on," I said. "What happened?"

"The two men the police caught at Du's place were flunkies who didn't know anything—not even the other guy's name. They said they were lured into the whole thing with the promise of big money if the plan worked. Otherwise, *nada*."

"That sounds like my job," I said. "Not the breaking the law part, but the contingency fee thing . . . but go on, tell me more."

"The police used the information you gave them when your GPS app showed the man with Du's phone making calls from Trafalgar Square. They confirmed his location with the phone company and then put out a call to the public asking for anyone who was taking pictures around there that day to mail or email their pictures to the police.

"They received thirty photos. Two of them showed a man talking on a cell phone. It was the same man in each picture. One of the photos even caught a glint of red, which is the color of Du's phone. Security cameras around the square showed the same man pacing and wandering around almost randomly for over an hour.

"So," I said, "how did they figure out who it was?"

"That's where Interpol comes in. They have a photo face-matching file that works like fingerprints. They put a close-up face-shot of the guy into their computer and in a matter of seconds five or ten names came out. One of them happened to be a man named Philippe McGregor, an expert in separating genuine art from forgeries. He's been a suspect in art thefts before but nothing could ever be proved . . . until now.

"Du identified the man in the photos as being the thug who thumped him on the head and bound and gagged him to a chair. After figuring out who he was they were able to match him with a smudged fingerprint they found on Du's phone."

"So they picked him up?"

"They arrested him last night at a hotel where he had registered under his own name."

Thor told the story well and I was impressed at how fast the police got it all figured out. Philippe must have thought that phoning from a busy public place would be a good way to be invisible because even if they traced his calls with GPS he would still be lost in the crowd. What he didn't anticipate were the tourists taking pictures all over the place. I imagine he was surprised when the cops knocked on his door.

"Apparently," Thor added, "he told the police he hadn't stolen the painting and had no idea where it came from. He said he had been hired to pick it out of a trash bin and then drop it where another person would find it. Beyond that he didn't even know who had hired him or who was going to pay him for his trouble."

"Thanks for the update," I said. "Anything new on the painting?"

"Nope, nothing yet. They said it would be weeks or months before they would get the results back.

"Thor," I asked, "when are you coming home?"

"Zach and I are flying back tomorrow night. I'll take Monday off and get my shop back open on Tuesday. This trip has cost me a small fortune. I'd better get some bucks from that painting or I'm going to send Du a bill for services rendered."

Speaking gently, I said, "Thor, he's family. He almost died. Please don't send him a . . . ."

Thor cut me off.

"Chill out, Mike," he said. "You're taking me way too seriously. I thought you knew me better than that!"

"Good-bye, Thor," I said. "I'll see you in a couple of days."

Thor closed out the call with, "'Ello, Mate," and "Ey Up Me Duck!"

He hung up before I could say, "What?"

I told Mona what Thor had told me but she didn't seem very interested in the crook part of the story, only the part about Du.

"You're the P.I.," she said. "You're supposed to be interested in stuff like that. But I'm a college librarian, so I think about things loftier than thugs and crooks . . . lofty thoughts that live high up in the top of ivory towers . . . ."

I groaned, knowing Mona was setting me up for something again.

"Mike," she continued. "You know why I'll never be a snob with my nose in the air? Because I'll be so far above you my nose will be pointing down!"

"Not so fast Your Majesty," I replied. "Looking down your nose at someone is just one more thing that snobs do, so you're a snob no matter how you look at it—or how you look at me—or whatever else you're looking at."

Mona started laughing. She started walking around the room with her nose in the air staring at the ceiling. Then she walked around the room looking down at the floor.

"I think I want to be the sort of snob who looks down her nose."

"Why is that?"

"Because then I can see you when I look down—and you are the most interesting thing in the room. Besides," she added, "I never realized how boring our ceiling is. Maybe if Brin painted a few stars on it . . . . ?"

"Mona," I interrupted, "if I don't lie down before dinner I'm going to keel over and fall asleep on the floor. Why don't you take a break from the laundry and we can take a nap together."

With imperfect timing, my phone rang.

"You gotta help me," the voice cried plaintively. "It's all coming down on me at once. If you can't help me . . . .

I could see it coming from a mile away.

" . . . I'm going to jump off the Holland Tunnel!"

My guts knew right away that there was something very wrong with this particular picture.

"You wouldn't want to do that," I said.

"Why not?"

"Because you wouldn't hurt yourself . . . you'd just get wet."

"Well, you still gotta help me."

"Okay," I asked, curious to hear his answer. "What do I have to do? How can I help?"

"I don't know if you can help me or not. It depends. Have you ever heard of snew?"

"I don't know," I said. "What's snew?"

"Nothing much," came the reply. "What's snew with you?"

It was Robert.

I have never felt so embarrassed in my life. I *knew* that joke . . . and I *still* fell for it.

"Welcome back, Mr. Maurison," said the voice as only Robert could say it. "Why didn't you call when you got in?"

"Because I was afraid you'd say something that would make me feel like an idiot . . . nice job, by the way."

"Thanks. I'm glad you liked it. Oh, I almost forgot, Chia would like you to have us over after you move in to your new place."

"Uh, Robert . . . I think you mean that Chia wants to have us over to your place after we move in to ours, right?"

"No. I got it right the first time. Let us know when would be a good day for us to come over. You can show us the pictures from your trip."

As I have said a thousand times, you can never tell with Robert.

Since I was now wide-awake, I decided I might as well phone the gal who had been double-stuffed by a TV.

When she answered her phone, she didn't sound anything like the woman on my voice mail.

"Hello, my name is Mike Maurison and I'm a Private Eye here in Manhattan. Are you the person who left a message on my phone earlier this week?"

"Yes," said a voice that was soft, feminine and very polite. "I'm sorry about what I said. I was so angry at Claude . . ." there was a pause. "Don't laugh. That's his name . . . really . . . I'm not mean enough to make up a name like that . . . Anyway, he did what I told you on the phone and I want you to find my TV and get my money back. Can you do that? I'll pay you . . . but not more than the TV is worth. Is that fair? I don't know if it's fair or not. I've never done this before."

"I'll have to think about it," I said. "I'll get back to you later, maybe tonight or Monday or tomorrow. I'll let you know. And good luck."

"That's exactly what Claude said. Thanks. Let me know."

After I hung up I told Mona about Claude, the girlfriend and the TV.

"I'm not sure I want to take the case," I said. "It sounds too complicated, too personal and I can see it taking up a lot of time. Plus, she doesn't have a lot of money to pay me if I go into overtime."

"How," Mona asked, "did the boyfriend pay for the TV?"

"With her credit card."

"And you don't get it?"

"Get what?"

"How to solve the whole thing and make her happy?"

"No. But I have a feeling you're going to tell me, right?"

"Right you are, Sherlock. Here's what you do. Phone her back and tell her to call her credit card company and tell them that the item she just purchased on their card was stolen. Most credit card companies provide insurance to cover stuff like that . . . it's part of their sales pitch. I'm surprised she didn't think of it already. She'll get her money back, her boyfriend gets some dishonest money and some pawn shop owner makes a few bucks. It's win-win except for the credit card company."

"My heart bleeds for the credit card company," I said. "I knew that . . . what you said . . . but I didn't think of it. Thanks for setting me straight. Your plan is good except for one thing. If I tell her this over the phone, she'll be happy but I won't get paid for it. It doesn't seem fair."

"The solution wasn't your idea so why should you get paid for it? It's my idea and I can do with it whatever I want, and what I want to do is mark it down as a charitable deduction. So go ahead . . . give her a call. Tell her it's on the house."

Out of the goodness of Mona's heart, I made the call.

"Duh," said the gal after I gave her the tip. "Why didn't I think of that?" Then, after a a pause, "Thank you Mr. Maurison, that solves everything. Thanks again. Good-bye."

She didn't even ask for my address so she could mail me a check.

Corinne fixed eggplant parmesan for dinner. I don't like eggplant.

Before the third and last bite hit my stomach, Mona and I said "Good-night" and disappeared into her room. We were so tired we gave the springs on her bed a rest.

Chapter 28
Moving Day
Sunday, July 28

Mona went to church, I didn't, and that pretty much sums up the morning. I didn't have any good reason not to go but I decided to stay home because, with the exception of my unplanned detour to Switzerland, I had been with Mona every day full-time since we got married.

I have spent most of my life on my own and although it's fun to be with Mona I've come to realize that I need some time by myself, too. Take museums, for example: There is no one in the world I would rather go to a museum with than Mona, but there are times when I need to be quiet, see some old friends and maybe have an imaginary chat with an imaginary grandfather, even if I'm only talking to myself.

So today I just sat around watching the "nothing" that's on Sunday morning TV when it isn't football season. I thought about getting a newspaper and doing the crossword but I was too lazy to walk down the stairs and back up again. There would be enough of that in the afternoon when we moved our things into the new apartment.

I haven't said much about it, but there were times on our honeymoon when I wished I had been able to go off on my own without Mona. It's not easy to wander aimlessly and mindlessly with another person. There is always the unspoken need to look for things to comment on or talk about—"Look at that steeple, it's so narrow, I wonder why?" or "What do think, should we eat here or keep walking?"—the sort of things that would never even cross my mind if I was by myself.

Sometimes, I suppose, Mona probably feels the same way,. After all, she's been living on her own for a long time, too. I don't think it means we don't like each other anymore. I think it is just that being married is a lot more complicated than I thought when we were talking these things over with Mona's pastor.

Before the wedding, my friend Sid said the hardest thing about marriage is deciding which way the toilet paper goes on the roller. That, he said, can be a real deal breaker. Sid should know. He and his wife never did agree on the toilet paper and now he's raising their two children by himself.

Mona and I agree on the toilet paper so I suppose that is a good sign, but here are other things that have started to annoy us about each other. They are all small things—little things that shouldn't matter but they do. I need to remember that it took me a long time to learn how to live by myself. Learning how to live with Mona will take some time, too.

Mona got back from church before 11:00 a.m. carrying two foot-long Heroes and a couple of sodas to share with her nephew when it came time to eat lunch. We had laid out everything we owned for Danny to load onto his truck. We were ready.

Danny arrived on time and the two of us carried Mona's dresser, chair, bed and books downstairs. There wasn't room left in the truck for anything else so we stuffed some bed linen, towels and blankets in between the larger things.

The drive to 81st St. only took a couple of minutes.

Loading and unloading things in Manhattan is easy. People simply stop their truck at the curb and the traffic just backs up until it finds a way to drive around it. Since it was Sunday, there wasn't much traffic to back up. The weather was sunny and warm so it was easy to haul everything onto the sidewalk and carry it up while Mona held the door open and stayed behind to watch the truck and things we hadn't carried up yet. We were done and ready for the second trip in less than fifteen minutes.

The second trip was to my place where we picked up the sofa, dresser, TV, microwave, my mother's pans, two knives and a grater. There was plenty of room for my clothes, books and my brochure collection as well. It was the sum total of everything I had accumulated over the past thirteen years. It looked almost pathetic sitting in the back of the pickup.

I turned to Mona and said, "It doesn't look like much, does it?"

"It's yours, Mike, and now it's ours. We don't need much. I have you and that is more than enough."

Suddenly Danny's pickup looked as though it was overflowing with priceless treasure—which is how Mona makes me feel when she reminds me how much she loves me.

The rest of Mona's things filled up the truck for trip number three and we were finished by 2:00 p.m. Danny re-parked his truck and joined us for lunch; our first meal in the apartment. Because the small table with four chairs that Pam was contributing to the cause hadn't arrived yet we sat on the floor and ate as though we were on a picnic. We were also waiting for Mona's parents to drop off two bookcases and something to put the TV on so we can watch it without lowering our heads like we're at church, praying.

After Danny left I said, "Let's celebrate the mess by eating out tonight."

"Are you kidding?" Mona said. "Our first night in our first home and you want to eat out? You've got to be kidding."

"You're repeating yourself," I said, "But I get the idea. We can do take-out."

Mona wouldn't be denied, so we walked down to the nearest corner grocery, bought a loaf of French Bread, canned spaghetti, Parmesan Cheese, a head of lettuce, a tomato, a bottle of wine and some Thousand Island Dressing.

"We can pretend we're back in France," Mona explained.

"Maybe we can make up for the day we missed being in Paris," I said optimistically.

One nice thing about our apartment is that the refrigerator works without buzzing like mine did for the past five years. The stove and oven work, too, and we even have a dishwasher. Once we got the towels out of a box, we took showers and discovered we also have plenty of hot water.

The bedroom came with off-white, short-napped carpet and the Living Room and Kitchen had new, laminate flooring. The first thing we set up was the bed.

As the day wound down to sunset, Mona heated up the spaghetti in one of my mother's pots. We spread a blanket on the floor. I found a spice candle in one of Mona's boxes. I lit it and placed it on a plate in the middle of the blanket. We poured the spaghetti into cereal bowls, broke the bread into pieces with our hands, drank the wine out of paper cups and toasted each other with *Prost*, *Mazel tov*, *Skål*, and *Vive la France*! It was so much fun we completely forgot the salad.

The apartment came with a communal satellite dish. After fiddling with the cable box for an hour we were able see something on my TV besides snow.

We went to bed early.

Chapter 29
Hat Trick
Monday, July 29

There wasn't anything to eat for breakfast so we ate salad washed down with diluted burgundy we pretended was grape juice. Before I left for my appointment with the hat man, we moved the two dressers into the bedroom so Mona could start putting her clothes away.

"Mona," I said. "I don't like mixing business with pleasure but the hat thing sounds like it could be a bit of both. Why don't you come along for the ride? You have the whole day free and your underwear won't complain if they're not put in the drawer until this afternoon."

"Mike," Mona said, "every so often you say the nicest, most romantic things. At times like those I feel loved and glad to be married to you. This is not one of those times."

"Why?" I asked with a wink. "Is your underwear more important to you than I am?"

I thought I was being silly, witty and wry but Mona didn't see the humor in it.

“Get out, Mike. Find the ‘Cat in the Hat’ man and don’t come back until you think of a way to apologize to my underwear . . . well? Why are you standing there? Go!”

She stood there, looking as beautiful as ever, but with her laser beam eyes aimed at the center of my forehead.

“Are you sure you don’t want to come?” I said, trying for a comeback.

Mona crossed her arms across her chest, turned around, walked into the bedroom and closed the door. If it had been a baseball game I would have been credited with a blown save.

I was not used to living in an apartment with a bedroom door that someone could close in my face while I was still in the apartment. I couldn’t decide if Mona wanted me to knock on the door or leave. After pondering a mental list of pros and cons, I decided to take Mona at her word and headed off for my appointment thinking how I could apologize to her underwear.

The hat man lived just a few blocks away on 92nd so I walked, hoping the exercise would settle things down in my stomach. I wasn’t used to arguing with Mona and this thing about her underwear was just one more piece of evidence that there was more to marriage than agreeing about the toilet paper.

The man with the missing hats turned out to be a retired NYPD officer. Just inside the door to his first floor flat was an old-fashioned six-foot tall hat stand tucked away in a corner next to a heavily curtained window.

Through the window, I could see the upper trunks of the trees that lined the street as well as the tops of heads belonging to people walking on the sidewalk. I noticed there were no hats hanging on the rack.

“Did I tell you that my name is Murray?” the man asked.

“Good to meet you, Murray.”

"What did you say? I don't hear very well. I can hardly hear the traffic noise outside. It's because of too much time at the firing range without ear plugs. You'll have to talk louder if you want to have a conversation."

I nodded. Then I said, "Okay." Then I yelled, "I'll try and talk louder!"

"Now I can hear you," he said.

Well?" he continued. "What do you think? How did someone get in here and get away with my hats—three times in a row?"

"I'll have to look around and see what there is to see before I can give you an answer. I'm not psychic. By the way, do you have any hats left?"

"I have lots of hats but I've locked them in a cabinet down in the basement where no one can find them. After I get the alarm system installed I might put some of them back where I can see them again."

There was a "Meow." I looked down as an orange and white tabby cat brushed against my leg, walked around the corner, sauntered down the hall and disappeared through a door.

Remembering Mona's words I asked, "Is that your "'Cat in the Hat?'"

I was hoping for a laugh or at least a smile but Murray continued to stand ramrod straight and as motionless as if he was a cadet standing at attention at the Police Academy. If he was smiling, he was doing a good job hiding it behind his clenched lips.

"Let me ask you a question, "I said. "Who do you think took your hats and how do you think they did it?"

"I don't know. I was a cop in the City for twenty-five years and I thought I'd seen everything there is to see but this just doesn't make sense. It could be some kids with nothing better to do. Someone might have made a copy of my keys. I don't know . . . I just can't understand why anyone would go to all the trouble to take a hat!"

"I was thinking the same thing, and why would they do it three different times?"

"That's what I hired you to find out," Murray said, still without a trace of friendly humanity on his face.

"Can I walk around and look?"

"Sure. Look anywhere you want. I didn't find anything and I don't think you will, either."

I checked the window, noting how dirty it was and how frayed and faded the curtain looked. The latch on the window, although old fashioned, looked solid and inaccessible from outside. The front door had a lock in the doorknob, a dead bolt and a chain.

"Were these all locked when the hats disappeared?"

"Yes, sir. They are locked when I'm in the house and, except for the chain, the other two locks are set whenever I go out. I do the same with the back door in the kitchen."

There were several rooms in the flat including a front-facing Living Room with its own street level window. In the back was a bedroom, a kitchen and a bathroom.

Behind the door where the cat disappeared, steps led to a basement area. Downstairs there was another bedroom and a poorly lit unfinished area with several cabinets, a bookshelf and a big pile of boxes up against the wall. There was also an old bed mattress, a few chairs and a five-foot stepladder piled up next to the boxes.

I heard some high-pitched mewing but the cat kept itself out of sight, apparently not sure whether I was a friendly visitor or not. When I looked at the downstairs bedroom, it was clean and empty except for a twin bed and a dresser.

"Does anyone else live here with you?" I asked.

"No, it's just me and the cat. Marlene died two years ago from breast cancer. She fought for three hard years and then, well, we both lost. So the answer is 'No.' Peppy and I are the only ones left."

This might be somewhat of a digression but my friend Robert's favorite television show is one where they show videos of people and animals doing things the show's producers think are funny—like college guys jumping off of roofs into swimming pools . . . and missing the pool—stuff like that. Robert tells me that they don't show a video if someone dies but if they only get badly hurt then that can still be funny and they'll show those.

The only things I liked about the show were the animal videos. Animals are strange creatures—especially house pets. Cats are especially funny and the videos showed them doing crazy things you'd never imagine a cat could do.

"Murray," I said. "I have three final questions. First, is Peppy a boy or a girl?"

"A girl. Is that important?"

"It might be. My second question is, do you ever let her outside?"

"Not often. But there are times when she slips out of the door. The first time she slipped out, I thought for sure I'd never see her again, but she came back, and every time she's gotten outside since it's been the same. She always comes back. You probably don't understand how important Peppy is to me. She was Marlene's pet and I never really liked having her around until Marlene passed away. Now she's one of the only things I have that . . . that . . . is like having part of Marlene still here with me . . . in the house. Oh, I miss her so much . . . ."

I waited for him to wipe the tear from his eye and then asked, "Was Peppy ever spayed?"

"I don't know. Marlene found him as a stray, just a kitten at the time. I don't know if she had Peppy spayed. Probably not, but I'm not sure."

"I agree with you. I don't think Peppy was spayed, either," I said, "and I think I know who took your hats and where they are."

Murray looked at me as if I had gone totally over the side of the boat.

"Follow me," I said with the same loud voice I had been using since we started talking.

We went down the stairs to the basement where I slowly and carefully began to move the mattress and the boxes away from the wall. Peppy magically reappeared and hissed at me like a snake.

"Peppy, stop that!" Murray shouted. "Be a good cat and be nice."

Peppy didn't look as though she was inclined to be nice. Her back arched and the hair on her back bristled as I slid the largest box away from the wall in the corner of the room.

I could hear the mewing even before I saw the four newborn kittens hidden behind the box. One kitten was lying on top of a felt Greek Fisherman's Cap; one was hiding under the brim of a beige slouch hat; and the other two were curled up inside an NYPD police officer's hat.

Peppy, who had stopped hissing as soon as the box had been moved, walked over and began going from kitten to kitten, licking each of them lovingly on the face,.

"Peppy is a mother," I said.

"Oh, my . . ." was all that came out of Murray's mouth.

Murray, of course, was too deaf to hear the kittens mewing and he had never considered the possibility that Peppy could ever be a mother. He also could not have known that Peppy was agile enough to take a running leap at the curtain and claw herself up far enough to knock a hat off the rack.

I had seen a cat do something similar to it on the TV show but I would never have thought of it or considered Peppy to be a suspect if Mona hadn't made the crack about Dr. Seuss.

Murray was embarrassed enough to pay me well for my trouble. He stuffed a little extra in my pocket when he realized he wasn't going to have to shell out a fortune for the security system.

Part of me wished Mona could have been there to share in the fun, but part of me was glad she stayed home because she probably would have figured the whole thing out before I did and that wouldn't have been any fun at all . . . at least for me.

As I left, my phone rang. It was Florence. Not a person named Florence, but the city in Italy.

The police needed to ask me some more questions as a sort of deposition on what happened during my abduction. The police had located the plane in northern Switzerland near Schaffhausen. From there the crooks could have gone anywhere—Germany, Austria, Lichtenstein or simply stayed somewhere in Switzerland. They had been flying a stolen plane and there was no way to identify them except through the photographs and videos taken by Mona.

They asked when would be a good time to talk and I said, "why not now?" I was a block from Central Park so I walked over and across to the park where I found a quiet bench and kept talking.

There wasn't much for me to say that I hadn't already told them but they were trying to build a criminal case and the prosecutor needed to clarify a few facts. As it turned out, they clarified a few facts for me, too.

The only one that really mattered was that the medallions were fakes. On the day of the theft, they had been on their way to being the central part of a Cellini retrospective at another museum near Florence. To his eternal embarrassment and permanent damage to his reputation, the curator of the museum that owned the medallions confessed he had done a bait and switch. The museum had kept the originals locked away in a safe and, unbeknownst to the other museum, sent copies of the medallions for the exhibit. The crooks had gotten away with the crime but only had fake Cellini's to show for it.

The Italian press was having a field day over the whole mess, so much so that my picture disappeared from the media like yesterday's news, which, of course, it was. As it turned out my fame had been short-lived and I had almost died for nothing—literally.

Yet the crime was still a crime and my kidnapping across international borders had put the fugitives in a tight corner. Personally, I had already washed my hands of the whole thing but if the police wanted to catch the bad guys and prosecute them I wasn't going to stand in their way.

Our conversation turned out to be so long my phone battery went down to five percent.

"I'm going to have to call it quits," I explained. "Time for one more question and that will have to be the end of it."

"Signor Maurison," came the question, "since you don't speak Italian how did you know they were arguing about you, especially if your head was covered by a jacket?"

"Because every time I heard someone say, '*questo idiota,*' someone poked me in the ribs with their foot. I may not understand Italian," I added, "but I know the word "idiot" in at least twenty-seven languages. As far as I could tell I was the only person in the car or the plane who was one."

"*Grazie,*" came the reply. "*buona giornata, Signor. Ciao.*"

The battery in my phone went dead and, for the first time in two weeks, I had perfect timing when it came to matters involving international law enforcement.

It was mid-afternoon when I got home. It seems strange to call our new apartment "home" but that is what it is and home is where I found myself walking in the door.

"Hello!" I called. "Anybody here?"

There was no answer. There was no Mona. She was gone.

There was, however, a table and four chairs sitting in the place where a table and chairs are supposed to go. Pam must have stopped by before Mona left.

There were also two bookcases against the wall and the TV was three feet higher off the floor than it was when I left. Mona's parents must have been here, too.

But where was Mona?

Our morning argument had seemed like a minor upset—although watching the bedroom door close in my face wasn't the best way for either of us to begin our day. Now she was gone . . . again.

I looked everywhere for a note or something that might tell me where she was but all I found was her clothes, either neatly hung in the closet or neatly folded in her dresser drawers. Her underwear was in one of the drawers and I paused for a moment to say, "I'm sorry."

I considered phoning her. I considered phoning her parents. I considered phoning Corinne but I didn't want to deal with her sarcasm again. I considered many things and finally decided to put my own underwear away in my dresser.

Mona walked in at 4:30 p.m.

I was so glad to see her that I said, "Mona, you're home!" as if it wasn't already obvious.

"Home is where the heart is," Mona said cheerily, "and if you have any heart at all you'll help me with these groceries. Three flights of stairs are more exercise than I counted on. This apartment is going to either make us very strong and very healthy or . . . ."

". . . it's going to kill us," I said, completing her sentence.

"That's not what I was going to say," Mona frowned. "You didn't let me finish. What I was going to say is that the stairs will either make us 'strong and healthy or . . . we're going to have Chia and Robert over for dinner tonight.' Did you get my note?"

"You were going to say all that?" I asked.

"You did see the note, didn't you?" Mona asked as she tapped her finger on a small piece of paper stuck to the refrigerator door with an "I ❤ NY" magnet.

"Why would I look for a note on the refrigerator?"

"Because that is where everybody puts notes. The refrigerator should be the first place you look when you walk into the house . . . or flat . . . I don't know what to call it yet . . . whatever it is that you walk into, check the refrigerator for a note."

"What does it say . . . the note, I mean."

"It says what I already said, that 'Chia and Robert are coming over for dinner tonight, and would you find some silverware and set the table.'"

"Sorry," I said. "I'll start setting the table now . . . ."

". . . after you bring in the groceries."

Mona was already taking control of the house . . . and me. I felt less like the king of the castle and more like one of the hired staff as I carried in the groceries.

"Chia said they would bring the pictures from their honeymoon in Puerto Rico and then we can tell them about our trip to Europe. I suggested that after dinner they take the first hour, we'll take the second hour, and then they can go home.

"One hour? That won't even get us past the first day!" I moaned.

"Maybe not, but the only photos we have to show are the silly ones we took at the Louvre and the ones I took of the crooks in Florence. That's not much of a show, Mr. de Mille.

"True," I said. "You can tell about Du and the painting and I get to tell about my close encounter with death and international intrigue."

Mona reached into one of the grocery bags and pulled out four small sirloin steaks, four potatoes, a bunch of asparagus spears and some basic cooking staples like butter, oil, salt and pepper.

"Steak and potatoes," I said. "Robert will like that."

"That's the plan," Mona said. "If you're good, someday I'll fix you something nice, too."

That was pretty much how it was until Robert and Chia showed up with a bottle of Pinot Noir and a bakery-made banana cream pie. The evening was looking better and better every minute.

Chia helped Mona mash the potatoes while Robert and I talked about his favorite TV show and how it helped solve the Case of the Missing Hats. Robert was so pleased with himself that he reached over his shoulder and patted himself on the back.

When he had finished patting, he pulled something out of his pocket and put it in my hand. It looked like a small piece of concrete or a strange sort of rock.

"I brought this from Puerto Rico as a present for you. It's a mineral found only in Puerto Rico. It is very valuable."

"What is it?" I asked.

"It's called 'supdock,' he said.

"What's supdock?" I said, as Robert rolled onto the floor laughing.

"What's so funny?" I asked, not knowing what or who he was laughing at.

"You sound just like Bugs Bunny," he said when he got himself back under control.

Robert had made me look and feel like a fool for the second time in three days.

The steak and asparagus were cooked medium rare and the potatoes mashed with enough butter and garlic salt to make them melt on our plates and in our mouths. It was a good dinner and Mona and I enjoyed the chance to share our new place with our best friends.

After dinner, we spent an hour looking at Robert and Chia's wedding photos and the ones they took in Puerto Rico.

When it was our turn, we spent an hour trying to untangle our way through the tragicomedy of Du and his painting. After pile driving the story into the ground Mona backtracked and started telling about my sleepwalking on the plane.

At that point I looked at my watch and said, "Oh, dear, look at the time," or words to that effect.

It was a fun evening and we decided that next time we would have Robert and Chia over to their place for dinner.

Chapter 30
Wow!

Tuesday, July 30

Today was the last day before Mona went back to work at Books and Things. She had given her two-week notice before we left for Europe but wanted to keep working until she started her new job at the Hunter College Library.

I was already getting back into the swing of the private eye business but since I didn't have any appointments on my calendar I lazed around in bed with Mona while the sun came up.

"Mona," I said, pillow to pillow, "I'm sorry about yesterday morning. I didn't know you were so sensitive about your underwear. I'm not trying to be sarcastic, I really mean it. There are so many things I never knew about you before. I think Pastor Cheryl was right. It's going to take a lifetime to figure each other out."

"Mike," Mona said from her side of the bed, "it wasn't the underwear. It's just that I've been with you every day for the past two weeks and I was looking forward to having some time to myself. The thought of going to work with you just pushed me over the edge. I'm sorry, too. I shouldn't have shut the door in your face. I needed to be alone and that was the only way I could get away . . . from you . . . That sounds really bad, I didn't mean it the way it came out."

I explained to her how I had been feeling the same way and we both agreed that things would get better once she went back to work.

Mona was also missing being around her old roommates.

As she put it, "Mike, I love you, but you're not Brin or Corinne."

"Something for which I will be eternally grateful," I said.

Mona laughed, I laughed, and whatever tension we might have felt vanished in a moment. As they say, married couples should learn how to kiss and make out, which is, of course, what we did.

"How should we spend the day?" Mona asked after we had gotten up and gotten dressed. "It's the last day of our honeymoon and I'm not planning on having another one anytime soon."

I knew what I wanted to do but I was having a hard time saying it aloud.

Ever since we left on our trip, I had carried a heaviness around in my guts, or in my soul or somewhere. It had to do with letting go of my fantasy life with my mother and other family members and friends—the ones who hang on museum walls around town.

When Mona and I were planning our dream trip to the great museums of Europe, I had been excited about meeting the people who lived in the paintings there. Because I had decided to give up those fantasies and start my life over again with Mona, I had found myself walking through the great museums of Europe, distancing myself from paintings I had always dreamed of striking up conversations with. I had missed the chance to meet them up close and personal and I knew I might never have that chance again.

I also missed talking with Mom, Grandpa van Rijn and Frieda. I felt disconnected somehow and alone. Mona had her parents, she had Pam and Danny, and I had. . . well, I had Mona. I was beginning to realize that Mona wasn't going to be enough.

"I'd like to visit Mom at the MoMA," I said. "And I'd like to have a chat with Grandpa at the Met. I think he'd enjoy hearing about our trip."

In saying this, I was taking a big risk. Mona could either embrace the idea or reject it. Deep down inside I felt as though our marriage and our future were on the line, ready to tip one way or the other depending on what Mona was going to say.

Mona had been making coffee, but she stopped and stood deadly still as she let my words sink in. She looked at me, not with laser-beam eyes but with soft eyes, dampening with what looked like tears. She walked over and put her arms around me, holding me like a mother holds her child.

Then she kissed me, not as a mother kisses her child but as one lover kisses another, full, and deep, as if to say, "You are mine and I am yours . . . wherever you go, I will go with you."

I had risked death, and Mona had given me life. I held her so tightly that she had to push me back with gentle hands in order to breathe.

"Let's go see Mom," she said.

So we did.

On our way, we decided to detour over to the Met to see Grandpa first.

One nice thing about having family and friends hanging on the walls of museums is that you can nearly always count on them being home when you stop by for a visit. We found Grandpa van Rijn in his usual spot, waiting for us.

"Good morning," he said as we stepped into the gallery.

His voice was clear enough for me to hear from thirty feet away.

"It's so good to see you," he added. "How was your trip? Did you get to Amsterdam?"

I looked at Mona and she looked at me.

"I hear him, too," Mona smiled. "Go ahead, tell him about our trip."

Mona and I stood and talked with Grandpa about everything, but mostly about his paintings. He remembered every painting we had seen hanging on museum walls. Some he groaned over, saying that he had thrown this one or that one together just to collect a fee from a patron. Others he was glad to hear were on public display so everyone could enjoy them.

"These are my children," he said, "and the painting on this wall is one of them."

"Strange, isn't it?" he mused. "That now I am my own child!"

"Grandpa," Mona asked. "If we had tried to talk to your paintings would they have talked back . . . like you are talking to us now?"

"Perhaps . . . perhaps not," he replied. "I talk with you because I know you and can trust you. We have feelings for each other in ways that most paintings aren't willing to have with the people outside. It's possible that one of my self-portraits would have recognized you and said '*Hallo*,' but I can't say that for sure."

I did my best to describe the painting Du had found in the trash bin behind his store. I asked if he remembered painting it.

"I painted more self-portraits than you or anyone can imagine. Some of them I refused to sell because they revealed too much about my soul. Some of these were so revealing that I burned them, or scraped off the paint so I could reuse the canvas."

"Did you sign all of them?" I asked.

"If you mean my drawings and sketches, No," he said. "Many of them weren't good enough to put my name on them, but paintings were a different matter altogether."

"What do you mean?" Mona asked.

"The ones I kept for myself . . . the ones I didn't feel comfortable letting others stare at . . . some of those I didn't sign because the painting itself was my signature. It was as if it was not just a painting but that there was actually a part of me living on the canvas in the texture of my hands, the sadness on my face, or the joy in my eyes. There was no need for a signature on those paintings. There were only a few of them that I didn't destroy and I have no recollection of selling any of the others. I have no idea what happened to them after I died.

"The one you described to me, the one with the fur coat and the red sash was one of those special paintings. I remember it well and I would enjoy seeing it again. It was one of the paintings I never signed."

Mona and I looked at each other. Du's painting had a signature. Our hearts sank as we realized that it was most likely a copy of the painting Grandpa had treasured as his own. Du's *Self-Portrait* had probably been painted by one of the more talented students in Grandpa's studio; a student who, whether from pride or from greed, forged his Master's signature in the corner.

"Grandpa," Mona said. "Thank you for what you did for the world and for what you have done for Mike and me. The world is a better place because of you."

The hint of a smile seemed to creep into the corners of his otherwise sad, wise and contemplative face.

"Grandpa," I said. "I want to thank you for trusting us and loving us enough to open your heart to us. You are a good man . . . and a good Grandpa!"

We said our "Goodbyes" and promised we would return for another visit soon.

"Well," Mona said as we left the gallery and headed for the museum exit. "That was exciting. Grandpa has never talked to me so much before. I feel like I'm now officially part of your family!"

"Did you hear what I heard?" I asked.

"If you mean the things he said about the self-portraits that he kept to himself, then 'Yes,' I heard all of it."

I nodded, lost in thought, like a Zen master pondering the imponderable.

Mona reached over and took my hand. She held it as we got on and off the bus that took us to West 53rd and she held it as we walked down the street to the Museum of Modern Art. As we went through the door to the museum, she dropped my hand so she could give Robert a poke on the arm.

Robert smiled and said, "Last night was fun."

That was all he said but, as usual with Robert, it was exactly right.

Mona took my hand again as we entered the Fifth Floor Gallery. Mom was waiting for us. For the first time I could remember, all five women in the painting turned their heads in our direction and every one of them smiled.

Mona gave them a little wave. We walked up as close to the painting as we could without the guard coming over and telling to back off. The painting is very large and we had to turn our heads up so high to see Mom that we instinctively backed up a few steps to get a more comfortable angle.

"Hello, Nesbitt," Mom said, calling me by the name she gave me. "So . . . now the two of you are married. I'm happy for you."

For some reason Mom had gotten more chatty than I could remember.

"As you know," she said, "I was never happy with your father. In fact, I wasn't very happy with myself, either. You were the one exception. You were my joy of joys and the love of my life."

Confusion stirred in my guts as I asked, "Then why, Mom, why? Why did you abandon me and run away. If you loved me so much why would you do such a thing? Why?"

Mona put her arm around my waist as we stood facing the painting side by side.

"I left you," Mom said, fighting back tears, "because I wasn't worthy of you. I treated you like dirt because I felt like dirt myself. Because I hated myself for so many things, I couldn't stand to be around you or your father anymore. Later, I found I couldn't stand to be around myself, either, until you brought me back to life in this painting.

"Since then I have rediscovered joy, happiness and peace for the first time in my life. Here, on this wall I am free to love you in ways I was never able to do when you were a child. Thank you so much for loving me . . . I still don't deserve it, but I am grateful for it."

It was as though she delivered a speech she had been practicing for a long time.

"Mom, I love you, and I'm glad you're happy."

Mona had to put her arm around my waist again.

"Mom," Mona said, "We've got to go. It's been a tiring day. Being here with you has been the best part. Mike and I are married and we are very happy.

"Personally," Mona said to Mom as she turned and kissed me on the cheek, "I am very glad you brought Mike into the world."

Mom smiled an enormous smile that would have ruined the painting if Picasso had painted it that way.

"I am too," Mom said.

I suppose mysteries, are called mysteries because . . . well, because they are hidden things that can't be easily seen or understood by the world. Mom was always a mystery to me but today she let me catch a glimpse of something she had kept hidden from me for all these years.

On the day I married Mona, I had been convinced that Mom was gone forever and that in one way or another I had killed her, perhaps more than once. Today, however, my mom gave me her blessing and with it, a second chance at life for both of us. Mona and I hope to be parents someday. If and when that day comes I have no doubt that Mona will be the mother for our child that mine was never able to be for me.

That will make my mom happier than anything else in the world.

Later that evening when it must have been past midnight in London I received a phone call from the Assistant Curator of the National Gallery. He had just received a preliminary report from the authentication committee that had been examining Du's painting.

"There's good news and bad news," he said. "The good news is that so far nothing has ruled out the possibility the painting is a genuine work by Rembrandt. The composition of the paint, the materials used in the canvas, the brush strokes are all consistent with original Rembrandts in a way that is almost self-authenticating."

"And the bad news?" I asked.

"The bad news is they have determined that the signature is a fake, added long after the painting had been completed—long after Rembrandt had died.

"The signature and the painting are causing a great deal of confusion and dissention within the committee. One member is suggesting that Rembrandt painted the self-portrait but never signed it. The rest of the committee isn't convinced and say there is no precedent for it. In any case, no one has come up with a reason why he wouldn't have signed it . . . at least if it was genuine."

"But," he added, "there is a lot more research to be done on the painting before their final report is issued, probably in another two months. I'll let you know."

When I passed the information on to Mona, she smiled that killer smile of hers and said, "Wow!"

Chapter 31
Back to Work
Wednesday, July 31

This morning Mona and I went back to work, Since our honeymoon is now officially over, today can be classified as the first "normal" day of our life as husband and wife. There will, of course, be many more like it but over time, most of the days will become blurred and indistinguishable from each other.

In contrast, each day during the last four weeks is etched into my memory like the Ten Commandments were carved into stone. Each day brought a new surprise and each day offered a new opportunity for Mona and me to "have and to hold" each other "for as long as we both shall live."

Today, when Mona and I walked out the front door together and headed off in different directions, it seemed as comfortably routine and familiar as seeing the guy who sells *faux* Rolex watches on the sidewalk across from the Plaza.

Today is a beautiful mid-summer day. The Verrazano Bridge is hidden in the haze and there are flower vendors on the street corners. As far as the tourists are concerned, Manhattan looks the same as it did in the books and brochures they read before they came. I, however, have been smushed in the mouth with a piece of wedding cake and, in some inexplicably mundane way, New York City has changed along with me.

Last night while we were asleep, I received an email from a man offering me a job investigating a parrot that flew in his apartment window and started rattling off a long string of Social Security numbers.

This morning I emailed back and said, "Sure, why not."

It's going to be another ordinary day in Manhattan.

More or less.

Books in the Mike Maurison Series

Book 1

I Want My MoMA

A Year in the Life of Mike Maurison, Private Eye

Book 2

To Have and To Hold

A Month in the Life of Mike Maurison, Private Eye

Book 3

Treasure Hunt

A Week in the Life of Mike Maurison, Private Eye

Book 4

Smoke and Mirrors

A Day in the Life of Mike Maurison, Private Eye

(available soon)

Other Books by James A. Tweedie

Long Beach Short Stories

The One Who Tells the Stories

(available soon)

All books are published by Dunecrest Press and are available on Amazon.com as paperback or Kindle

Made in the
USA
Middletown, DE